I0762025

A Beaumont Bros Circus Mystery #3

THE YULETIDE KILLER

TABI SLICK

This is a work of fiction. Names, characters, places, events, and incidents are either products of the author's imagination or are used fictitiously. Any resemblance to persons living or dead is entirely coincidental and not intended by the author.

Published by SWC Indie Press

www.SWCIndiePress.com

Hard Cover Edition, 2022

ISBN: 978-1-7345568-8-9

Printed in the United States of America

www.TabiSlick.com

❀ Created with Vellum

TRANSITIONED UNIVERSE
BOOKS BY TABI SLICK

Tompkin's School: For The Extraordinarily Talented
Tompkin's School: For The Dearly Departed
Tompkin's School: For The Resurrected

~

The Unforgivable Act
The Detective's Nightmare
The Yuletide Killer

~

Timur's Escape

To stay in the know about upcoming series visit:
www.tabislick.com/join

At length an oak chest, that had long lain hid,
Was found in the castle — they raised the lid,
And a skeleton form lay mouldering there
In the bridal wreath of that lady fair!
O, sad was her fate! — in sportive jest
She hid from her lord in the old oak chest.
It closed with a spring! — and, dreadful doom,
The bride lay clasped in her living tomb!
Oh, the mistletoe bough.

— THOMAS HAYNES BAYLY, *THE MISTLETOE BOUGH*

CONTENTS

1
THERE'S MAGIC IN THE AIR

Halifax, Nova Scotia

"LET HIM HANG!" A grubby man shook his fists at the weak prisoner as he passed, toted off in a barred caravan on its way to the gallows.

Hundreds of angry spectators lined the cobblestoned street, a fresh blanket of snow sogging their muddy boots.

"Rot in hell!" Another shouted.

"What of his partner? Is there any word of Madam Onay?" a young reporter in plaid trousers asked the officers guarding the procession. "Have you found her yet?"

"Lies. He's the one who done it." An old woman shoved the reporter aside.

The young man slipped on the ice and tumbled into the fresh blanket of snow that layered the ground. But nobody noticed, save for a shadow in the crowd. A mysterious figure in a black hooded cloak snaked his way through the mob and snatched up the young lad before vanishing. Not one saw where they went, nor did they care. Instead, all eyes followed their celebrity prisoner as the town's very own serial killer was brought to the gallows near the water's edge.

John Walsh grasped the bars from within the cage, a sneer upon his boyish face, which was blanketed with fresh cuts and bruises. "Do your eyes deceive you?"

A basket of rotting food smacked the iron bars, and a scrap of lettuce fell at his shoeless feet. John bent at the waist and plucked it off his toe.

"Death is coming for us all. It's already here," he whispered.

The cart jerked to a halt, and an officer pried the door open. "Out, you."

The shackles rattled in perfect harmony with that of a heartbeat as John Walsh, the murderer of many, including the town's most beloved bachelor, Irvin Talmage, Jr, was pulled from the vehicle. A woman spat at the prisoner's face, and the wet goo sloshed down the scar under his left eye. He locked eyes with her, a smile spread across his face, and he winked. His grey irises flashed emerald green, sparkling with magic.

The woman pinked and backed away. "He's not a man. He's the devil!"

"HANG THE DEVIL!" The mob shouted.

The officers ignored their cries and continued to guide John Walsh up the wooden platform. The chief inspector sat nearby along with the affluent Talmage family, all clad in black mourning clothes for their only son and heir. The chief inspector kept a watchful eye out for any means of escape. His job was on the line, after all. Mr Talmage, Sr, would make sure of that.

The hangman wasted no time. As soon as John was on the stage, he pulled the noose over the prisoner's dishevelled hair.

"Yes, let me hang awhile," John shouted with glee before the hangman pulled the lever.

The crowd bellowed back in approval, and the trap door swung open. The noose snapped tautly, and John's limbs quivered until they stopped. The bluish-grey body hung slack.

Silence filled the circle around the gallows. A young girl sucked in a quick breath of air. The hangman checked the pulse and gave the chief inspector a nod.

Minutes past and right when the crowd turned to leave, a hand twitched.

"What was that?" Someone asked.

"Did it just *move?*" Another piped in.

John's eyes snapped open, sending a gasp through the crowd. The chief inspector leaned forward in his seat.

"Miss me?" John grabbed the rope around his neck with a chuckle and swung his legs as if he were on a child's swing.

"What in God's name?" Mr Talmage let out a guttural roar.

"Not God. It's only me," John said with a laugh. "But you can't kill me. You can't kill me dead."

"Get him down!" The inspector cried.

"As you wish." John Walsh snapped his fingers. The rope flickered with magic before it unwound itself from the gallows.

The minty sulfuric stench of black magic lingered in the air around John. He landed without a sound in the snow-covered mud.

Men and women screamed alike, piling upon each other to get away. Officers drew their weapons and raced for the prisoner. The chief inspector yanked a pair of handcuffs from his belt and pushed through the madness.

"Oh here, allow me." John grinned once the chief inspector approached him, bringing his free wrists together.

"Wha—?" The chief inspector's eyes went wide, still heaving from the run over. He doubled over to try and catch his breath.

"You can't kill me, but I can't leave yet," John Walsh said with a mad chuckle. "So be a dear and take me back to my cell."

When the inspector didn't move, John rolled his eyes and grabbed the handcuffs. The iron shackles snapped themselves into place with a flash of green magic.

John sighed. "Ah, that's better. Now, would you be so kind as to escort me back?"

Not wanting to take any chances, John Walsh was quickly removed from the failed execution to the darkest cell the chief inspector could find. No one could fathom how it happened, but the rumours of John Walsh's devil magic spread like wildfire throughout the town, almost as swiftly as the chief inspector removed of his duties and replaced with another unfortunate soul.

A Few Nights Later.

IT WAS a quiet winter night for the little town of Halifax, and all were safely in their beds. Save for one in the black hooded cloak who marched down Bishop Street. His path was illuminated only by the coiling fire that hovered over his gloved palm.

Something scuttled in the shadows. The figure in the black hooded cloak stopped in his tracks just outside an old, abandoned home. An owl hooted, but all was still. Finally, he pushed his way through the wrought iron fence. It squealed shut behind him, and the snow crunched under his boots as he made his way into the two-story house that smelled of rot.

"Hello?" A weak voice cried from the adjacent room. "You can't leave me here!"

"Loscht," the cloaked figure whispered and clenched his palm into a fist. The flame extinguished in a puff of smoke.

The wood-panelled floor groaned as the cloaked figure made his way into the mostly empty room on the left. Cobwebs covered everything except for a mirror placed in the centre. A circle of symbols was drawn on the floor around it in white chalk.

But the cloaked figure wasn't alone. There, tucked away in the corner, sat the young reporter. His plaid trousers were torn, revealing crimson welts that blistered his legs.

"Please." He tugged on the rope that tied his wrists to the wall. "I've told you everything I know. And I haven't seen your face. I promise I won't tell anyone. You can let me go."

The hooded figure turned to his prisoner. A mask of bones concealed the cloaked figure's face. The poor young reporter sobbed, but there was no use. It was time. The cloaked figure had the last ingredient the spell required, so he laid out his offerings on the floor within the circle of symbols.

"With this chalice of thieves, I call upon thee," the cloaked figure chanted to the mirror. "Frau Perchta, hear my plea!"

The figure stood still. His breath hitched at the anticipation of conjuring the ancient witch. But moments passed, and the mirror remained still.

"Frau Perchta, *please*!" The cloaked figure gripped either side of the mirror and brought their masked face closer to his reflection. "Set things right, and I swear on my life, my heart will be yours."

The room fell silent. Nothing moved, and the cloaked figure's shoulders slacked in despair. Then a sudden shimmer caught in the reflection. A drum thumped from somewhere in the room. The conjurer whirled around to find the source, but the young reporter in plaid was the only other person in the room.

Candlewicks flicked on, suddenly lit with fire illuminating hundreds of melted wax candles strewn about the dusty room. The cloaked figure turned to the mirror.

"O, the mistletoe bough!" A sing-songy voice echoed through the glass. The conjurer's hooded reflection melted into liquid. It danced to the rhythm of the drum. The glass churned like a sea of lava until two eyes of coal blinked back. *"How sad her fate, a dreadful doom. The bride lay clasped in her living tomb!"*

Sharp teeth lunged at the cloaked conjurer, escaping the mirror for a second before it puffed into dust. The glass lapped upon itself once again. It squirmed like mealworms until it morphed into a beautiful woman with delicate features and ruby lips. Her lustrous mane was crowned with a head of goat horns. She gazed with a predatory eye back at her conjurer in place of his reflection.

"You came!" The conjurer in the black cloak bowed low.

"But of course, my pet." Frau Perchta's plump lips spread to reveal razor-sharp fangs. *"Tell me, what is it your heart desires?"*

"Chaos." The conjurer glanced down at the tip of his boots that peeked out from under his long, black robes. "And revenge."

Frau Perchta's fanged smile deepened, and her harsh cackle sent tremors down the mirror's frame. It rattled the glass, and a whimper reminded the cloaked figure that he wasn't alone.

"Silence!" The cloaked figure snapped his fingers. A needle and thread stitched the young reporter's lips shut.

He shrieked, wide eyes as he tried to shake the needle away, but soon his cries were muffled by the thread.

The conjurer returned his attention to the mirror. "Please, Frau Perchta. I'm desperate."

Frau Perchta winked back. Her rosy cheeks faded into grey, and her hairline receded up to her goat horns. Her once youthful face pruned until it was not a fair maiden staring back from the mirror but an old hag with hollowed cheekbones and a wrinkled brow.

"Oh, my poor little pet," she crooned. *"Now that I can accommodate. But first, is the flax spun? They always forget."*

The conjurer motioned to the items at his feet. A holly branch, a black candle, and three small bundles of freshly spun flax surrounded the golden chalice.

Frau Perchta sucked in a quick breath in anticipation, and her coal eyes lit up.

"Good little pet." She batted her eyelashes back at the conjurer. *"And what of my groom?"*

The conjurer stepped back so Frau Perchta could see, the cowering young reporter tucked away in the corner.

Frau Perchta's harsh cackle echoed as she jumped with glee. *"Bring him to me!"*

The poor young reporter trembled, cowering back, but there was nowhere to escape. The cloaked figure yanked him off the ground and snatched the rope that bound him.

"Your sacrifice," the cloaked figure said to Frau Perchta as he shoved the reporter into the circle.

The reporter stumbled, falling to his knees. His hands caught his fall, splotched with red bruises from the attempts to free himself. A fresh blanket of tears streamed down his desperate face.

"Ah, he will do nicely." Frau Perchta admired the broken lad. She flicked her eyes up to her conjurer in the black cloak. *"Now, get me out so we can have our fun."*

The conjurer reached for his boot and brandished a sharpened blade. He moved towards the reporter like a cat about to leap on its prey into the circle. The reporter tensed as the cloaked figure neared. The figure scooped the chalice off the ground next to the reporter, and he sighed with relief but winced at his swollen lips still sewn up.

The cloak around the conjurer's wrist fell back to reveal a fair-skinned wrist, and with one swift motion, the conjurer sliced into his own flesh as if he'd done it a thousand times.

"Spiegelgrab, spiegelgrab," the conjurer recited the spell as the crimson droplets filled the chalice. "Von Frau Perchta, dem Hexengeist. Free thy spirit, let it rise."

The conjurer repeated the chant thrice until the chalice overflowed and then whispered, "*Zupf!*"

The reporter's eyes widened when a berry plucked itself off the branch on the floor in front of him. The berry floated up and hovered over the chalice before it crushed itself into powder. Red crumbles tumbled into the chalice, mixing with the thick blood. It popped and sizzled. Crimson and green smoke billowed up from the mixture.

"*Yes, yes, that's it!*" Frau Perchta hissed.

"Accept this blood offering of ivy and gold!" The spun flax flitted up into the air just as the berry had. It snapped with light and twirled into a braid before melting itself into the mixture of blood.

"*Easy now, don't let it spill,*" Frau Perchta cooed, her reflection giddy as the conjurer yanked the young reporter's head back and lifted the chalice to his sewn-up lips.

The reporter made a noise, and his mouth tightened. The conjurer gripped the reporter's jaw, snapping a thread.

"*Schwa glutsivam,*" the conjurer ordered the chalice, and it lifted on its own out of his gloved hands, tipping over.

Red blood mixed with gold flax funnelled through the air and snaked its way into the reporter's mouth. He coughed, his throat closing against the liquid that poured between the threads that secured his lips.

"Move this bride from here to there so you may rise." The conjurer shoved the poor lad towards the mirror who let out a muffled scream.

It echoed with Frau Perchta's frantic laughter, no longer within the confines of the glass. The old hag evaporated into a cloud of black smoke that seeped out of the mirror.

"And with my heart's desire known," the conjurer lifted his voice above the drums that quickened their beat. "Take my body as thine own!"

The mist sprung out in all directions, surrounding the conjurer like spiderwebs. The cloaked figure's head flung back from the force of the smoke that poured into the whites of his eyes. Frau Perchta consumed the conjurer, taking hold of his body for herself.

The drum halted its thumping. The conjurer's head snapped forward, his eyes shimmering green from behind his mask.

Frau Perchta sighed from within her new body, stretching his arms up overhead. "Ah, that's more like it."

Footsteps thudded against the floor. The possessed conjurer turned just as the reporter attempted to flee the room.

"Not so fast, my bride," the conjurer hissed, snatching him back by his collar. He brought the reporter's face to the mirror. "It's time for you to hide in your living tomb."

With one swift movement, the conjurer shoved the poor lad into the mirror. The glass turned liquid once more and absorbed him entirely.

Frau Perchta leaned her new body's masked head to the side as the reporter stumbled in the reflection. The reporter turned to try and run away again but slammed against the mirror he was now trapped in.

"Close with a spring!" Frau Perchta snapped her new body's fingers. "*Brechteram!*"

The reporter's eyes widened before the glass shattered into a million pieces. Little bits of his broken reflection rained down onto the floor with a plunk.

"Now, then," Frau Perchta said through the cloaked figure's body. She brushed a piece of glass off his shoulder, now reflecting spatters of the reporter's blood. "It's time to play, my pet."

A scraping noise followed by a high-pitched squeal came from the nearby window. Frau Perchta twisted her new neck towards the sound, where a tiny sliver of moonlight sprinkled in through an opening in the drapes.

The witch raced for the window frame, his black gowns swishing against the floor, and slid the drapes aside. A quiet street covered in a fresh sheet of snow twinkled back, but otherwise, all was still. It must've just been the wind.

Frau Perchta gazed out at the new playground with a smile as the conjurer's plan for revenge surfaced in their mind. Yes, it would be a glorious night, but not for the little town of Halifax.

2
THE CHRISTMAS WITCH

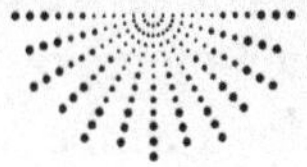

Deadman's Island,
On the outskirts of Halifax

EMMA SHOT UPRIGHT. Forgetting she was in the top bunk of the caravan, she hit her head hard against the ceiling.

"Ow!" She rubbed her forehead, lying back down.

Her heart still thumped rapidly from her restless dreams. Her clothes clung to her in a chilling sweat. What sort of magic had she witnessed last night? It was her first time out with the circus to scout for the new recruit, the one Antoine sensed had power like their own. They searched for whomever it was so they could extend an invitation to join a life where magic was disguised as mere trickery.

Goosebumps swept down her arm at the memory of the skeletal face in the mirror. It seemed as if it looked right at her before the smoke burst through the glass, devouring the cloaked figure in its wake. She couldn't tell if the cloaked figure was a man or a woman, but whoever it was sent a shiver down her spine. If this was the powerful being

Antoine sensed, she wasn't sure she wanted to tell him. What if it was the dark witch in the mirror? The one who devoured the poor man in the torn plaid trousers and was now out traipsing around Halifax in her conjurer's body?

Emma knew they'd all had a past with darkness, but this seemed like a new thing altogether. One she wanted no part in. The face of nightmares that reflected from that mirror was forever etched in her memory, and she was confident she'd be unable to sleep for a while. And who was in the cape that had conjured it?

"Nein!" Franziska cried from outside.

Emma sat up once again, this time taking care not to bump her head, and swung her legs over the side of the bunk. She climbed down the wooden ladder. The small caravan was only big enough to fit two stacked bunks on either side of the long rectangle with one foldable cot tucked out of the way for Artus, the youngest of the Beaumont brothers, to sleep next to the panthers. Absinthe and Kizmet would always protest if he didn't sleep close to them. It was cute, really, but Emma much preferred the sleeping arrangements during milder weather when they could sleep in their own separate tents. It was difficult enough to sleep with Timur's snoring without the slew of nightmares witnessing the previous nights' events would likely bring.

A loud bang shook the entire caravan. Emma swayed, nearly stumbling over her own feet. What was going on out there? She stuffed her boots on and wrapped herself tightly in a wool blanket before turning the latch to the caravan's door. It squealed open. The bright light flooded in, and she squinted.

"WATCH OUT!" Artus cried from somewhere overhead when something sharp and scruffy smacked her in the face.

"Careful, Artus, you hit poor Emma." Franziska rushed to her side. "Are you all right?"

"Yeah, I'm—" she scrunched her nose, fighting a sneeze as she stepped out into the morning light. "—ah, I'm fine. What's going on? And what *was* that?"

She looked over her shoulder to find the source. One side of a long garland made of evergreens and holly berries lay on the ground by the caravan's back wheel while the other dangled from the roof. Artus stood on top of the vehicle with a hammer in one hand. Timur stood on the opposite end, struggling to secure the garland.

"Isn't it wonderful?" Franziska clasped her porcelain hands together, bringing them to rest on her lips. "We wanted to decorate for the season before Antoine returns."

Her snow-white hair caught the sunlight just right, reminding Emma of diamonds as they lay in perfect ringlets cascading from a high bun on the top of her head.

Franziska turned to Emma. "We were going to surprise you too, but Artus here"—she waved up at him with a grin — "couldn't catch the garland!"

Artus ran a hand through his long, black hair with a sigh. "*Es tut mir so leid, mein Schatz*." Artus winked, swinging his arm that held the hammer across his waist and bowing low.

Franziska harrumphed. "You are most certainly not sorry, and I'm not your *darling*. I should never have taught you that word."

Emma giggled at their banter before taking in the sight of their work. She'd never had a proper Christmas. Not really. In her old life, she'd never had the opportunity to celebrate. Her father was always drunk and her mother always said she didn't deserve to partake in any Yuletide festivities. She'd been forced to spend her holiday working in the butcher shop alongside her abusive father. She grimaced at the memory. After running away from her terrible life as the butcher's daughter and joining the *Beaumont Bros Circus*, she swore that she would never touch a meat grinder again.

A thrill of excitement rushed through her at the thought of finally experiencing her first Christmas with her new family.

"Where's Antoine?" Emma asked, picking up the fallen garland from the fresh powder of white snow that blanketed the campsite and the nearby forest of Deadman's Island.

She looked up just in time to catch Franziska's wince. Something was going on, and from the way she glanced at Artus, it wasn't good.

"He went to town to fetch the last ingredient for my homemade stollen," Franziska replied and masked her face with a smile. "It's a Christmas tradition! It wouldn't be the same without it. Oh, and one last patrol. He's so very close to finding the poor soul."

She returned to the campfire; a black kettle sat perched on the burning logs next to a frying pan of steaming eggs.

At the mention of patrolling, the black coal eyes of the lady in the mirror flashed within Emma's mind, and her breath hitched. How was it possible for someone to come out of a mirror only to possess another? And what were those symbols the hooded figure had drawn in blood? It seemed like magic, but not one that anyone should have. To Emma, it looked more like witchcraft.

She wracked her memory just trying to recall the name the hooded figure had called the old hag. It sounded German, but she couldn't quite remember. A Frau something. Burlap perhaps? Should she even mention it to the others? Her gut instinct was that she should, but a part of her didn't want to worry Franziska and ruin a perfect morning. And what if they thought she'd gone mad?

But if she didn't, and something terrible happened, she would never forgive herself. She would just have to swallow her own fear.

"Franziska?" Emma asked, mustering the courage to ask

as she tossed the garland up to Artus, who caught it in one fell swoop.

"Hmm?" Franziska glanced up while picking up the kettle to fill the tin mugs with black coffee.

She took one of the filled mugs and stretched it out towards Emma, who took the proffered mug before taking a seat across from her circus mum. Breathing in the rich and nutty aroma as it steamed from the cup, she smiled as it warmed the chill from her bones. She squeezed the tin handle in to calm her jittering nerves.

"What is it?" Franziska prodded, furrowing her slender brows with concern. "Is everything all right?"

Emma bit her lip. "Do you believe in witchcraft?"

Franziska blinked several times. "Well, I believe there are those who practice, I'm sure, but do I think they hold any real power? Nein, none at all. Why do you ask?"

Emma took a hasty sip of the coffee, gasping as the hot liquid burned the roof of her mouth. "What about"—she gulped, her stomach doing a million backflips — "a Frau witch? One that can be released with a spell?"

The older woman's eyes widened as a wide grin spread across her face. "A Frau witch? Like Frau Perchta?"

Emma nodded. Her cheeks burned when Franziska erupted into a fit of laughter, and her heart plummeted.

"What's so funny?" Artus asked, leaping down from the caravan, followed by Timur.

They joined the women around the fire. Emma grimaced, now wishing she'd never opened her mouth.

Franziska wiped the tears from her eyes, handing the two men their mugs of coffee. "Oh, Emma was just reminding me of an old fairy tale from my childhood."

Timur took a seat beside Emma and produced a vial from his pocket with crimson liquid, tossing a few drops in the mug. His eyes flashed blood-red with anticipation before locking eyes with Emma. "Would you like some?"

Emma swallowed hard. It'd been so long since her last transition, she almost forgot the full moon would be upon them soon, and if she didn't partake in the vampire's ritual, she'd lose herself like she had when she first received her powers.

Though it was this darkness that gave her the strength to leave her old life, it was also what took a piece of her soul. A pit formed in her belly at the memory of her first kill after giving in to the demon within. She couldn't risk it. Not with whatever was possessing that hooded figure on the loose.

She grabbed the vial. "Thank you."

As she took a sip of the coffee sprinkled with hints of metallic, the moon pulled at her heart, urging her to abstain. But with each swallow, the tug lessened until it became a tiny hum in the distance.

"What fairy tale?" She asked with a defensive edge to it.

Franziska's features softened. "You asked about Frau Perchta, the Christmas witch."

"And what is this Christmas witch?" Artus asked, scooping a helping of the eggs onto a plate. His two panthers must've smelt the food while hunting because as soon as Artus sat down, the two felines leapt from the surrounding woods and took their positions at either side of him.

Artus arched a brow as Kizmet and Absinthe gave him an expectant side glance. "Oh, did you want some of this?"

Kismet let out a moan, and Artus slumped his shoulders, unable to say no to their begging eyes, and tossed them both a few bites.

"Well, from what I remember, the tale goes like this. There once was a goddess," Franziska began, leaning forward in her seat and widening her eyes. "A beautiful white maiden born, she was. Each Yuletide, she guided the departed safely from the land of the living to their afterlife. This journey took every soul across the bridge of decision and through the underworld.

But on one Christmas night, the world changed for the goddess forever. A hexenmann—or, rather, a man witch in English—known as Krampus, the son of Hel herself, was sent to seduce the poor maiden and turn her against mankind."

"Upon their first kiss," Franziska continued, "a spell upon Krampus's lips cursed the goddess. It turned her heart to coal. On that day, she fell from grace and was stripped of her beauty. It transformed her into the image of Krampus, the Christmas demon. Her skin aged a thousand years, her beautiful mane fading to grey, and a pair of devil horns replaced her crown of holly upon her head."

Franziska pointed her index fingers on either side of her forehead, twisting her eyes as she made a growling noise.

Artus snorted and nearly spilt his coffee as the rest of them laughed.

"Why was she cursed?" Timur asked.

"Jealousy, of course." Franziska rested her hands in her lap. "Eons ago, Hel, the queen of the underworld, was cursed to remain in Niflheim, unable to roam the land of the living for all eternity. She wanted Frau Perchta's powers, the ability to travel between worlds again and only by turning the maiden's heart as black as rot could she succeed."

"What happened after Krampus turned her? Did Hel get what she wanted?" Emma gripped her coffee mug so tightly her knuckles turned as white as the snow that surrounded them.

"She got that and more." Franziska's eyes sparkled with delight. "It is said that Hel created her greatest weapon that day. Frau Perchta rises from the dead during the twelvetide beginning on the twenty-fifth day of December seeking hearts that are as lazy and deceitful as Krampus was to her."

Emma's face turned ashen, remembering what the hooded figure had requested. Revenge. But upon who? Then she remembered that it wasn't the twenty-fifth yet. Chills swept down her arms, realizing that part of the myth must not have been true.

Franziska leaned forward. "And there's nothing that upsets Frau Perchta more than leaving a mess for her to clean. They say that if, when the season is over, your garland isn't put up, and your flax isn't spun, she'll creep into your bed on the twelfth night of Christmas, gut you of your stomach, and replace your bowels with hay!"

Emma's back stiffened.

"Oh, but not to worry," Franziska said, letting out a lighthearted chuckle. "It's just a children's story meant to scare the youth into obedience."

"It's quite the story," Artus replied.

"That it is!" Franziska shook her head, chuckling to herself. "I hadn't thought of it in years."

Timur cleared his throat. "It reminds me of the ones told to keep the humans from the Ubir Janissary camps during the Ottoman Empire."

This took Emma by surprise, and the three of them gaped at the old vampire. They all knew he referred to vampires as Ubir and that he'd once been a soldier in the Janissary Corp but had no idea they had specific armies filled with vampires. It was also quite uncharacteristic of him to share his past so openly.

Timur stopped mid-sip, glancing between them. "What? Is Franziska the only one who can be nostalgic during this time of year?"

Emma bit back a smile. Jokes weren't his strong suit.

"Well, I think not," Franziska said with a nod. "It's all very sentimental. But I must ask, Emma, wherever did you hear of Frau Perchta?"

"I can't imagine too many know of her in these parts," Artus commented in between bites of food.

Not knowing what to say, Emma folded her lips over her teeth. She feared they would make fun of her, but she was sure it was Frau Perchta that the hooded figure conjured last night.

She finally expelled the breath she'd been holding. "I think I saw her. Last night."

Five pairs of eyes, including the panthers, froze on her. Emma's cheeks flushed with heat, and she lowered her gaze to her coffee, now cold.

Franziska frowned. "What do you mean? Where? How?"

"Last night while on patrol," she began, refusing to meet their inquisitive stares. "When we split up, I saw something."

She finally lifted her eyes, pleading for understanding. "At first, she was just in the mirror, but someone in a black cape began to chant. The window was opened just a crack, and I could hear the words they spoke. German, I think. I can't be sure, but I know the name. I heard the hooded figure call the hag in the mirror Frau Perchta."

Artus and Franziska shared a concerned glance.

"Emma," Franziska replied, her voice soft and patient. "It was late. Maybe it was just your imagination?"

"Besides, Antoine would've sensed if someone supernatural was nearby," Artus added. "That's what we were out there for."

"I swear it's true." Emma's heart sank as her fear became a reality. They didn't believe her. Why couldn't they trust her enough on this to take her word for it? She knew what she'd witnessed.

"Or perhaps it was the full moon's effects?" Timur offered, his eyes drawn downward and hidden behind his chin-length curls, but Emma was confident she saw a flash of doubt cross them.

She blinked back the moisture that sprung up as a knot of betrayal formed in her stomach.

"No." She stood. "I know what I saw."

"Frau Perchta is just a myth." Franziska rose from the log beside the fire, raising her hands gently as she tried to persuade Emma.

Just then, the slosh of hooves against the snow-covered path pulled their attention to the approaching steed.

"Whoa there," Antoine, the eldest of the Beaumont brothers, hollered and pulled the reins in to slow the horse from its gallop.

He trotted up to the campfire and dismounted with a flourish and let his horse graze alongside Clement, the other steed which was Emma's favourite.

Antoine stretched his tall, lengthy frame before tucking his black top hat in the crook of his elbow.

"Antoine!" Franziska rushed to his side, greeting him with a kiss.

When she stepped back, Emma couldn't help but notice the briefest of whispers shared between them. What was going on? Did something happen on his morning patrol? Before she could ask, the moment was over, and their furrowed brows and frowns were replaced with strained smiles.

Emma glared at Artus, trying to demand answers with her eyes, but he flicked his gaze back down to his coffee. Why were they keeping her in the dark? And from what?

"My, what do we have here?" Antoine stood back to take in the caravan's holiday dressings.

"Doesn't the caravan look wonderful?" Franziska asked.

"It's absolutely divine," he agreed, slinking his arm around her waist and spinning her around in a warm embrace.

Franziska let out a gleeful laugh. "Timur and Artus helped

me with the garland and the wreath I made this morning, of course—oh, but did you get the nutmeg?"

"Of course, my dearest." Antoine snuck a small parcel from his pocket.

Franziska's eyes lit up as if he'd just proposed. "Oh, Antoine, you've truly saved Christmas."

"I know who your new recruit is," Emma said, gaining Antoine's attention. "Well, at least *what* it is, anyway."

"Sorry?" Antoine drew his eyebrows together.

"Emma," Franziska sighed.

"Did I miss something?" Antoine glanced between the two women before eyeing his brother, Artus, and the vampire Timur for answers.

"A lot." Artus shook his head, passing Antoine a plate of food as he brushed by. He whistled to Absinthe and Kizmet, still lounging by the fire. "Come on, you two, let's go find somewhere fun to explore."

"It's a witch called Frau Perchta." Emma lifted her chin. "I saw someone conjure her last night."

Antoine shook his head. "Emma, I found who we've been searching for."

"What?" Emma glanced between the rest of the circus members, but she seemed to be the only one who was shocked by the news. "And you all *knew?*"

The sudden stab of betrayal sent her eyes watering. Not only did they not believe her warning of Frau Perchta, but they'd kept secrets from her and for what?

"We didn't want to worry you," Franziska said as if sensing her spiralling thoughts.

"Worry me? I'm already worried, and you won't listen," she cried. "So, if I'm not to worry about Frau Perchta, then what?"

"From the fact that soon we will no longer be safe in Halifax," Antoine said, gravelly.

Emma furrowed her brows and swatted a tear away. "What do you mean?"

She hated this public display, more frustrated than anything that once again she felt like the outsider to the group. Though a part of her knew it was only because they cared about her, it still wasn't fair.

"I've discovered that the one I've sensed is a prisoner of Halifax, and..." he trailed, setting his hat on the log beside Timur and picking up an extra mug of coffee. "Well, he's not keeping his power a secret. Which poses a true threat to us."

"They're calling him the devil," Franziska added.

Timur grunted, slurping his mug. The tangy notes of his blood creamer prickled Franziska's nose, and she grimaced.

"The devil? Why?" Emma's heart clenched.

They'd just started practising a winter performance that included her. She'd finally get a chance to stand alongside her family and show off her light manipulation to the world under the pretence of a magic trick. She'd promised Detective Barnaby Grey a front-row seat. She hated the thought of leaving before she'd had the chance to keep it.

"Because of his power," Antoine replied, taking a sip of coffee. "It seems they tried to have him hanged for his crimes, but he didn't die."

"He got away?" Emma asked.

Antoine shook his head. "That's what's more disturbing. Though he appears to have the power to do so, he let them take him back to prison. The town is now calling for him to be burned at the stake for the use of magic."

"And if we're discovered...." Franziska looked away, unable to finish that thought.

Antoine cleared his throat. "If we are, then we could be next."

Emma shivered that had nothing to do with her standing ankle-deep in snow. The whole situation reminded her of a modern-day witch hunt. Her stomach knotted up at the image of the entire town coming after them with fiery pitchforks.

Though she was confident Detective Grey would do something to stop that from happening somehow. Perhaps he'd be able to convince the town that they weren't a danger to them. At least Detective Grey understood that those with magic were better together. The Beaumonts didn't succumb to the darkness as often as they did before when they were alone because now they had a family. A place to belong.

"We won't leave right away," Antoine continued. "It is our duty to reach out to the prisoner, though we'll have to be much more careful now. Once we've done that, I'll make arrangements to leave as soon as possible."

"But where will we go?" Franziska asked.

"I don't know," Antoine replied. "We'll have to wait and see what the future decides to reveal to me."

Emma was sure the future included death. The image of the witch with goat horns possessing the cloaked figure flashed in Emma's mind once again. She cringed at the memory of the witch killing that young man in plaid by shoving him into a mirror before it shattered. What had she called it? A living tomb?

The thought of what this witch might do next sent a shiver down her spine. It wasn't only them who were in trouble. With such a powerful witch on the loose, the whole town was at risk. Then another thought made her swallow hard. What if the witch was the very prisoner they were visiting?

The implications of what this could mean for them sent her mind racing. But what could she do? Antoine and Franziska didn't even believe her.

"It will take some time to figure out how to get to the prisoner, won't it?" Franziska asked.

"I'm afraid so. He will most likely be heavily guarded." Antoine took a seat as he discussed the various possibilities of sneaking into the Halifax jail.

Emma barely heard them as her mind sprung to life with a half-baked plan.

"This city is in grave danger," she said, and the two closest circus members looked at her. "Frau Perchta *is* real. First, I'm going to prove it, and then I'm going to stop her."

Before any of the Beaumont circus members could respond, Emma bounded towards Clement. They watched in stunned silence as she snatched the reins and mounted the unsaddled horse. She didn't care, she just had to get to town as fast as she could.

"Ya!" Emma nudged the steed gently with her heel, and the horse broke into a gallop away from their camp.

She left the others in a dust of snow as she aimed for the main road. She knew what she'd seen and, even if the circus didn't believe her, she had a pretty good idea of who might. Their lives, along with the whole town, depended on it.

3
HARK THE HERALD

Barnaby Grey's Flat,
Grafton Street

"BALLS!" Wilson groaned and scratched out the error in his note before crumpling the paper altogether and tossing it into the growing pile in the bin next to the desk.

It hit the corner of the overstuffed container and tumbled to the wood-planked floor. Wilson flared his nostrils with a huff, picking the paper back up. A mess wouldn't help him in his investigation one bit. Quite the contrary, if he were to leave the waste out of place, it would nag him to all ends.

With the meticulous precision of a doctor, he folded the piece of paper and smashed it in with the rest of the rubbish. He was in the middle of tracing out the last known sightings of Madam Onay, the woman he believed to be John Walsh's partner-in-crime in the murder of the town's beloved bachelor and heir to the Talmage fortune.

After the arrest of John Walsh, she'd vanished into thin air, or so it would seem, and he was confident this was an indication of her guilt. Although he'd been heavily drugged by some type of narcotic that made him see what his partner Barnaby called 'magic', he *swore* he'd seen Madam Onay with them. John Walsh had to have some sort of accomplice there waiting in that alley while he lured the two detectives there. He was certain it was her. He just needed to find her so he could prove it and have her arrested.

Of course, John Walsh had been less than forthright every time he went to question him at the Halifax jail. And now, since his failed hanging, the authorities moved him out of the police station to a top-secret cell. No one had any clue where it was, which, of course, could only mean one place; the prison located underneath the Governor's mansion and impossible to visit without suspicion. The town was convinced John Walsh had demonic powers and now called him the devil to make matters worse.

Wilson rolled his eyes. They were all fools to believe in such theatrics. It was probably all orchestrated by Madam Onay anyway. It would only take a mixture of a potent hallucinogen and an incompetent chief inspector. Thankfully he'd been replaced since then, though he had yet to meet this new inspector to gauge if he was any better.

But that could wait. According to the *Acadian Recorder,* the clock was ticking down the days to the second attempt to execute John Walsh. He was to be burned at the stake for the use of magic. Wilson ground his teeth at the preposterous idea. Magic didn't exist, and the barbaric punishment was entirely unnecessary. If he could just find Madam Onay and dispel the town's belief that John Walsh was the devil, then the two could be tried together in an orderly fashion.

He just needed to determine her daily routine and those who knew her best, then he was certain he'd be able to locate exactly where she was hiding.

"The murder of the foundry's heir, one Irvin Talmage, Jr."

Wilson jotted down on the fresh piece of paper in a neat scrawl, tacking it to the map on Hollis and Prince Street. "Then she ran south"—he traced the map with the tip of his index finger — "back into the Halifax Club, through the secret door into the auction house, and out onto Granville before 'disappearing'."

At least that's what Barnaby swore happened, but Wilson knew she must've used the same drug that John Walsh had. She could've easily dosed them with it if it were airborne—while wearing some sort of protective apparatus—and kept running until the effects set in. Then while he and Barnaby were hallucinating, she would have vanished out and intp the throngs of people on the street.

"Definitely plausible because"—Wilson scribbled 'sighting' on another piece of parchment before stabbing it onto the map — "Mr Kirkham of the Acadian Recorder said he'd spotted her minutes later."

So, not magic as Barnaby would like to think, Wilson thought to himself with a smug chuckle.

"Ahem."

Wilson barely glanced over his shoulder at Barnaby. He stood by the front door, his thick fingers gripping a giant book in one hand and his bowler hat in the other.

"Don't you look dreary," he said, noting the unusually dark suit his colleague donned before he flitted back to his work. "Not that I'm complaining; your garish vests aren't quite easy on the eyes."

"Did you forget?"

"Hmm? Wilson stabbed another tack into the mass of paper and scribbles blanketing the map.

"The *funeral*? It's today."

Wilson arched an impeccably trimmed brow. "And?"

"*And* you need to be preparing."

"For what?"

Barnaby guffawed. "Oh, I don't know, perhaps the *funeral* for the Talmage's only son?"

"And why do I need to be in attendance?"

"Well," Barnaby scoffed. "It's not as if the whole town will be there or anything."

His sarcasm wasn't lost on Wilson, but he still didn't see how that had anything to do with him. If the whole town was there, why bother? It wasn't as if the family would be left wanting.

When Wilson didn't budge from the desk, he continued, "I guess to you it is only the son of the foundry owner, but to the town, he was a very beloved young man. So, it wouldn't be right to miss it. Some would even call it a slight."

"Fine." Wilson rolled his eyes. "But the obituary stated it would commence at half-past ten, and it's barely eight."

"Yes, and I was hoping to run an errand along the way, but I guess there is no need for you to accompany me there." Barnaby placed the hat atop his head. "But I do hope to see you at the service."

"Yes, yes, but dear Barnaby!" Wilson called after Barnaby just as he was about to close the door behind him.

Barnaby sighed, pausing at the door.

"I am curious." Wilson turned to face his old colleague with a sheepish grin. He placed his elbows on top of the map, resting his fingers under his chin. "Will the service be so dull as to require that piece of fiction in your possession?"

"This?" Barnaby glanced down at the leatherbound book. "It is part of my errand. And *The Complete Compendium of Bestien and Magic* is not fiction. If you must know, there are beasts in this world and I intend to educate myself as best I can. I'd suggest you do the same if I thought you'd listen to me."

With that, Barnaby spun on his heel and slammed the door on his way out. Wilson shook his head. He worried about his friend. If the town got wind that their resident private detective was caught up in the supernatural, he feared what they might do. But, unfortunately, his colleague was determined. There was little good he could do now aside from concentrating on the investigation at hand. So, with a shrug of his shoulders, he returned his attention to the map before him.

BARNABY LET OUT a puff of air, aggravated by Wilson's constant taunts. He'd teased him ever since Barnaby started studying the paranormal. But, after that day in the alleyway, when Emma had helped him say goodbye to his dear nephew before he moved on to wherever ghosts went to in the afterlife, he knew in his heart magic was real. No matter how many times Wilson repeated his theory that they'd been drugged with a smidge of Lophophora cactus, or some other concoction known to have hallucinogenic properties, Barnaby didn't believe this for one second.

For one, he had no idea how one would get their hands on the plant as it was predominantly native to South America. Secondly, it couldn't have been this due to their lack of vomiting and other common side-effects of the devil's root. And lastly, they'd seen *and* heard the same things. A hallucinogen couldn't do that. At least that's not what Dr Larson said when Barnaby sought him out for consultation to further his argument against Wilson's theory.

Little good it did. Wilson still refused to believe him, and the book didn't help matters much. But it wasn't all for not. His efforts had led him to find the exotic bookshop tucked away on a quiet corner just off Sackville. He would never have found it if it weren't for his stubborn efforts in finding irrefutable proof that magic existed. However, Barnaby began to think that Wilson still wouldn't believe even if he witnessed the Beaumont circus perform. He would simply say it must be an illusion or some other reasonable explanation. But not even that would happen, as it would take a miracle to get Wilson to step even a foot in the same room as one of those circus folk without him putting one of them in handcuffs.

Barnaby shook his head at the mess of it all, buttoning his sack coat and tightening his wool scar before he pushed his way out the front door and onto Grafton Street. The crisp winter air greeted him, and hooves clapped against the cobbled street, punctuating the otherwise soundless morning. Not even a foghorn called from the bay.

The sun beamed down overhead as if to mock the town of Halifax as all prepared to mourn their beloved Irvin Talmage, Jr. Yes, today would be quite a difficult day. But, first, he needed to get to *Engel's Exotic Books & Herbal Emporium* before the funeral. He'd found something while doing his usual early morning reading from the book he'd bought from them that required clarification that couldn't wait.

He shivered, his breath trailing behind him in puffs of white smoke as he bounded down the powdery white sidewalk towards the shop owned by the Engel's, a brother and sister sibling duo. They'd recently opened the store, the only shop he knew of in town that offered a variety of rare books from all over the world curated by Mr Roderic Engel himself. His sister, Gertrud, ran the herbal counter, and together they managed the business that Barnaby had stumbled upon in his search of occult literature.

At first, meeting them, he couldn't believe the two were siblings. Mr Roderic Engel was a petite fellow, and Gertrud's slender frame towered in comparison. Yet, they shared the same unusual white hair for their age and identical bulbous tipped noses. Barnaby thought it resembled much of

Franziska's features and wondered if there was any relation. But, of course, that would be too much of a coincidence.

The shop was a marvellous commodity where one could even purchase a variety of teas to sip on while perusing the many rows of shelves filled to the brim with volumes.

The section dedicated to myths and legends was his particular favourite which is where he'd found the rare book he now held in his hands. Surprisingly enough, neither of the Engel siblings gave him any strange looks when purchasing the compendium. They seemed even eager to answer all of his questions about the supernatural as if they were true believers. It was one of the reasons why he felt at ease seeking their counsel on the chapter he'd just read on a bestien species called a Hexengeist—or rather a 'witch spirit'—and he had many questions. He had to translate a lot of the book from German, which made reading and understanding two very different things. Good thing he still had a rudimentary grasp of the language.

His shoe slipped on a bit of ice while turning to cut down Prince Street when he caught a glimpse of crimson hair. It took a second glance to realize it was none other than Emma flying by horseback through the sleigh tracks that zigzagged down the street.

"Detective Grey!" She hailed, coming to a halt in front of him. Her voice was breathless, and her countenance was as frenzied as her hair was frizzy.

Barnaby blinked several times before it finally clicked that she was addressing him. "Emma! This is quite a shock. Is everything alright?"

"Yes. Well, no. I was hoping to speak to you about"—the girl shifted to put her back to a group of women in mourning shrouds as they swept by — "something supernatural."

The women glanced back, and Barnaby swore if eyes

could kill, he'd surely be dead. They were probably a few of the townsfolk who believed all magic was dark and evil now that John Walsh had exposed his power. They were calling him the devil. The prisoner was creating such a terrible name for the magical community. Not that he knew too many in that community, but he knew enough to know that not all with magic were bad.

"But perhaps this isn't a good time." Emma bit her lip and clasped her hands behind her back.

"No, no, no." Barnaby smiled, shaking off the thought of giving those judgmental women a piece of his mind. "For you, I've always a spare moment. However, we should probably not stand out here in the cold and look! You don't even have a coat. You must be positively freezing."

"It's fine," she said with a nervous laugh, her eyes darting about as if something would leap out and snatch her at any second. "I naturally run a bit warmer as the full moon nears."

Barnaby frowned, not certain what she meant by that, but chose not to ask as she seemed all in a bother about something. "Come, I know a place close by where we can speak in private."

He took the reins from the young girl, guiding them down the street to the front of the shop. He tied the horse around a post and motioned for Emma to follow him inside but stopped in his tracks when he turned to the door.

A large piece of paper was tacked to the entrance with the words' Devil Worshipers' written across it in red ink. He bit his cheek, letting out an aggravated sigh. The gull of people and their prejudices. He stormed to the door and ripped the hideous message down.

"What is that?" Emma asked, poking her head around to see for herself.

Barnaby crumpled the paper before she could read it.

"Nothing," he said, straightening his jacket. He pushed the door open. "Right this way."

The little bell jingled behind them, and the wind howled in the distance when the door clicked shut. They were welcomed by the warmth of the shop. Rows of towering shelves stretched up to the ceiling and framed the single aisle leading to the front counter where books and tea could be purchased.

To their immediate right, a few tables and chairs stood in front of the glistening bay windows and a few reading nooks, while to their left stood more rows filled to the brim with books.

"Be with you in a minute, Detective Grey!" A woman's pleasant accent and deep contralto greeted them from somewhere behind the tall counter.

Emma glanced around in search of the woman. "Who was that?"

"Miss Gertrud Engel, one of the siblings who own the place."

"How did she know it was you?"

"I find it best not to ask." Barnaby waved towards the tables. "Why don't you have a seat, and I shall order us some tea?"

"Thank you," Emma said.

Her eyes watered for a second before she blinked the moisture away and promptly found a seat next to the window.

What could possibly have upset Emma so that she would rush here all the way from Deadman's Island by herself? Was it the townsfolk? Had their campsite been attacked? His eyes flitted upwards, praying none of the Beaumont circus members was hurt.

The hair on the back of his neck prickled at the anticipation of more bad news. But first the tea. Something of the chamomile variety seemed prudent.

"Detective Grey, you're back!" She popped her head out from behind the counter, her milky-white hair swept back into a stylish bun that accentuated her diamond-shaped face and angular cheekbones.

"How are you, Miss Engel?"

"Splendid, and how is our fine detective?"

He pinked. "I'm well, thank you. You're too kind."

"And you're too bashful," she added with a radiant smile, wiping off a brown powdery substance on her nose that dotted her otherwise flawless skin. Probably the culprit of mixing spices.

Her infectious joy sent Barnaby's heart racing. But then he remembered the hateful sign still wadded up in his pocket, and his stomach knotted. How could he deliver such bad news to such a kind and beautiful woman? The thought of it gutted him.

"How did you find the compendium?"

"Enlightening, to be sure." He returned her smile, deciding it best not to mention the note. "Though I do have some questions for your brother. Also"—Barnaby rested his fingertips on the maple counter and eyed the first thing with chamomile on the menu drawn up on the chalkboard behind the towering woman — "might I have today's special?"

"But of course." Gertrud winked, her chin rising infinitesimally before bustling about the counter for teacups and saucers. "It's my very own blend with a touch of lavender as well. Just the one?"

"Two, please."

"Ah, wonderful." She winked again, and he flushed at the implication.

"My niece," he blurted.

"How lovely," she replied. "I'll bring them to you."

Suddenly feeling hot, he couldn't bring himself to look Miss Engel in the eye as he fumbled for a few bills.

"Thank you." He tossed the money onto the counter and raced back to where he left Emma before he could embarrass himself further.

She hadn't moved an inch since he left her, sitting stiff-backed at the table. Her eyes darted wildly out the window, seemingly unaware that her knee repeatedly bounced under the table. As soon as she spotted him, she scooted the chair back. It nearly toppled to the floor.

"I really can't sit like this, not with that thing out there." She leaned towards the exit. "I must show you where I saw it."

Barnaby rubbed his forehead. "Emma, please. I don't have much time for my errand before I must make an appearance at a *funeral* this morning so let us sit until you've caught me up with whatever it is that's distressing you."

"I'm sorry." Emma dipped her head down, flushing.

"Don't be. I'm always here for you," he said, motioning for her to sit back down. "It's really the least I can do after you helped me say goodbye to my dear nephew."

He placed the book on the table between them. Just then, the tea was brought on a tray by the lovely Gertrud. If this were any other time and Barnaby wasn't in a rush, he would've prodded Emma to see if she saw the resemblance between Miss Engel and her guardian, Franziska. But now was not the time.

"Now," Barnaby began once Gertrud was out of earshot. "You said this had something to do with the supernatural, yes? Do tell me."

Emma's lip trembled, her eyes growing distant as if she were reliving whatever had befallen her. From the sweat that built up near her brow, Barnaby couldn't imagine it was anything good.

"It isn't"—Barnaby's voice faltered — "I mean, no one's died, have they?"

Emma swallowed hard. "Sort of. I don't know, but I think so. It's..."

She trailed, setting her tea back on its saucer. She looked back out through the window at the pearly white street before locking eyes back on Barnaby with a renowned focus.

"You believe in ghosts now, of course," she said, more of a statement than a question and leaned forward. "But do you believe there are... spirits?"

Barnaby drew his eyebrows inward. "Aren't they one and the same?"

"No. I mean, yes, they are, but I was more referring to *evil* spirits that can possess people."

He blinked. If he hadn't seen the power the *Beaumont Bros. Circus* had for himself, he wouldn't have humoured this conversation. But he had, and he knew that if the good power like the circus existed and the evil that was John Walsh who murdered his nephew existed, couldn't there be other forces of evil out there? But to possess people, that was a foreign concept to him. Before he'd started reading the compendium, of course.

"What type of evil have you witnessed?"

"I'm not quite sure what kind, but I think someone was murdered last night."

Barnaby shivered. "Are you certain?"

"Yes." She sucked in air. "You know that Antoine has this ability, the one that allows him to sense those with powers and sometimes locate them?"

Barnaby nodded, despite this being the first he'd heard of Antoine's ability.

"Well, we were out scouting out this one particular power and"—she blinked rapidly as if she could hardly believe what she was about to say — "I saw someone in the window of this abandoned house."

"It wasn't the old McLeod House, was it? Across from the Governor's grounds?"

That house had always given him the jitters ever since he'd heard the rumours of how it had become abandoned. After the father died, the McLeod family were never the same. The mother grew mad. She killed her three children in a heartbroken rage before she plunged the dagger through her own heart.

No one could bring themselves to renovate the place, so there it stood, vacant and ominous. A pillar to the madness that had created its state. It was said that one could still hear the moans of the children at night. Perhaps some type of poltergeist. But, honestly, he didn't understand why the Governor hadn't yet seized the place and torn it down. He and Wilson would pass by it often whenever they had a question for Dr Larson. His office was a few buildings down the street.

"Maybe?" Emma shrugged. "I can't be sure, but none of the other homes was as barren or rundown as this one."

Barnaby's back stiffened. "Then it must be the one."

"Anyway," Emma continued, drawing Barnaby's thoughts back to the table. "This man, or woman, I really couldn't tell from the disguise they wore, was standing in a circle of strange symbols drawn on the floor in front of a mirror."

"A *mirror*? How odd."

She nodded. "The man in the cloak recited an incantation that made a witch come out of it."

Chills swept up Barnaby's arms. He'd just read something in the compendium about a witch spirit that could be trapped within mirrors. But was it possible for them to escape them? And, if so, what kind of witch spirit was it? He couldn't remember but figured it'd be rude to start digging through his book while Emma was talking, so he sat quietly and listened.

She went into great detail about the previous night's events. Barnaby's stomach quivered at the mention of the blood being forced down a poor lad's mouth before he was shattered in a million pieces of glass. When she finally finished, he rested his elbows on the table. He fiddled with a bit of his goatee that was starting to come in while he thought.

After a few moments, he asked, "And what did this spell sound like?"

"I don't know." She clutched her teacup so tightly Barnaby was certain they'd go numb.

"It was foreign to me, except for a name." Emma widened her eyes. "Frau Perchta. That's what's possessing this... this practitioner or whatever you call a human who does magic."

"A mage? Or a witch?" Barnaby's stomach somersaulted at the thought of someone practising such dark magic in their little town. What sort of danger would this bring upon them?

It didn't help that most of Halifax's citizens were crying for a witch trial. If they knew a human practitioner was in their midst, how much worse would it get for Emma and her circus family?

He would help her any way he could, but he couldn't remember anything about there being a Frau Perchta in the compendium. Indeed, there had to be something that could help, though, right? After all, Frau Perchta was a Germanic name, and the compendium mostly contained bestien from that region. Perhaps Mr Engel would know.

Emma sat her teacup down with a clink. "When I told the others, they barely listened to me at all and just made a joke of it."

"Why would your family, of all people, make light of what you saw?"

Emma bit her cheek. "Franziska says this Christmas witch is just a fairy tale. An old ghost story told during yuletide to scare children into being good so they don't get gutted of their stomachs."

"Uh… erm." Barnaby brought a fist to his mouth and coughed against the hot tea that rushed down the wrong pipe.

He wasn't certain what she meant by 'gutted', but it didn't sound good. He cleared his throat, trying in vain to relax his sudden rock hard stomach.

"They tell this to *children*?"

"That's what Franziska said." She rested her elbows on the table. "And Antoine just went on about some kind of devil and the town's growing fear of magic."

"Ah, yes. That." He sighed.

"They think it's unsafe for us here and will probably move us away soon, but they don't understand. It's not safe here for *anyone*. Especially those without magic."

He frowned. "Why?"

"Because I heard what Frau Perchta wants. She's going to kill more people, Barnaby." Her voice cracked as tears brimmed her eyelids. "And I've no idea who or how to stop it. What if she comes after you, the town, or even that Detective Wilson Davies?"

She shook her head at the thought and Barnaby couldn't help but be moved. Her concern for him and his colleague who had once hunted her pulled at his heartstrings. The poor girl rested the weight of the world on her shoulders, a responsibility he firmly believed wasn't hers. She cared too profoundly, more than Wilson deserved, and was much too young to be burdened with such things. He pulled a kerchief from his breast pocket and handed it to her.

"I know this is all sounding strange." She dabbed her eyes.

"But I know that if I showed you the house and you saw the symbols that you'd believe me."

"I do," Barnaby said softly.

"You do?"

He nodded his reassurance. "I don't know what type of supernatural creature you saw, but I do believe you witnessed something terrible."

The glare from the window warned him time was getting late. He checked his pocket watch. There was barely an hour before the service commenced, which meant he wouldn't have time to stop by the McLeod House and get answers to his questions—if he could still remember what they were with the horrific thought of Frau Perchta and missing stomachs so fresh in his mind.

"I'll tell you what"—he clicked the gold clasp of the watch closed — "If you allow me a few hours, let's meet this afternoon. Then we can investigate the house together. Does that sound agreeable?"

Her features lifted, a sparkle of hope in her eye. "Of course. Thank you, Detective Grey."

"It's Barnaby to you, my dear," he reminded her.

"Yes, Detective Barnaby. And thank you for the tea."

She rose to her feet when he stood, but he waved his hand. "No need to rush off, I know the owners, and I'm sure they won't mind at all if you pass the time perusing for a while. Enjoy."

She tucked back into her seat. "Until the afternoon, then."

With one last wave, he retrieved his book and headed back to the counter to consult Mr Engel. He'd entirely forgotten his previous inquiries, save for one at the forefront of his mind. Was it possible for a human to have the power to conjure a spirit out of a mirror to possess them? And who was Frau Perchta? Was she a beast like the ones he'd read about in the compendium?

If so, he was confident nothing good would come out of a possessed human performing witchcraft around town. But, nevertheless, he was determined to find out everything he could about the subject. Whatever Emma saw, now that he was made aware of it, was his responsibility to solve. Even if the thought of true witchcraft sent him on the verge of losing his breakfast.

4
HERE WE COME A-WAILING

St. Paul's Episcopal Church,
Argyle Street

BARNABY HUFFED with disappointment as he made his way down the deserted sidewalk to the church. It turned out that while having tea, Mr Engel was off on an errand and wouldn't be back in the shop until the afternoon. He hated having to wait so long to get answers about Frau Perchta. The whole thing would eat at him all through the service.

"You're late," Wilson chided Barnaby, who scrambled around the empty Grand Parade to meet him at the foot of the stairs. "I've already received one too many dirty looks for one day."

"Yes, yes, I know. But, unfortunately, it couldn't be helped. Has the service started already?"

Wilson arched a brow at Barnaby when he attempted to obscure the compendium under his jacket. He didn't need to tarnish his name by giving the townsfolk any reason to think him mad.

"No, I believe they're all still congregating in the antechamber. Well, not everyone. I had to console this woman, a Miss Lauretta, who was absolutely beside herself with grief. Did you know she was uninvited to the funeral?"

"You mean the fiancée of the deceased?"

"That's the one."

Barnaby shook his head. "No, I didn't know that. I wonder why?"

"Who knows. The politics of that family astound me. Particularly their distaste for me when we both know I was a crucial part in putting their son's murderer, John Walsh, behind bars."

"But you forget about the ones you falsely accused," Barnaby added.

"I call those calculated risks. Besides, if they don't like me, they still know me as your colleague. Good thing this town of yours still likes you."

Barnaby grinned sheepishly. "Yes, I suppose it is."

"Well, chop, chop, then." Wilson clapped his hands and turned to ascend the stairs up to the church's double doors. "We are the last ones to arrive, and may I remind you that *you're* the one who desired to attend this performance."

Barnaby muttered to himself about it not being a performance but thanked the stars that Wilson didn't hear him. He froze on the last step when the bright blue hue of Wilson's shoes glittered in the sunlight.

"What on earth are *those*?" Barnaby demanded.

Wilson sighed at the top of the stairs and looked down at him. "Shoes, dear Barnaby. They are my shoes. Now, can we get on with this?" He gestured to the door.

"A bit *'garish'* as you like to say for a funeral, don't you think?"

"They are my lucky shoes." Wilson glared and yanked the door open for them.

The door thudded behind them. An itchy silence met the two detectives as a hundred pairs of eyes stared back at them. The foyer outside of the sanctuary was a sea of black veils and suits, the restless crowd cramped shoulder to shoulder waiting for the cathedral to open. Why would they make everyone stand out here? Barnaby didn't think it right, but what other choice did they have?

"Good morning," Wilson greeted a tearful Mrs Talmage with a bow and removed his top hat.

"My condolences," Barnaby added.

The poor woman barely looked up from her handkerchief, but her husband, Mr Talmage, wrapped his arms around her trembling shoulders and glared daggers at them. Barnaby grimaced, wondering if perhaps he'd been wrong about being in the town's good graces while they manoeuvred to the only space left in the stuffy foyer.

"You mean to tell me," Barnaby hissed, keeping his voice low when they were out of earshot from the Talmages. "That you can believe in lucky *shoes,* but when it comes to magic or John Walsh having any superpower whatsoever, you deem it preposterous?"

"Well, I—"

What was probably about to be a poor joke made at his own expense was quickly brought to a halt when Mrs Talmage shouted and broke away from her husband.

"THAT'S ENOUGH!" She swung her arms and stormed towards the doors leading into the sanctuary. "They can't keep us from paying our respects to our only son any longer."

"We must wait until the priest has summoned us." Mr Talmage's stiff frame moved as fast as he could after his determined wife.

She swung the double oak doors and stopped. A blood-curdling scream from the elderly woman sent a chill running down Barnaby's spine. The two detectives pushed past the curious crowd descending upon the poor woman to see what caused Mrs Talmage to produce such an awful sound.

The ceiling vaulted high above them, combined with the stained glass that depicted various scriptures, made for a rather grandiose impression. But it was the pulpit splattered with crimson droplets that oozed from the body slung over the top of it that caught Barnaby's attention and made him wish he'd never stepped foot in that bloody sanctuary.

"Dear God." He shuddered, growing still at the sight of uniformed police officers swarming the podium.

Mrs Talmage fell in a heap in the middle of the aisle, her eyes frozen on the body being peeled off the maple top. Even Mr Talmage seemed unnerved, resting his hand on his distraught wife's shoulders to provide support but unable to tear his eyes from the lifeless corpse. Whispers of this being the devil's work swept through the congregation. The priest moved about the congregation to share calming sentiments, but whispers of the devil's work spread like wildfire stirring up fear.

"See?" Wilson slapped Barnaby's back as he marched towards the crime scene with a confident stride. "These are my lucky shoes."

"Wilson!" Barnaby gaped after his partner, stunned by the terribly indelicate joke and ashamed at his apparent delightedness at the prospect of a new case.

They were detectives, but that didn't mean they had to be barbaric vultures. He shook his head and quickly bounded after Wilson, if only to keep him from embarrassing himself. However, now was not the time for theatrics. As he neared the podium, the damage to the body became clearer, which promptly brought Barnaby to a screeching halt at the foot of the crowded platform.

He sucked in air, the wild brown hair and a green scarf

tied around the dead woman's forehead triggering a memory. "Madam Onay!"

The very same woman Wilson was searching for, the one he believed to be the partner of John Walsh in the murder of Irvin Talmage, Jr, along with Barnaby's nephew and a few others. And, by the looks of the corpse of Madam Onay displayed at the exact time of the Talmage's funeral, Wilson probably wasn't the only one who thought so.

"You know this woman?" A man with reddish-grey mutton chops said.

Barnaby remembered him from the last town hall meeting as the new chief of police, Chief Inspector Plundell.

"Er... yes, sir. Well, sort of." He cleared his throat, tugging at his collar. "She worked at the Halifax Club as a..."

A kerplunk followed by a grunt drew the inspector's attention to the officers attempting the feat of moving the limp body. It flopped unceremoniously onto the stage floor at their feet. Barnaby let out a puff of air, glad he didn't have to admit to the chief inspector that he'd gone to see a psychic. It was one thing to admit to Wilson that he believed in magic, he didn't want the whole town to know just yet. Not until he had solid proof, at least.

"Careful, there!" Chief Inspector Plundell snapped at the officers, his cheeks reddening under his mutton chops. "This is still an active crime scene. Don't want you harming the evidence."

The inspector scowled, pivoting back to face Barnaby. "Well?"

"Uh, well y-yes, I do believe we've—"

"This woman's stomach has been cut open," Wilson called to them.

The chief inspector and Barnaby both turned on the detective, who now knelt beside the open.

"What do you mean cut open?" Barnaby asked breathlessly.

Wilson had brandished a pair of tweezers from a secret bed in his sapphire shoes.

Barnaby rolled his eyes. "Of course, you never know when you'll need to pull *that* from your boots."

"See, here." Wilson ignored his jibe and brought the tweezers to the woman's bodice where just at the naval, a small tear had been made.

He pulled at a small thread with the tweezers, and the cloth fell away, revealing a bruised chest so black and blue that it didn't resemble anything like a human body.

"Now, I'll have to compare my analysis with Dr Larson," Wilson continued, "but notice the crude yet delicate stitching around the entire lower abdomen?"

The purpling skin was cut jagged in a large circle, stitched tightly shut in most areas, but Barnaby quickly averted his gaze at the innards that peeked out from a corner of the woman's abdomen where the killer must've lacked time to finish.

"Our killer was in quite a hurry," Wilson said as if reading Barnaby's mind.

"What the hell do you think you're doing?" Chief Inspector Plundell addressed Wilson with indignation.

"I'm working, of course," Wilson replied.

Barnaby tuned out the two as they bickered about which one of them had jurisdiction as his conversation with Emma echoed in his mind.

Frau Perchta... guts you of your stomach... it's just a fairy tale... told at yuletide to scare so that they don't get gutted of their stomachs.

Barnaby held his belly, the contents of which lurched. Could it be? Was the culprit who did this the very demon Emma had just described to him? His mind spun at the possibility, pulling at his collar at the sudden heat. He would be in desperate need of a stiff drink and a cigarette once this was over.

"AND AS I TOLD *YOU*!" Chief Inspector Plundell shouted back at Wilson, gaining Barnaby's attention. "I am the chief inspector, and your disruption and disrespect to *my* crime scene—"

"Inspector, please." Barnaby stepped up beside his friend. "He only meant to help. We see now that you have things perfectly under control."

Chief Inspector puffed up, his chin lifting.

"We what?" Wilson's eyebrows shot upwards.

Barnaby sent a meaningful glance towards Wilson that he hoped conveyed that he should just play along.

"We only wish to pay our respects." Barnaby motioned to the body, glancing downward, which he instantly regretted when something sour reached the foot of Barnaby's tongue.

He gagged and withdrew his kerchief to cover his nose and mouth.

Get control of yourself! He chided himself, a death grip still around the compendium in his free hand.

"Ah, yes," Wilson said, picking up on the cue. "Paying our respects, of course."

"Hmph." The inspector narrowed his eyes, distrusting of the detective's sudden change in demeanour. "Well, as it were, I'm going to need both of you to clear off."

"Though, it does seem to me that you may require our particular set of skills after all," Wilson said, clapping his hands together in excitement.

Barnaby let out an involuntary groan. That's not what he intended at all. Paying their respects was supposed to be a way out of the sanctuary, not further intruding on the crime scene. Barnaby enjoyed an exciting new case as much as the rest, but he preferred his presence to be desired, whereas

Wilson thought himself something of a genius. And at times, he was. He often saw what others couldn't, which was almost always welcomed, but by the jaw-clenched expression glaring back at them from the inspector, Barnaby feared now was not one of those times.

"I've heard about you." The inspector's face pinched as he jabbed a finger at Wilson. "I know the mess you made of the tin box phantom, and I won't have the likes of you meddlin' in my crime scene."

"Wilson, let's go." Barnaby motioned towards the exit that was now being emptied of mourners by the ushering police.

He didn't know how much more of the stench of death and decay he could take. His stomach quivered every time his eyes glazed over the body. No, he was definitely not suited for this type of detective work.

"Victim is female, approximately thirty," Wilson began, proceeding to ignore them both to continue his investigation. "It appears her clothes were ripped open before the fatal wound was executed."

"How do you know?" Barnaby glanced at the shredded dress, immediately regretting it when he spotted crude stitches. Dry blood crusted at the seams and smeared all across her bruised belly.

"Look at the fibres of cloth underneath her fingernails." Wilson waved his hand at the body.

The inspector huffed and took a reluctant step in closer to take a look. A tiny sliver of fabric stuck out in the dimly lit room.

"They match her dress, indicating she was still moving when her clothes were cut." Wilson smiled triumphantly. "And the jagged pattern left from what I can only imagine being a very dull knife indicates a struggle from the victim herself. One that, unless she were a ghost, could not have been done by the victim postmortem."

"Could she have been a ghost, you think?" Barnaby asked in a hushed tone.

"A what?" The inspector tilted his head and frowned.

"Nothing. He said nothing at all." Wilson glared at Barnaby.

"Well, *if* your hypothesis is true," the inspector said, crossing his brawny arms across his uniformed chest. "Then what, pray tell, do you believe to be the cause of death?"

"Isn't it obvious?" He arched a brow. "She was stabbed with a knife. The woman struggled, as is evident in her defensive wounds on her arms and hands, but ultimately hit something sharp, which is why she has a very nasty bruise at the nape of her neck that probably threw her unconscious during the struggle. Which is why the bottom right side of the cuts to her abdomen is much smoother than the rest."

The two followed his gesture towards the stitching. Barnaby gasped. He hadn't seen it at first, but there it was. A smooth expertly cut incision in a sea of jagged slices of skin. Then the sour taste returned, and he quickly looked away from the ugly scene.

"Honestly, inspector," Wilson said, "if you didn't see it before, I don't know why you're insistent upon my leaving. This case needs me."

"Hold on, *detective*," the inspector said, putting as much disdain on the word detective as if it were a curse. "Your theory is that her stomach was cut while she was still *alive*? You couldn't know that!"

Wilson flared his nostrils, and Barnaby knew his colleague was growing impatient with the inspector's interrogation.

"Are you not the chief inspector?" Wilson cried, flailing his arms emphatically. "How could you not know the difference between the pool of blood of someone who's been cut while still alive and one who's already dead? This is outrageous. What do they even teach the police here in this city?"

"Now you listen here," Chief Inspector Plundell raised his voice, bowing up to Wilson though he still stood four inches short of the detective's six-foot stature. "I won't have you trespassing on *my* crime scene and insultin'—what in bloody's name are you doin' now?"

Wilson squatted next to the dead body and sniffed the length of the woman's arm, garnering him a dirty look from the chief inspector.

"Incense," Wilson muttered.

"Nonsense? Yes, I quite agree." Chief Inspector Plundell was so red in the face and neck Barnaby was sure his head would explode.

"No, not 'nonsense', *incense*. There's a great deal of the scent on her." Wilson straightened, stepping away from the body. "From the sweet resin and balsamic aroma, I'd say a blend of Frankincense and Myrrh, to be exact. And a touch of wet dog indicating she recently spent some time in a basement somewhere. That should be a good starting point."

Barnaby's mind spun at the mention of the incense. Hadn't there been a chapter on it in the compendium? He dug his fingers into the spine of the leatherbound book at his side, itching to open it up but knew better than to do so right then and there in front of a room of police officers.

"Is there perhaps a lower level here?" Wilson spun around in search of a possible door.

"Why?" The inspector arched a brow and tapped his foot.

"Well, seeing there's a lack of blood spatter on the stage, I can't imagine this being the place our killer performed their antemortem surgery."

"Blood spatter? What is this, a bloody *painting* to you?" the chief inspector exclaimed.

Wilson took a long, deep breath inward, reminding

himself that very few took his theories of analysing blood seriously.

"No, not at all. Blood can be very telling as I've discovered on numerous crime scenes I've solved in the past. I wrote a whole study on it that I'm sure was publicised somewhere. Have you not read it?"

The man just stared at him blankly.

"Ah, well, it's your loss." Wilson shrugged. "Anyway, do you know where I could find the basement?"

"No. There's no lower basement here." Chief Inspector Plundell bit his cheek as if he regretted even providing that tiny bit of information. Then, the clink of metal got Barnaby's attention as the inspector unhooked his handcuffs from the side of his belt. "Now, you have five seconds to clear out, or I'll be doing it by force."

"My apologies, inspector," Barnaby said, grabbing Wilson's arm, determined to drag his partner down the aisle if he had to.

Wilson yanked his arm free. "That won't be necessary. I've already gleaned everything of importance from this scene. I bid you a good day, inspector."

Barnaby rolled his eyes but let out a sigh of relief when Wilson followed him towards the exit. They were halfway to the door when Wilson spun on his heel.

"Oh, but inspector!" Wilson lifted a finger to his lip.

"Wilson!" Barnaby groaned.

The chief inspector gazed back at them with wary eyes.

"I would check the victim's mouth."

Barnaby gawked. "Wilson, you can't think this is connected to who murdered the Talmage's son, can you?"

There were two items always present in each of the murders in the tin box phantom case. One was a tin box of teeth and the other a note between the lips of the victims.

But this couldn't be the work of John Walsh as he was already in prison. A copycat, perhaps?

"Why, of course not." Wilson looked down at Barnaby while the inspector reluctantly checked. "But can you think all this a coincidence? Madam Onay was at the scene where Irvin Talmage, Jr was murdered, and now she's found slung over the pulpit on the same day as the man's funeral?"

"Well, the thought did occur to me, but that doesn't mean—"

"I can't believe it." Chief Inspector Plundell swore.

The detectives looked up just as the inspector pulled a crumpled piece of paper from the woman's mouth.

"What does it say?" Wilson asked, his chest thrust out as if he somehow knew already.

The inspector unfolded the paper and cleared his throat. "It just says *'For Irvin'*." The inspector glared at Wilson. "But how did you know?"

"Just as I suspected," Wilson whispered to Barnaby before addressing the chief. "I didn't, but it only stands to reason someone would want to further avenge the death of the town's most beloved Irvin Talmage, Jr. Good day!"

"If I find out you had anything to do with this—" The inspector shouted after them as Wilson reached for the door.

"Oh, don't be silly," Wilson called over his shoulder. "I'll have this case solved before your next cup of tea. And I expect a handsome reward when I do."

With that, Wilson waltzed out of the sanctuary with a determined spring in his step. Barnaby shook his head, closing his eyes for a moment while trying to pull his thoughts and patience together. He promised himself he would not try to dissuade Wilson from inserting himself upon this case—not that he could anyway—but Barnaby was confident this was the work of whoever was possessed by Frau Perchta. He feared that because his colleague didn't believe in magic and had no idea what he was going against, he would very likely end up dead.

"Wilson," he said, bounding after the detective who was already halfway to George Street. "Wilson, I can't advise that you take on this case."

"Why, because of Chief Inspector *Plundell*? The bumbling fool." Wilson chuckled.

"No, it's because of the witch who did this."

Wilson gave him a curious glance. "You couldn't possibly know who did this when we haven't even eliminated all of the suspects. Although come to think of it, we haven't even made a list of who might've done it, so carry on. Wait a minute, did you say a *witch*?"

Barnaby sucked in air to catch his breath. He underestimated how heavy the compendium was and how fast Wilson was walking. "Yes, I've been reading about these creatures known as two-legged beasts. They can possess any human who can then take on whatever abilities these spirits have. I can't be certain. I haven't read anything that can do what we just saw in there yet, but this morning Emma—"

"Not *her* again. If I see that murderer one more time, I *will* have her arrested."

"Please, Wilson," Barnaby said, referring to the case of the butcher's daughter that put Wilson on the tail of Emma and the circus back in London. "I've heard all about that night, and I can't blame the child. She had no control over what she was back then. Besides, those vile humans were no parents, I can tell you that for certain."

Emma had grown up in quite a terrible household. Her father, the butcher, was an abusive drunk and her mother, from what he was told, was horrid as well. It had been Emma's first full moon to shift into a powerful winged creature and killed them both without any recollection of doing it in the first place. Though it was a terrible thing she did, he couldn't help but feel sorry for the poor girl. It wasn't her fault she'd been born into such unfortunate circumstances. Thankfully the circus had helped her control her power.

"No, dear Barnaby," Wilson replied, interrupting his wandering thoughts. "What's certain is the utter nonsense you've wasted both of our precious time with. Any more talk about witches and magical beasts, and I'd say you might need to have your head checked by Dr Larson."

Wilson upped the speed of his impossible pace back towards Barnaby's flat.

Barnaby huffed. "Just because you don't believe in something doesn't make it any less real."

He pulled out his silver Swiss pocket watch to check the time and slowed, letting Wilson speed ahead. He would need to meet Emma in front of the McLeod House soon, and he didn't have time to deal with his colleague's antics.

"Are you coming?" Wilson turned back expectantly.

"No, I don't think so. I'll meet you later. I've decided it might be best that I solve this case on my own."

"Ah, do I sense a wager?" Wilson sauntered back down the hill, hands in pockets. "If I solve this case before either you or the inspector, then there'll be no more talk of this *supernatural* stuff?

Barnaby sighed. "I don't have time for this, but fine, I'll humour you."

"Splendid!" Wilson clasped his hands together, a glint in his eye.

He was enjoying this too much for Barnaby's liking.

"And if I win, you shall agree to owe me whatever I want no matter if it's going to Deadman's Island and witnessing the Beaumont's powers for yourself?" Barnaby arched a brow at Wilson, who took a pronounced swallow. "What are you so nervous about? Do you think it's likely that you could *lose?*"

Wilson shook his head, reaching for Barnaby's right hand to shake on it. "Of course not. You've got a deal."

After the two detectives shook once, they promptly went their separate ways. Barnaby trotted back down George Street with a new sense of purpose, bounding past the church that still swarmed with police and mourning bystanders. He kept his gaze averted when the officers hoisted a blanket covered stretcher out of the church and quickly took the first right onto Barrington.

He was determined now more than never to figure out what sort of spirit Emma saw last night and why this witch would kill Madam Onay "for Irvin". Was the one who conjured the witch connected to the Talmage family? And would they kill again? If so, who would be next? The many unknowns tormented him and urged his feet to move even faster. He had to find answers, and he prayed he'd find some at the McLeod House.

5

DO YOU HEAR WHAT I HEAR?

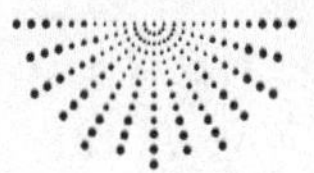

The McLeod House,
Bishop Street

Emma paced the sidewalk in front of the rotting house, and the sun glared directly overhead, signalling midday. She'd spent as long as she cared to cooped up in that shop, she'd nursed her tea until it grew cold, and by noon she couldn't take the indoors any longer.

She'd found a discarded burlap sack to shield her shoulders from the cold and took the brisk walk to Bishop Street. The daylight made the deserted house all the more ominous if that were possible. The door creaked in the breeze, barely hanging to its last hinge. Two second-story windows stared back at her like black, hollow eyes and a curtain, shredded and torn, lapped out of the second story like claws. It caught on a sharp piece of jagged glass at the windowsill, and the whole house howled.

A shiver ran down her spine as the glittering sun reminded her there was nowhere to hide. Yes, it was definitely worse during the day. She turned about-face and walked the length of the gated home for the hundredth time, kicking the snow. Where was Barnaby? He'd promised to meet her here but couldn't remember if a specific time was mentioned. Perhaps she should return to the Engel sibling's shop just in case?

"Oh good, you're here."

Emma spun around. Her heart skipped a beat at the sudden noise. Barnaby crossed the street, the curious book she'd seen him with at the bookshop still in hand. What type of book could be so important that he'd take it everywhere with him?

"I'm sorry, I didn't mean to startle you," he said, resting the book on a stone pillar in the fencing around the house's scraggly front yard. "I hope I didn't keep you waiting long. There was a terrible incident at the service."

"Is everything all right?"

"Nothing you need to worry about." Barnaby gave her a tight smile before turning to face the abandoned house. "Now, show me where you saw this possession take place."

"It was just over there." She pointed to the windows on the ground level. "I'd heard something within and, since we were scouting for magical power, I thought I'd check it out."

Emma led the way through the metal gate. It squealed shut behind them.

"And did you smell anything?" Barnaby asked when they reached the window.

"I don't think so. Why?"

"Oh, it's nothing." He peeked over the windowsill into the house, the light from the sun barely illuminating the floor within. "And what about the symbols? Where were they?"

"They should be on the floor right there." Emma peeked into the room, but the wooden floorboards were swept free of all evidence. Her heart raced, and she clenched her fists. "No, this isn't right."

She ran to the front porch and jumped over the fallen door. Her foot caught on the edge, and she nearly fell but luckily caught herself on the rotten bannister. Dust billowed up, and she coughed.

"Perhaps it was a different room?" Barnaby followed her inside.

She wiped her hands off on the skirt of her dress and walked to the room; she swore she saw the whole thing happen. The floorboards creaked with each step, sending her heart aflutter.

"It was this one, I'm sure of it," she said upon entering the empty room.

Besides a dusty old dresser shoved in the corner of the room, it was empty.

The window remained the same, save for the missing curtains, but Emma distinctly remembered them being drawn. Had they been removed? What an odd thing to do. And what was that smell? She covered her nose as the rot of wood mixed with something sweet and earthy met her nostrils.

Barnaby sniffed and suddenly sneezed. "Pardon me."

"You smell it too?" She studied the floor for any signs of the symbols. There had to still be some kind of residue on the floor. Her shoulders hunched when she didn't even spot a shard of glass from the broken mirror.

"The scent is potent for sure."

"I don't remember this smell before." She shrugged in defeat. "Of course, I was outside, and it was very late."

Barnaby set the book down on the little dresser and walked the length of the room.

"There's no point. It's all gone," Emma moaned, her ribs

tightening at the thought that maybe she'd just imagined all of it after all.

"Perhaps," the detective said, lifting his forefinger. "But I'm sure if we look hard enough, we'll find something. Glass can be swept up, but chalk is not so easily cleaned, and these floors have been scrubbed."

She lifted her eyebrows. "How do you know?"

Barnaby motioned to the centre of the room exactly where the symbols had been. "See how the dust has been disturbed here in a circular pattern? As if someone wiped something away with a wet rag and then swept more dust over it."

Emma studied the faint dust pattern that could be anything.

"It's not much to go on," Barnaby continued. "But I'm sure we'll find something more substantial after giving this room a good once over."

She met Barnaby's kind smile with awe. She didn't know why Barnaby was being so nice. He had no reason to believe her. But she was grateful all the same. Ignoring the sudden eerie sensation that they were being watched, she scoured the room in search of any sign of a bloody piece of glass or a bundle of flax.

They rattled each loose board, even scooted the dresser out from the wall in case something was tucked behind it, but no matter what nook or cranny they searched, they only discovered more cobwebs and a handful of rats.

"This is useless." Emma threw up her hands and rested an elbow on the top of the dresser.

Barnaby knelt in the centre of the room, bent over with his cheek resting on the ground. He had one eye shut with the other one peeking through the floorboards at something.

"Take a break if you must," he said, his voice strained. "A thorough investigation can take time."

She crossed her arms and winced at the thought that she might've wasted the detective's time. Why was he so determined to help her still? It was apparent that even if she was right, there wasn't any evidence left.

As her spirits plummeted further into a hole of doubt, she eyed Barnaby's book on the dresser to distract herself.

"The Complete Compendium of Bestien and Magic by Dr Heinrich—" she gaped at the name and grabbed the book, bringing it closer to be sure she read the author's name correctly. "This book is by Dr Heinrich E. *Kunstler*? Where did you get this?"

Barnaby sat up and narrowed his eyes. "From Engel's Emporium. Have you read it?"

She brought the fingertips of her free hand to the engraved last name. "No, but I think I know who wrote it."

"Oh?" He stood, wiping the dust off his slacks.

"I recognized the name. Franziska's father was also Heinrich Kunstler. I wonder if this might be the same? Although it would be quite a coincidence. Can I read it?"

"Of course," Barnaby said. "Though, I do think I shall be finished here soon. Although, I must say, whoever you saw last night did a good job of concealing their activities."

Emma flushed. "I'm sorry."

"Don't be." Barnaby waved her comment off. "It just won't be as easy as I'd hoped to figure out what kind of bestien we're dealing with without seeing the markings firsthand."

"Bestien?" She hesitated on the pronunciation, glancing at the book's title. "What is that?"

"It's German for beasts. Magical spirits who live in the underworld, but on occasion get a foothold into our world." Barnaby scratched his head. "I'm still very new to all of this, but thankfully Mr Engel is quite knowledgeable on the matter. He's the one who pointed me to this book when I first sought out the shop, you know."

He stopped, cheeks turning a shade of pink when he must've realized he was rambling.

"Anyway, take a look for yourself." He turned to examine the back wall again.

Emma placed the book back on the dresser and flipped open the monstrous volume. She turned to a drawing of a short, fuzzy creature with pointy batlike ears and an upturned nose. She covered up a giggle, wondering how this cute little thing could be considered a beast.

A Koboldgeist. She read the handwritten title at the bottom along with the summary of what it was.

The Koboldgeist is a Faen Bestien—the word 'bestien' was scratched out in what she assumed was Barnaby's handwriting and replaced with the word 'beast'—*this goblin-like spirit can only possess those that walk on two legs but prefers children.*

Emma gasped. What a horrid thing to do, possessing little children. She read on to find out if this creature had any particular reasoning.

They have a desperate desire to be helpful, often found tending fires and tending to chores long after everyone has gone to bed. This bestien is considered harmless and will relinquish the child once they've shed their youth.

Well, at least it wasn't dangerous. She wondered how a child even got possessed by one of them in the first place. Or even how Kunstler discovered such a thing. She turned the page but instantly regretted it when her eyes fell upon the next drawing.

A wrinkled, old woman with a hooked nose and hollow cheekbones stared back at her, reminding her of Frau Perchta's reflection.

"What is it?" Barnaby asked.

She must've made an involuntary noise but was too

distracted by the image of the witch's razor-sharp teeth to notice.

"It looks just like her," she whispered and picked up the book to show him. "This is very close to what I saw in the mirror. Except she didn't have talons for fingers or purple skin like this one."

Barnaby studied the page, taking the book.

"The Hexengeist," Barnaby read the heading, bringing his index finger to the page and skimming the description. "It's a witch spirit, either a Hexenmann if it's a male or Hexenfrau if it's a female spirit, that possesses humans with the ability to cast spells."

"Like a witch."

Barnaby nodded. "It also says it usually requires a verbal wish that matches the desire of the Hexengeist that's being conjured, an incantation, and a blood sacrifice."

His voice faltered on that last bit, and Emma sensed he knew more than what he was letting on.

"So, there are many different types of bestien," he said, more to himself than to her. "You're sure this is what you saw?"

"Something like it."

"I wonder if this book mentions anything about Frau Perchta." He was about to shift through the pages when a clink from the wall beside them caught their ears.

Emma narrowed her eyes. "Do you hear that?"

"I'm afraid so."

They turned towards the wall, suddenly noticing a large frame that swung on the hook it hung from, nearly covering the space between the ceiling and the wall. Dust puffed into the air from the canvas as something scurried behind the wall. Barnaby's face whitened, and he took a step back, but Emma moved closer. She placed her ear against the wall to listen.

Something small scratched against the wood from behind the framed artwork. She clenched her hands into a fist and knocked.

"Careful!" Barnaby hissed.

The hollow echo of the knock confirmed her suspicion. "There's more to this room. Quick, help me remove this picture."

"I've got a bad feeling about this, Barnaby said, placing the compendium back on the dresser and removing his coat. He folded it on top of the book before making his way to the other side of the frame.

Together they heaved the large painting from its hook, and the bottom of his splintered free, crashing onto the floor with a loud thud.

Emma winced, meeting Barnaby's wide eyes.

Barnaby sighed. "So much for keeping everything undisturbed when whoever was here last night returns."

"If they return," she corrected as they sat the frame down next to the mess. "And I'm sure we'll be able to put things back as they were."

"It's a door!" Barnaby gasped, and Emma followed his gaze to the space on the wall where the painting was hung.

If they hadn't been looking for it, they would've never seen it. The door blended into the wall, a tiny rectangle gap and a tiny metal ring flush with the wall the only clues that there was another room beyond.

"Would you do the honours?"

She nodded, a thrill of adrenaline shooting through her, and she pulled the metal loop for a door handle. The hinges creaked as the door swung open, giving way to pitch darkness. Not even the light from the windows or the cracks in the walls penetrated this room.

Barnaby hesitated but inched to the threshold ever so carefully. "Hello?"

Nothing. And then a screech and a shuffle sent the two jumping back. A rat scuttled across Emma's shoe, letting out an involuntary scream. She sighed, resting a hand on her chest and laughed.

"Just a"—Barnaby gulped, looking a bit faint — "a rat."

"I wonder what's in here? Why would a secret room be here, anyway?" Emma asked, not bothered by the rat as much as Barnaby seemed to be.

"I don't know, but *I* wonder if perhaps it'd be best if we leave? Or at least come back with a lamp. It's impossible to see in there."

She looked over her shoulder at the detective who wrung his hands. "Why would you need a lamp when you've got me?" She winked and snapped her fingers.

A spark flickered from the tips of her fingers, and the energy of the sun rushed through the window in a spiral of light. It zigzagged about the room before engulfing her hand.

"See?" She said, holding a ball of energy that sparked in the palm of her hand.

Barnaby's mouth fell slack. "It's... beautiful!"

"It's part of my power." She smiled and turned to the secret doorway.

Leading with her ball of light, she stepped over the threshold. The windowless space danced with light and illuminated a room no bigger than a closet. A rolled-up rug leaned against the back wall, and crates filled with rotted junk blanketed the space, but what caught Emma's eye was the wood-framed mirror tucked in the corner. It was missing its mirror and looked exactly like the one Frau Perchta appeared from before it shattered.

"That's it!" She pointed to the glassless mirror.

Barnaby squeezed in to get a closer look. He studied it for a moment before he glanced down. "And what do we have here?" He motioned to a box on the floor behind the mirror.

The contents rattled as he hoisted it up. "The shards of glass you mentioned when the spirit escaped."

He picked a sliver up and brought it up into the light. Something dark-tinged the sharp tip. "Blood, perhaps?"

"The glass flew everywhere." Emma shrugged. "I'm sure a few must've nicked the conjurer. But do you see the knife they cut themselves with? Or the chalice?"

"I don't believe so, but if you remember what these symbols look like, I believe I know who might be able to help identify them."

"The bookshop owner?"

"Yes, now if I could just get a spare piece of paper and a fountain pen."

"The last page of the compendium is empty. Why not draw it there?" Emma asked.

Barnaby grimaced as he searched his pockets for a pen. "I hate the idea of further defiling the book, but I suppose that would work. Ah!"

He marched to the dresser where his sack coat lay and removed a pen from its inner pocket before bringing the compendium over to Emma.

"Now, do you think you could remember the symbols exactly?"

She nodded, taking the pen. The ink glided across the page as she sketched out the curling 'u' shapes and eyeball looking symbols. Barnaby peered over her shoulder while she drew for a moment before tidying the place back up.

"Done." She set the pen down.

A crash from behind her sent her whirling around.

"Guess there's no fixing that." Barnaby had the frame back on the wall, but the bottom piece once again fell off. He tossed the lop of wood aside to make it look like it'd fallen on its own.

A floorboard creaked from the front room, and they met

each other's wide eyes. Another step echoed, and they froze. Someone was there. Was it the witch coming to get them? Emma didn't want to wait and find out. Barnaby brought a finger to his lips when she opened her mouth to speak. He motioned for her to follow him to the shattered window. Emma was sure whoever was there could hear her thumping heart.

Barnaby propped his foot on the windowsill and heaved himself over.

"Ow!" He groaned when his pant leg caught on the crooked glass framing the windowsill, sending him catapulting into the snow below.

Emma's breath hitched, glancing over her shoulder at the footsteps headed her way. A dark shadow stood in the entry of the foyer, just far enough that the face was concealed, but from the belted frock coat and top hat, she guessed it was a man and definitely not the witch from last night.

"You there, halt!" The shadow called after her.

Emma scurried through the window, clutching the outstretched harm. Barnaby assisted her down onto the field of ice and snow-covered weeds, and they hurried towards the back of the house.

"This way." The detective wheezed, clearly out of breath.

Emma hardly heard him over the thud of blood pumping through her eardrums. She quickly caught up to him. Her foot skidded when Barnaby pulled her around the corner just as the stranger leaned out the window. They pressed their backs stiff against the house's rough exterior and held their breath. Her heart clenched, nearly bursting as she tried to keep quiet.

A few breaths passed, and then an audible crunch. Emma's eyes flicked up to Barnaby's, and the concern in his expression matched the fears that rushed through her mind.

What if they got caught? Would they get arrested? Or worse, was it someone working for Frau Perchta?

Slow footsteps chomped closer and closer, a quiet and predatory step. Emma clasped a hand over her mouth. Her chest ached both from holding her breath and the fear of not knowing who would round that corner. Her muscles quivered, but then the footsteps stopped. Several minutes passed and, when no one appeared, they both let out a breath.

"I don't know if they've left, but they haven't followed us, so I think it's safe." Barnaby pointed to the back fence. "We can take our leave that way."

Emma's shoulders slacked, relieved nothing lunged at them. But where did they go? She didn't have time to answer that as the detective was already halfway to the fence. She raised after him. He swung the gate open, and she stopped in her tracks.

Her eyes went wide, and Barnaby turned back when she didn't follow.

"The book!" Her stomach dropped as if she'd fallen from the second floor of that rotting house.

Barnaby wrinkled a brow, glancing back.

"I-I'm sorry, Barnaby. I'll fix this." She turned to march up the back door praying whoever had caught them was already long gone.

A hand on her shoulder stopped her.

"It's not safe yet. We don't know if whoever that was is gone, and I'd hate for you to get in trouble for trespassing," he said, guiding her back down the snow-covered path and out the back gate. It clanked shut behind them. "We'll just have to check back later for it. Don't worry."

Her cheeks burned. How could she have forgotten something so important?

"But what about the bookshop? How will you get answers from Mr Engel about the symbols?"

"Do you think you could recall the symbols you drew?"

She nodded.

"Then we'll just have to hope that's enough for Mr Engel. I'll return later when it's safe to get the book."

When Emma's expression remained tense, he pressed on. "Don't worry. Being a detective is as good as any cover in this town. We'll just have to hope that the book goes unnoticed until then."

With that, they retreated down the sidewalk towards the bookshop. The success of finding some sort of evidence of the previous night's events sent a light flutter through her chest but was dimmed by the disappointment of losing the book. She hated that it might further delay a way to find whoever conjured up such that evil spirit. A shudder ran down her spine. What would the witch do now that she was out?

6
THE POISON & THE PUNCH

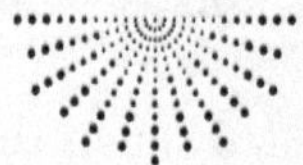

The detective's flat,
Grafton Street

Wilson whistled to himself and marched up the steps to Barnaby's flat building. He couldn't believe he'd gotten his old colleague to agree to his terms. He chuckled to himself, his chest puffing with the certainty of his impending win.

"Good morning, Mrs Mable," Wilson greeted the landlady, holding the door open for the grouchy old woman bundled up in a thick wool coat and a ridiculously furry hat.

Wilson wrinkled his nose when she passed by. The hat smelled of rat droppings. He held his tongue when she scowled back at him. He was in too good of a mood. He wasn't even sure what excited him more. The prospect of Barnaby putting a rest to his talk of ghosts and magic or the thrill of a brand new case. Either way, he couldn't wait to begin his investigation and bounded up the rickety stairs to the uppermost floor.

Once inside the apartment, he took a seat at his desk

strewn with maps and notes he'd made to track Madam Onay's whereabouts. He brushed the mess aside. There was little secret as to where she was now. He grabbed a clean notebook and pen to make his list. He needed to gather all the people he could think of who knew Madam Onay and who might've spotted her at the scene of Irvin's murder.

Faces and their names flooded his mind, and he had to get them out so he could narrow it all down. It was the best way to figure out what was known and to address the gaps. Though he was glad, Barnaby wasn't around to see him using a notebook. The teasing would never end as he claimed to never need one. He often didn't, but in this case, when there really were dozens of suspects, he would stoop to using the crutch.

Grabbing a pen, he focused on the task at hand. First, he had to acquaint himself intimately with Madam Onay's world to find the most likely group suspects. Once he had those, he'd then be able to interview each of them in turn.

"Barnaby is certainly one who knew her." He smirked, scribbling his name at the top and adding a note 'psychic consultations' as the description of their acquaintance.

Just the thought of how many times his old friend had visited her at the Halifax Club for a psychic reading made his head hurt. The poor fellow should've saved his money. It was all a gimmick, after all, based on a mixture of limited observations and farfetched assumptions.

Not that he actually suspected his colleague of murder, but if he did, Barnaby would quickly be eliminated simply on the grounds of his lack of motive. He didn't think Madam Onay had anything to do with John Walsh killing Irvin. Instead, he stubbornly believed John Walsh had some sort of power. A preposterous notion, of course.

There was the other point that Barnaby couldn't have murdered Madam Onay because he was in the apartment all morning. Not to mention the amount of vomit that would be present if Barnaby had even attempted to make an incision. Barnaby certainly didn't have the stomach for murder, but Wilson had to cover all grounds. He was nothing if not thorough.

Scratching off Barnaby's name, he continued the list with a more thoughtful approach.

Victor, the butler at Halifax Club.

He scrawled the name, the memory of how protective the butler was over the late Irvin Talmage, Jr coming to mind. But could he have avenged Irvin? It was possible. Especially since the butler was also Madam Onay's last known employer. The ones closest to the victim were usually the most culpable.

Mr Dods, the dockmaster.

This one he put under Victor's. He recalled the way Barnaby and the dockmaster bonded over both seeking Madam Onay out for their fortunes. He rolled his eyes and also scratched this name off the list.

Mr Kirkham of the Acadian Recorder. The newspaper reporter had only seen Madam Onay once but thought it prudent to find out if he knew anything else.

He then remembered the distraught fiancée of the deceased, Miss Lauretta. Could her delicate build allow for the strength required to beat another as much as Madam Onay's was? Not to mention Madam Onay was a great deal taller, and it would've required much strength to hoist her frame from wherever the original crime occurred to the scene at the funeral.

Nevertheless, he added her name to the list for the sake of thoroughness and moved on.

Finally, he scribbled in the most likely to have had a hand in Madam Onay's untimely demise.

The Talmage family.

And, of course, their inner circle, whoever those persons might be. The note read 'For Irvin', which indicated a revenge murder and who better to avenge his death than one of his own kin? Particularly Mr Irvin Talmage, Sr what with Irvin junior being his only son and all that. Mr Talmage had arrived at the scene of his son's untimely death so quickly from the *Talmage & Sons Foundry* it was almost as if he'd been there all along. Definitely suspicious.

But would Mr Talmage have been so foolish as to leave that note in Madam Onay's mouth? Why would the killer put something that could be so easily traced back to them? One's handwriting was like a picture into one's soul. Every stroke was unique to the one holding the pen. Perhaps rational thinking was too much to ask in the heat of committing revenge. Better safe than sorry.

He circled this last name, promising to speak with each one of the family members and their closest friends, whoever they may be. This would be no easy task, however, given his tense relationship with them. But first, he needed to pay a visit to Dr Larson to examine the body for any clues. And hopefully, get his hands on that note.

He checked the time. It had only been a few hours, plenty of time, he thought for Chief Inspector to get the body to the mortuary. What a fool that man was. From the moment he was hired, the guards at the station had been much more reluctant to allow him to visit John Walsh. There was always an officer keeping a watchful eye on him as if he were a conspirator when he did.

"Hmph." He snorted.

What a ridiculous notion that one. But of course, this turn of events with the murder of Madam Onay changed *everything*. If she were the one working with John Walsh, as he suspected, then they would not need to worry about the prisoner escaping. His partner was dead, and such was his means of escape. Wilson was confident of this.

He stood from the desk, deciding he shouldn't delay his visit with the doctor any longer. He fetched his frock coat once more and made his way to the tiny home office on Bishop Street. He was just about to pass the Governor's mansion when a loud thud like wood crashing came from the abandoned house across the street.

"Did you hear that?" A young constable asked who'd stopped in his tracks just a few paces from Wilson.

"Indeed," Wilson replied. He narrowed his eyes at the foreboding two-storey before turning back to the constable. "Probably just a tree squirrel, but if you have a spare moment to investigate, that might be vigilant of a capable officer such as yourself."

The young man—not but twenty by the lack of wrinkles and barely a shadow on his chiselled chin—straightened his belted frock and gave a stern nod.

"Of course, sir," the constable said before dashing across the powdery white road.

Wilson shook his head at the naïveté of the rookie and continued down the street. He hoped for the sake of the young cadet that there wasn't anything dangerous waiting for him inside. Perhaps something more exciting than a rodent, of course, but nothing too treacherous.

"Dr Larson?" He called upon entering the office.

Having grown accustomed to the doctor never being in the front room, he didn't bother waiting for a reply and marched around the counter guarding a wall of medicines. The top of the desk was cluttered with prescription receipts and jars of various pills sitting out in the open for any hoodlum to grab. He wondered if the doctor would ever consider hiring a secretary.

The door behind the counter was wide open, so he

waltzed through and down the narrow corridor to the end. Faint voices came from behind the last entry, the doctor's examination room, but he paid no attention to them and turned the handle. For the briefest of moments, a thought to knock crossed his mind before he quickly stifled the idea. Better not set a precedent of such things, he thought and sauntered into the room.

"And you are certain—" Chief Inspector Plundell stood on the near side of the examination table, his back to the door.

The old doctor peered around the inspector and rolled his eyes when he spotted Wilson. He removed his spectacles and wiped his bushy white eyebrows. "Detective Davies, what an utter surprise."

Wilson smirked at the doctor's derisive tone.

"*You*? Again?" The chief inspector scowled, pointing a knobby finger at him. "I warned you not to interfere with my crime scene."

The gangly detective waved a hand about the room. "And is this your crime scene, inspector? I was under the impression that this was Dr Larson's examination room."

Chief Inspector Plundell flushed, giving his reddish-grey mutton chops an even more crimson hue.

"Now, Dr Larson"—Wilson folded his hands behind his back and paced about the room — "do go ahead and answer Chief Inspector Plundell's question regarding your certainty that the gipsy was still breathing when her killer sliced open her stomach."

The inspector's mouth fell open, and the doctor rubbed the bridge of his nose.

"Pretend like I'm not even here." Wilson bent at the waist and eyed the many books the doctor collected on the bookshelf beside him. Mostly filled with volumes on human anatomy and chemistry.

"Doctor, he can't be right, can he?"

"Well, Chief Inspector," the doctor replied, returning his spectacles. "To tell you the truth, I'm not certain of much anymore, except for *that*. There is undeniable evidence the trauma committed to the victim was all premortem."

"Aha!"

The two men glared back at Wilson from the examination table. He caught their ugly stares and raised his hands. "My apologies for my involuntary celebration that my findings were, indeed, correct and thus confirms that my deduction skills are still sharp."

The doctor returned his attention to the ashen woman on the table. "She fought viciously against her attacker but ultimately was made incapacitated by whatever caused this."

Dr Larson gently placed his hands on either side of the woman's neck and lifted. Purple abrasions blanketed the back of it. Wilson pretended to be busy reading *An Inquiry into the Causes and Effects of the Variolæ Vaccinæ*. It was an older edition than his own copy, which occupied some space in his vast library back in London. Oh, how he missed the cleanliness and comfort of his own townhome. And he had yet to hear from Hubert, his butler, which warranted a smidge of concern. He wondered if the old man missed him.

"How terrible," the inspector said in awe. "Especially to have gone out this way."

"Indeed. But what's more strange is this," the doctor said, which drew Wilson back into the observation at hand. "When I removed the stitching the killer performed on her navel, I found her stomach to be missing and replaced with this."

Wilson took a step closer to the table when the doctor reached a gloved hand to the bit of cloth covering Madam Onay's midsection. Both he and the chief inspector gazed intently as he pulled the fabric back to reveal a gaping bright yellow hole where the woman's bowels should've been.

What is it?" The chief inspector's jaw fell slack.

"It appears to be finely cut hay," Dr Larson said, taking a pair of tongs off a nearby tray. "I thought it best to wait to remove it until *you* were present, inspector."

Wilson rolled his eyes at the slight.

"Rightly so." The chief inspector straightened.

"At a glance, I thought perhaps—ah, yes, it appears my suspicions were right."

With the hay removed, the light overhead illuminated a completely vacant cavity. No stomach. No intestines. Nothing remained inside the woman's chest aside from her ribcage.

The chief inspector sucked in air, and Wilson approached the body, tired of his façade of disinterest.

"So, this is why our killer stitched the victim back up." Wilson rested his hands on the side of the cold examination table.

"They were right." The inspector gasped, taking a step back.

Wilson frowned. "Who were?"

"What do you mean *who*?" The inspector cried. "You must've seen them this morning, the protestors with the 'devil worshiper' and 'kill the devil' signs. This is his work."

"Who's work? You mean 'the devil'?"

The inspector lifted his chin. "Indeed I do."

"Hogswallop," Wilson scoffed.

"Has to be. Only the devil himself could do such a thing to this poor woman."

Wilson groaned, pacing the room to try and drown out the absurdities that were flying from the inspector's trap.

"Even if she might've been a conspirator in the Talmage murder, nobody deserves to this kind of brutality. I mean, if it wasn't the devil, then who else could've done it?"

"Yes, inspector, who *else*?" Wilson prodded. "An astute

question, one we should evaluate. Who else could've removed a victim's stomach? I'll tell you who, anyone with the knowledge to know why a stomach is so important to a murder case."

The inspector's expression blanked.

"Bullocks, he doesn't even know!" Wilson pressed the sides of his temple before continuing. "The stomach is a crucial element that, if studied, can give clues as to the cause of death. But the more important question we should be asking is why else would the killer need to do this?

Perhaps we have ourselves a killing for science. Isn't there a college of medicine in these parts? Surely this could've been done by the hand of a student. Possibly in the hopes to get a lead in their courses. Back in London, there are rumours of a black market for such things."

"Then why go through the trouble to remove and replace it with hay?" The inspector asked.

"In this case, a medical student is unlikely," Dr Larson said as he set his tools aside. "The stitching is all wrong. No student of medicine would do such sloppy work. It's too... hesitant. Too radical as if their hand trembled. If it *were* done by a student, perhaps a first year would be this horrendous. But as it were, I don't believe first years require such in-depth evaluations of human anatomy."

"And then there's the problem with the note." The inspector reached for his back pocket and pulled out a wilted piece of paper.

The very one that had been shoved into the victim's mouth. Wilson's muscles clenched, and he opened his mouth to express how imperative it was that the note be stored in its own clean and sealed container for preservation, but the words refused to form. Instead, Barnaby's voice of reason echoed in his mind, telling him not everyone had such a high standard for handling evidence. Besides, if he digressed into rules of methods, he'd be distracting from the real purpose of his visit.

He huffed. He hated it when his colleague was a voice of reason.

"Where was that found?" The doctor asked.

"In the woman's cheek," the inspector said, placing it on the table beside the corpse.

Wilson's fingers itched to grab it, but there was no way to do it without being spotted by either the doctor or the chief inspector.

"It reads 'For Irvin' suggesting a revenge killing."

"Hmm, if revenge, then I'd suspect she was poisoned." Dr Larson shrugged. "It'd explain why the entrails were removed, but it's hard to tell without the stomach to analyse."

"Then," Wilson mused, "our killer would've known why he needed to remove this crucial piece of evidence,"

The doctor gave a sad nod.

"And so a medical student would still fit the bill," Wilson whispered to himself.

Chief Inspector Plundell narrowed his eyes. "Wouldn't there be visible signs on the woman's mouth or at least some sort of skin reaction if she were poisoned?"

"Do you *ever* read, inspector?" Wilson gawked at the sturdily built officer. "Or have you truly not seen the effects of a simple dose of strychnine in the entirety of your profession? It astounds me that in this day in age, an officer of your calibre hasn't heard of at least the most common of poisons, say, arsenic? Which is impossible to detect without an autopsy. Can you really not know this?"

"I think I've heard quite enough from you, Mr Davies."

"*Detective* Davies," Wilson corrected.

The inspector jabbed a knobby finger at him. "You and your self-proclaimed title should do well to learn when to respect those of a higher authority."

"If you two gentlemen can't behave yourselves," the doctor said, raising his voice to match theirs. "I will have to ask you both to leave my examination room."

The detective and chief inspector glared at one another for a moment. The inspector shook with rage at Wilson, who remained calm and collected.

"Of course, doctor," Wilson said, returning his attention to the residing town physician and mortician.

"To address both of your concerns," Dr Larson began. "Yes, there are many chemicals that can cause visible abrasions."

A triumphant smile grew upon Chief Inspector Plundell's face as he turned to Wilson to revel in his victory.

"However"—the doctor motioned to the woman's cavity — "Detective Wilson is also correct in that not all poisons would have an exterior reaction. The most concrete evidence of detecting poison and identifying the type is by evaluating the stomach."

Wilson lifted his chin, mimicking the inspector's lofty posture, who slumped in response. He knew it was childish, but he couldn't help feeling the tiniest bit smug. Here was a man of law and duty incapable of seeing what was right before their eyes. Of course, it was a kill of vengeance but also a kill of intelligence. An image of the killer was becoming all the more distinct.

There were three things he knew for sure. Firstly, that the killer had a connection to Irvin Talmage, Jr and his untimely demise. That they had a knowledge of Madam Onay's involvement with John Walsh, and, thirdly, they had the expertise to poison their victim, remove the stomach and all the evidence of the crime.

"And if you had this… stomach," the inspector began, gesturing towards the hole in the body. "How would you know if it were poisoned?"

"I would have to boil it. If the victim were poisoned, the toxins would be extracted in the heat." The doctor glanced between the inspector and the detective. "It's imperative that if it's found that it be brought to me immediately. And soon. The longer time that's passed, it will nearly be impossible to tell."

"One question, Dr Larson, if you'd so indulge me." Wilson raised his index finger.

"What is it?"

"Can you approximate how long Madam Onay has been in this postmortem state?"

The inspector remained silent, his expression vacant, but his posture defied his disinterest as he tilted forward.

The doctor shrugged. "From her temperature now, minus the average temperature of someone still alive, I'd say maybe five… six hours at most?"

"Thank you," Wilson said, turning towards the door. "You've done a fine job here, and I shall bid you both adieu."

"Where are you going?" The inspector turned and arched a ginger brow.

Wilson paused at the doorway. "I'm going to have a word with our murder suspect."

The inspector widened his eyes. "You can't know that yet."

"Well, of course not. Not for certain, anyway. We'll never know until I speak with him. Ta-ta!" Wilson waved and bounded down the hallway towards the lobby.

Quick steps followed him. "You're not addressing anyone without the accompaniment of me."

Wilson glanced over his shoulder at the inspector. He was quite out of breath trying to keep up, and the detective smirked. It almost reminded him of Barnaby, but he didn't know who he preferred as an assistant more. Barnaby or the inspector.

On the one hand, Barnaby wouldn't contradict him at every turn. Nor did he have the power to arrest him. But on the other, the inspector wouldn't misinterpret science for folly. He shrugged, figuring he hadn't the slightest of choice in the matter and increased his stride around the counter with the inspector huffing and puffing behind him like a petite-sized bad wolf.

"Have a good day!" a faint voice called behind them, but the detective was in too much of a rush out the front door to pay the third person in the front office any attention.

THE INSPECTOR STRODE UP to the Talmage's giant manor on the corner of Spring Garden and Dresden Row near the public garden, hot on Wilson's heels. "Do you honestly expect the Talmages to answer any question so soon after the botched funeral?"

It took them little time to get to the three-story structure of stone, brick, and pine. It was nearly as lavish as the Governor's house. Save for the fact it lacked the grandiose castle-like turrets on either side of the mansion.

"No," Wilson said, pulling the knocker and letting it clang against the door. "But I do hope to glean something from their reactions. Particularly that of Mr Talmage."

"Of course, he was my first suspect as well," the inspector said quickly.

"He's but a few on my lengthy list."

"I shall require you to give up that list, of course."

"Of course." Wilson gave a closed-mouth smile. He had no intention of relinquishing his list of suspects to the likes of him.

The door groaned open, and the butler peeked out from within. "Yes?"

The old man had large, puffy circles framing foggy eyes that stared out into the distance, not even making eye contact.

"Hello, good sir," Wilson began, folding his hands behind his back. "I am Detective Wilson Davies, and this is my associate—"

"I'm no such thing!" The inspector shouted and cleared his throat. He turned to the butler. "Forgive him, I'm Chief Inspector Plundell, and this is *my* associate—"

Wilson rolled his eyes. Barnaby would never interrupt him like this. How embarrassing?

"—really more of a trainee, actually. Anyway, I have a few questions for the Talmages. Are they in?"

"Just a moment." The butler shut the door on them.

The two men stood on the stoop in silence. The wind whipped at their frock coats and nipped at their hats.

"I expect you not to utter a word, you hear?" The inspector said.

Wilson sighed and glanced upward as snow sprinkled down from above.

"Unlike Detective Grey," the inspector continued, "you've not proven yourself to this town. In fact, from what I hear, you've made a fool of our police and even almost had an innocent man hanged!"

"That is still up for debate."

The inspector opened his mouth to further their argument when the door swung open once more.

"The master will see you in the drawing-room," the butler said in a monotonous tone.

A shiver ran down Wilson's spine when they entered the grand hall, the warmth of being indoors melting the chill from his bones. He admired the bifurcated staircase below the vaulted ceiling. It framed either side of the grand hall before uniting in a single set of steps leading down to the ground level. The last few rows of steps flared out, an elegant touch in Wilson's opinion.

The butler guided them around a giant ladder right in the centre of the room upon which a servant stood at the very top and dusted the antique chandelier. They passed the stairs and were led through the right of two doorways. A spacious front facing room with a slightly shorter ceiling, but still just as grand as the front hall.

Another elaborate crystal chandelier welcomed them, dangling above an array of sofas, one occupied by a tearful middle-aged woman in a black satin gown. Wilson recognised her from the funeral as Mrs Talmage. Two other much older women sat on either side and comforted her.

Of the two older women, he knew the one on the left as Mrs Peaston, Mr Talmage's secretary. Her salt and peppered hair was severely parted down the centre and slicked smooth into a tight bun at the nape. He noted that she still wore the same nasty frown on her wrinkled face as when he first met her at the foundry when he came to question Mr Talmage about the brightsmith who'd been killed along with the Talmage's son. How close was Mrs Peaton to the Talmages, anyway? Fairly close if the way she swooned over Mrs Talmage was any indication.

He was certain he'd never met the woman to Mrs Talmage's right. She was more advanced in age than Mrs Peaton, with pure white curls that peeked out underneath a pearled hair net.

"Chief Inspector Plundell, sir," the butler addressed Mr Talmage, who stood at the fireplace with his back to them.

He didn't look up, his dull eyes affixed to the flames that lapped within the firebox.

The inspector marched forward and stretched his hand towards the stiff, suit-clad gentleman. "It's a pleasure to finally meet you, Mr Talmage. I'm just sorry it isn't under better circumstances."

Mr Talmage turned away from the fire, furrowing his greying brow when he locked eyes on the inspector, which highlighted the dark circles under his eyes. He shook the inspector's hand but made no effort to respond.

Wilson stepped further into the room and cleared his throat.

"And his associate, Wilson Davies." The butler bowed before retreating through the doorway.

"Detective Wilson Davies, at your service." Wilson removed his top hat.

Sniffles mingled with the crackle of the lit hearth as four pairs of eyes fell upon the gangly detective. Mr Talmage blinked several times before they widened in recognition.

"How *dare* you bring him here!" The greying Mr Talmage brushed past the inspector and stormed towards Wilson. The vein in Mr Talmage's forehead stuck out. "This man is not allowed to step even a foot into my house."

"Well, I believe that's a bit too late." A wide grin spread across Wilson's face but faltered when no one else laughed. Pity, a sense of humour could cure almost anything.

The expressions of the older women matched the ferocity of Mr Talmage's reaction, save for Mrs Talmage, who hardly seemed to register anyone else in the room. Her wet gaze fell on the drenched kerchief she held in her trembling hands.

"Now, Mr Talmage, I assure you," the inspector said in an attempt to reason with him. "I will be handling this case with great care."

"You won't be handling anything with *that* buffoon!" He waved his hand at Wilson, who frowned.

"I beg your pardon, but the only buffoon in this room is —" Wilson didn't have time to finish that statement before Mr Talmage's knuckles met his square jaw.

The detective stumbled back into a fauteuil armchair, one of the posh French ones with the intricate wooden frames and embroidered upholstery. Wilson would have admired it had black speckles not been impeding his vision. His back slammed against the velvet cushion, the force of which sent the whole chair tipping onto its back legs before keeling over. The detective hit the ground with a loud thud, and then everything went dark.

7
DECK THE HALLS

THE RINGING in Wilson's ears muffled the shouts and exclamations that filled the drawing-room. He slowly came to, and the fuzzy room grew clearer. A hand stretched out to help him up. He gripped it with one while he messaged his jaw with the other. It cracked, and the tender skin below his lip smarted at the touch, but when he withdrew his hand, there was no sign of blood which was something.

He groaned as he rose back upright onto two sapphire-shoed feet.

"Are you okay?" A deep, gruff voice asked.

Wilson blinked the black spots away, the chief inspector's reddish-grey mutton chops coming into view. The officer and the woman with the pearled hair net were both at his side.

"Yes, fine." Wilson gasped. A sharp stab in his lower back sent a spasm through his body. "I guess I should've expected that."

The chief smirked and slapped him on the back.

"Irvin, please," came Mrs Talmage's soft voice.

Mr Talamage was at the mantle once again, his back

turned away. His response to his wife was too low for Wilson to make it out, but he saw the effect. Mrs Talmage shut her mouth instantly, her lower lip shaking as fresh tears swelled. Mrs Peaton didn't even look one bit bothered by Mr Talmage's outburst. She barely glanced in the direction of the commotion, her hands on Mrs Talmage's shoulder to comfort the poor woman.

"That is the only warning you'll get," Mr Talmage said, his tone calm.

"Please, let us keep things peaceful," said the chief.

"Well, it's a bit late for that." Wilson brushed himself off and straightened the collar of his frock coat. "I guess that's one way of treating a renowned detective who's solved hundreds of cases such as Madam Onay's—well, not exactly like Madam Onay as each case has its own particular flavour created by the uniqueness of the murderer—"

"Oh, just like you *'solved'* my son's murder?" Mr Talmage whirled around, his eyes glaring with rage.

"Indeed, I did solve it." Wilson broadened his shoulders and took calculated steps towards him. The slight flicker in the older man's eyes made the corner of Wilson's lip turn up just a smidge. It was the look of uncertainty, possibly in anticipation of Wilson's retaliation for the punch. He wouldn't, of course. Not when there were more pressing matters at hand. "Our killer is behind bars now, is he not?"

Mr Talmage scoffed. "I've read all the reports. Everyone knows that there was a second party."

Wilson arched a brow at this confession. "And pray tell, who do you think this second party could've been?"

Say it, he thought. *Say you knew about Madam Onay's involvement. It would make it so much easier for the chief inspector to arrest you.*

Mr Talmage guffawed and turned back to his place at the mantel.

"Chief Inspector Plundell." Mrs Peaton's rose, glaring daggers at Wilson while directing her words at the officer. "While we are grateful you're taking it upon yourself to assume an active role in this morning's… disturbance, you must understand that this is not a good time for the Talmage's."

"I understand, madam," the inspector replied, all the colour draining from his pink face. "But we've found new evidence to suggest the killing of Madam Onay is connected to the murder of the Talmage's son."

Mrs Talmage froze just as she was about to blow her scarlet nose for the hundredth time. "What do you mean?"

All eyes turned to the distraught woman, and Mrs Peaton sat back down onto the velvet chaise next to her.

The chief inspector cleared his throat, giving Wilson a look to warn him to keep his mouth shut. The detective sighed and decided to do what he did best and stick to observing. For now, at least.

"There was a message left on the…" the inspector's voice faltered and glanced among the women present.

Mrs Talmage widened her eyes in expectation.

"On the dead body?" Mrs Peaton finished.

"Mrs Peaton, you're too crass!" The woman in the pearled hair net scolded. "Do you not see Mrs Talmage's disposition?

"Please, Mrs Tilcott, as if hiding the truth would do her any better." Mrs Peaton rolled her eyes at the elderly woman.

Mrs Talmage burst into a fresh round of sobs, and Mrs Tilcott embraced her, sending a glare at Mrs Peaton.

"She's no tact whatsoever," Mrs Tilcott muttered, just barely loud enough for Wilson to hear.

He studied Mrs Tilcott in the pearled hair net with intrigue. Despite her advanced age, she held herself with the posture of someone half her age. A cane was unnecessary from the way she moved to the window, but still, she grasped one in her right hand, which he found curious.

Could this petite woman indeed be the same Mrs Tilcott whose cat the late Irvin Talmage had once babysat? And whose cat had been killed in such a ghastly way? It must've been as he couldn't imagine there being another Mrs Tilcott in Halifax with who the Talmages acquainted themselves so closely with. Just think of the confusion. The elderly woman must've had a strong stomach, remembering Barnaby's description of how she'd found her feline.

The chief inspector cleared his throat for the umpteenth time. "The killer left a note on the body indicating it was for the late Irvin."

"For Irvin?" Mrs Talmage echoed before her eyes glistened, and her shoulders shook with the sudden sob that came forth. "My Irvin."

"I just need to know where each of you were this morning before the funeral," the inspector concluded.

Mr Talmage paced behind the chaise, running a hand over his balding head and muttered something to himself.

"We were all here preparing for the service," Mrs Peaton said, her severe eyebrows drawing together.

Wilson arched a brow. What an intriguing set of dynamics this ensemble had. An affluent businessman, his wife, a widow, and an old cat-lady—only two of which had any relation—all under the same roof the morning before the funeral. What a captive alibi. Could they all be in on it?

"Well, not all of us," Mrs Tilcott piped in from the window overlooking Spring Garden Road.

And the plot thickens. A slight grin spread across Wilson's face.

Mrs Peaton gave the old cat lady in the pearl hair net a ferocious stare that not even the dim-witted chief inspector missed.

"And who was that? Chief Inspector Plundell pulled out a notebook from his pocket.

Of course, he used a pen and pad out in the field like a novice. Wilson tapped his foot on the carpet, wondering if anyone would notice if he took his leave to go nosy around the house. There was something Talmage's weren't saying that made the hackles on his neck stand upright, and he wouldn't rest until he found out what it was.

Perhaps he'd find evidence of Mr Talmage having any medical knowledge in his study? Or Madam Onay's blood splashed upon a bit of clothing? If Madam Onay had been dead only for about five to six hours, as Dr Larson suggested, then that would put the time of death one hour and a half before the funeral, give or take. If this was Mr Talmage's doing—or anyone else's in this room—then that wouldn't have given them much time between slaying the gipsy, moving the body from wherever the actual deed was committed, and changing clothes before the funeral. Perhaps it even occurred in this very home? Did they even have a basement?

A sharp sniff echoed as Mrs Talmage blew her nose. "She must be speaking of Irvin's fiancée, Lauretta."

"Don't speak her name," Mr Talmage spat.

"And where was this Lauretta?" The chief inspector asked.

"Who knows where that poor unfortunate was," Mrs Peaton cried and lifted her chin. "No one in this room would. She was certainly not good enough for our Irvin, given her class. Which is why Mr Talmage couldn't approve of their engagement."

"Precisely," Mr Talmage agreed with his secretary. "And where is this note about our son anyway? I'd like to see it."

Wilson took a slight back step towards the doorway. As intriguing as family dysfunctions and parental disapproval were, he really was more interested in finding out what the

Talmages were hiding. His experience taught him that all aristocratic families, particularly one as powerful as this one, had dark secrets.

"Of course." The chief inspector reached for his back pocket only to remove a bit of lint. "I had it with me… it was right here!"

Mrs Peaton pressed her lips into a thin line.

"Do you mean to tell me that you, the *chief inspector*"—Mr Talmage waved a hand of the poor officer — "who has come here on the very day of my son's funeral to ensure confidence in us that his ability to uphold justice can be trusted, has *lost* a key piece of evidence?"

With the Talmages, Mrs Peaton, and Mrs Tilcott's attention all on the chief inspector, Wilson took this opportunity to duck out of the room. Their shouts echoed out into the grand hall, which was now, thankfully, empty of servants. He darted for the second doorway nearby and peeked his head inside. A massive dining table filled the entirety of the room.

"Not this one," he muttered to himself and dashed past the grand staircase to the other side of the hall, where he repeated the process.

A blue drawing-room, a green one, a library, and a conservatory all occupied various sections of the west wing. Deflated and about to give the upstairs a try, Wilson spotted a narrow door in his peripheral just to the left of the staircase. He paused at the foot of the grand staircase and checked over his shoulder. A maid flitted by, too occupied with whatever errand she was on to notice. Now or never.

He bit back a smile and waltzed to the tiny, mysterious door and reached for the handle to turn it. The latch clicked, and the spindle turned a smidge, then stopped. He rattled the handle a few times, but it was safely locked. With a quick glance in either direction, he lowered himself onto his knees. He winced as the harsh marble pressed against him.

The mortise lock was impressive, to be sure. From his inspection, he could tell it was one of the more advanced ones with a lever tumbler lock. And, judging by what he could see of the lock system that glistened in pristine condition, he suspected it to have five levers. It had to be new as only those models came with such enhancements. But why would the Talmages require security on such a tiny door that looked more like the entrance to a coat closet? And why was it replaced with one so new? He would just have to wait and see after he picked it.

It would be tricky and, for the ordinary fellow, impossible. Particularly with his time constraint. Good thing he wasn't normal, and luckily from the shouts and protests that echoed from the drawing-room, he could tell they hadn't noticed his departure.

However, it was only a matter of time, and he still needed to get to Dr Larson's to fetch the killer's note. The chief inspector was the real buffoon. He'd left it behind without even realizing it. If only he'd been able to take it without them noticing, that would've been genius. But alas, he had to leave it behind, creating a reason for the inspector to follow him in a hurry. Now Wilson had to get to it before the inspector figured out where he'd left it. But first, this door.

He reached into the breast pocket of his frock coat and sighed with relief when his fingers grasped a small purse. He'd almost forgotten it was there. It housed his tools for this exact occasion which he'd hardly had the use of in some time. The cylindrical apparatus with 'a' shape at one end slipped into his fingers like an old glove, and he inserted the longer end into the lock followed by a small picking wire. It slid into place, and he turned the apparatus counterclockwise, listening for the click of the iron curtain.

Ping.

He smiled and adjusted his position on the floor, his

steady hand keeping the t-shaped tool still while carefully manoeuvring the picking wire.

Cling!

The first door opened. A few more clicks, and he hit a false door. He sighed, having to start from the top. He wouldn't make the same mistake twice. Then, turning the apparatus back clockwise, he closed and reopened the curtain and attempted once again.

"Click on one"—he wiggled the metal again, his breath catching as each tiny movement rattled into place — "click on two."

He bypassed three to avoid getting trapped again and moved on to four which snapped open with ease. A final click followed by the satisfying slide of the deadbolt when it opened sent a jubilant smile upon his lips.

"Aha!" He chuckled and pocketed his tools.

Wilson turned the handle and nearly skipped with delight through the tiny door. The brightness of the grand hall vanished, and in its stead, a vat of darkness replaced it. He pulled out his lighter and snapped the flint wheel. Sparks followed by a flicker of fire illuminated a narrow hall. Wilson squinted, adjusting to the dim light. He was shoulder to shoulder against the walls that stretched up on either side of him. The forest green runner stretched onward, guiding him forward.

He marched a mere ten paces, and the hallway opened up to a larger room, the ceiling only a foot higher than in the hallway. Shelves encased the entire oval room, and each filled with an array of books. A small fireplace with more books on the mantel stood behind a mahogany desk and tufted leather sofa.

"A second library?" His mouth fell slack and the extraordinary sight.

It wasn't until he reached the desk that he realized it was

so much more than a library, but an office that much resembled his own. He scanned the surface of the desk, choosing to ignore the abominable mess upon it, in search of anything resembling handwriting. A letter, perhaps. Anything with Mr Talmage's script on it would suffice.

Adrenaline pumped in his ears, unable to deter the thrill of not knowing if or who would be waiting for him when he emerged from the secret office. He hoped no one, but there was always a risk when chances of opportunity were snatched.

He lit the candlestick on the edge of the desk and snapped the lighter shut to free his hand. A ledger sat open underneath a blanket of papers and trash. With a swat, he tossed the mess aside and studied the handwriting, but he couldn't be certain it matched. The thought of stealing it ran through his mind, but of course, that couldn't't' go missing as it would raise too many suspicions. At least to those who knew of this room's existence. He was fairly confident Mr Talmage would be one of those.

While carefully shuffling a few newspapers, pamphlets, and binders in the hopes of finding scraps with scribblings that matched the handwriting on the ledger, he spotted a framed certificate on the wall. Tucked within one of the glass cabinets, this shelf was intentionally void of books. He leaned his head to one side, abandoning his search and approached the odd display. With the candle in hand, he lifted it enough to see the frame upon the ledge and tsked.

"Why, Mr Talmage, you astound me." There on the ledge, the cursive print of a certification as a medical practitioner glared back at him. The signature revealed it was issued to none other than Irvin Talmage, Sr.

Wilson shook his head. Why go through all that schooling only to spend the rest of your life doing something else entirely? Perhaps an unwanted inheritance and 'family business' were to blame? Whatever it was, this was evidence that Mr Talmage had the knowledge to remove Madam Onay's stomach. He also had reason to avenge his own son's death and could've easily seen Madam Onay at the crime scene. A perfect suspect. Almost *too* perfect, but still worth investigating.

Footsteps from overhead alerted Wilson that he was wasting precious time, and he snapped into motion.

"Where is he?" An angry voice shouted.

Wilson's heart skipped a beat, finally spotting a tossed laundry list in the wastebasket. He grabbed it and ran down the narrow hall. He blew out the candle and swiftly removed himself from the forbidden office under the stairs.

"There! A woman cried to his left.

He hastened away from the door and into the grand foyer, his heels tapping against the marble floor.

"Where've you been?" The inspector cried, looking every bit as livid as the anger in his tone.

"Forgive me. I was in need of the lavatory." Wilson tipped his hat to the angry band that barged towards him but didn't stop. He darted towards the front door. "Now, I really must take my leave. A detective's work is never finished."

"Stop! Stop right there this instant!" The inspector and Mr Talmage shouted together, but it was no use.

By the time the inspector reached the exit, he'd already extricated himself from the manor into the bitter northern wind that bristled down the street. The clap of hooves pulling carriages and the muted call of a ship's foghorn welcomed Wilson, and, seeing it pertinent to forgo the captain's carriage, he made haste once again on foot towards the doctor's.

His pulse pumped high at all the excitement of nearly getting caught. He was happy to have an excuse to use his lockpicking skills, but it had taken him much too long. Was he losing his touch?

The thought of this formed a pit in his stomach that tormented him all the way to the medical office and pestered him even more when he retired at Barnaby's flat for the evening.

8
A WITCH CAME DOWN AT CHRISTMAS

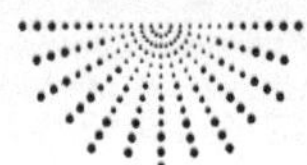

Engel's Emporium,
Albemarle Street

Emma followed the detective all the way back to the little brick and mortar shop. She hoped above all that the book would still be at the McLeod House and that she'd have enough time to go back and get the compendium for Barnaby.

The sun hung low behind the Citadel, casting shadows across the cobblestoned street. Nightfall would come all too soon, and she knew Franziska would be upset if she didn't return before then. A shiver ran down her spine. It was definitely getting late.

"Hey there, Clement," Emma whispered to the horse, still tied up in front of the shop.

She stroked his white and grey speckled coat. Clement shook his mane with a snort.

"I know. We'll be done soon."

Of course, she couldn't really understand Clement. Only

Artus had that power, but from the way the horse stomped his hoof, she could tell he was ready to go home. She sometimes wished she had Artus's magic ability over her own. At least then, she wouldn't have to drink blood to contain her beast. But then, there was something alluring about light and dark all within one if just its poetic symmetry.

"Coming?" Barnaby asked from the stained glass door.

"Yes." She gave Clement a final pat on the back and followed the detective into the shop.

She rubbed her hands together in the warmth of the shop. So distracted by her own thoughts, she'd forgotten how cold she was.

The shop was surprisingly busier than it had been earlier in the day, with a few women seated by the bay windows with noses in books or steaming cups of various herbal blends. A few men patrolled the aisles for their desired editions. These must've been the few townsfolk who didn't mind a little mysticism. It put a smile on her face. Even Barnaby drew his eyebrows upward, but he didn't comment on the crowd.

"Hello again, Miss Gertrud," Barnaby greeted once they'd reached the tea counter. "Is he in now?"

"He's in the back," the towering woman behind the counter replied in a thick accent.

"You can—" The woman named Gertrud stopped when she met Emma's gaze.

Emma couldn't help but stare. She looked so much like Franziska, with her slender build and snow-white hair she wore in two puffs on either side of her head.

"Have we met?" Gertrud tilted her head to the side and sniffed the air.

The words stuck in Emma's throat, and so she simply shook her head. She flushed and peeled her eyes away.

"Hmm, well, best follow me then." Gertrud waved for

them to move around the counter towards a door off to the side.

She unlocked it with a key at her hip. Emma wondered what was so important that they had to keep it locked.

The air grew thick, almost foggy, when they passed over the threshold into the dim storeroom. Emma breathed in the air and coughed. The taste of something sharp and rustic hung in the air. She glanced at Barnaby, but he didn't seem to smell it. Instead, he breathed in the air with a neutral expression as if he didn't smell the stench at all. Emma made a face that went unnoticed in the murky room.

Dozens of lamps illuminated the little room, which housed even more books. They were perched within glass encasements beside an array of towering boxes stacked upon each other. They stretched up all the way to the ceiling. A rusted globe dangled on the edge of one box, tossed among dozens of broken clocks. All of this crowded around a giant apothecary case that covered the entire wall on the far side. The drawers had colour coated knobs and tags. It reminded her of how the mistress would organize her drawers at the lace shop she worked when she lived in London. Though she doubted these ones housed any thread or lace.

"Roderic," Gertrud addressed the petite man seated on a stool. His back was to them, hunched over a desk next to the apothecary case.

"Yes? What is it?" He glanced over his shoulder.

Smoke billowed up from the cigarette tucked in the crook of his mouth. His owl-like eyes glazed over them from behind half-moon glasses before returning his attention to his paperwork. He resembled too much like the owl statue perched on his desk for her liking.

"Detective Barnaby Grey has returned," Miss Gertrud said, approaching her brother. The keys at her waist rattled.

"You remember him, yes? The one who purchased the *compendium?*"

The way Gertrud emphasized the word 'compendium' made it sound like there was only one. But that had to be wrong. There had to be more copies of it, yes? Emma assumed there had to be. Otherwise, why would they sell it? Of course, it was an unusual bookshop.

If it were the only copy, then it must've been a fortune. How could Mr Barnaby have ever afforded something like that? Her stomach tightened once again, the guilt of losing it becoming even more unbearable.

"The compendium, you say?" The metal stool squealed as he shuffled his feet and spun the seat around to face them.

His white hair poked out beneath a velvet smoke cap. Its gold tassel fluttered against his cheek. He tossed it out of the way with a flick of his hand. When his eyes fell upon Emma, he widened them, peeling his spectacles from his nose and stood. The short man stood almost at eye level with her. A second later, the cigarette dropped to the floor.

"Oh!" He exclaimed when the ashes sparked and hit a bit of exposed skin at his ankles. "Forgive me."

He thrust the heel of his shoe down onto the end of the cigarette in big, dramatic stomps before picking it up.

"Are you all right?" Barnaby asked.

"Yes, yes, yes," the owl-eyed man said, straightening. "I'm fine. I shall take it from here, sister. I'm sure three are customers out waiting for your celebrated teas."

"Of course," the much taller woman replied and turned to leave, but not without giving Emma a conspicuous side glance and a sniff.

Did she smell bad? Emma folded her arms across her chest just in case. And why were they staring at her like that?

"Detective, my sister says you've been enjoying the compendium thus far."

"Yes, indeed, but I do have a few questions. Do you have a few moments to spare?"

"Yes, yes, many moments." The short man gave a quick bow and returned his half-moon glasses to his nose. "And who is this young lady you've brought with you?"

His eyes widened once more when they locked on her.

"E-Emma," she stuttered.

"Emma," he repeated.

He removed the space between them and stretched a hand out in greeting. Emma glanced at it nervously but then took it. When their hands touched, a spark zapped, and the bookshop owner clasped hers in both of his.

"What are you doing?" She cried when he sniffed the length of her palm, ripping her hand away before she could find out.

"I do apologize. I didn't mean to alarm you." Roderic lifted his hands up. "It's just, I haven't experienced the scent of true magic in some time."

Emma and Barnaby both gaped at him.

"You know what I am?"

"Well, no. Not exactly," the odd shopkeeper said. "Magic has a very distinct smell, but what variant of magical creature is almost impossible to identify unless you've come by it before and *you*, my dear, I most certainly have not been in the presence of before."

"Smells? Variants?" Barnaby spluttered, drawing his eyebrows in.

Emma thought he might faint from how confused he looked, and she imagined he had a great many more questions than she did.

"I think I will need a cigarette after all."

"Of course. Have a seat." He gestured towards a few overturned crates near his desk for them to have a seat on.

Barnaby gave a grateful nod and took the proffered cigarette with an eager hand.

Emma shook her head when Roderic offered her one. "Can you really smell magic?"

"Can you not?" Roderic lifted his white eyebrows, too white for his age. She shook her head, and he tucked his ink pen behind a pointy ear. "Curious. Quite curious."

"What's curious?" Barnaby asked between puffs.

A wide grin spread across Roderic's face. "That someone emanating so much magic can't even smell it herself."

Emma's mouth dropped. She smelled of magic? What did that smell like?

"Magic at its core is made up of two known variants," Roderic began. "Where is the compendium? I believe there's a chapter on this in there."

Barnaby swallowed visibly and rubbed his knee with a free hand. "I—"

"I forgot it," Emma piped up. "I was just looking at it, but we were in a rush which is why we've come here."

"Ah, that's unfortunate." Roderic glanced about as if looking for something but sat back down on the stool. "I'll just have to remember, then, won't I?"

He leaned forward, his owl-eyes sparkling. They all mimicked his posture in curiosity.

"As I said, there are two aromas that are known. The scent of the begapte or, in English, the gifted, and that of the geistige bestien, your 'spirit beasts'"—he put this in air quotes — "which we refer to as bestien for short. Begapte, like myself, tend to have some sort of citrus-based notes. Bestien have a woodsy aura."

"Even the kob… kobulars?" She winced, knowing that didn't sound right.

"Koboldgeist?" Roderic offered.

She nodded.

"Yes, yes, they do!" Roderic chuckled and slapped his knee. "Those little ones smell like hickory. So much so it could burn off your nose."

"If bestien are spirits, then what are begapte?" asked Barnaby.

"We're magicians, of course. Gifted with bestien-like magic but are not possessed like the bestien. Those beasts are rarely able to do much damage without possessing a willing human or magical vessel."

Barnaby and Emma shared a fearful glance.

"In addition to the citrus or woodsy smell, all who possess magic have a very…" he paused, his owl eyes darting off into the distance as he searched for the right word. "A sort of sulfuric undertone, but it's diluted."

"And what's mine?" Emma asked.

"That's what's so puzzling. I've never smelled anything like yours in my whole life. You both have the scent of human and of spirit." He stuck his bulbous nose into the air and took a long sniff. "It's neither woodsy nor citrusy, but both and neither all at once."

He sniffed again. "Floral, too. A deep, spicy aroma like an opulent stargazer lily. Not a scent among either creature. Still, it's magic. Powerful magic, in fact. So, tell me, what is your power?"

Emma swallowed hard, wondering how much she should reveal. She had the odd sense like she could trust him, but she wasn't used to telling other people about her magic. Her heart thumped, and her hands tingled with the quiver of power that ached to be let out. Was it better to just show him?

She dug her fingers into her palms and took deep, long breaths. Then, squaring her shoulders, she focused on the energy around her that sizzled with static.

The lamps spoke to her, and she angled her hand towards the one on Roderic's desk. She wiggled her fingers.

Snap!

The light within the glass went out before it sparked to life midair and hung for a moment above the lamp. Roderic followed it with awe as it zigzagged across the room.

ZING!

Warmth zizzled in her fingertips. The fire flickered around her fingernails and crackled, growing even brighter.

"Marvellous," Roderic gasped, admiring her glowing hands. He folded his hands in prayer and rested them on his chin.

"To be honest, I don't know what I am," Emma said, waving her hand back at the lamp, sending the ball of light back. My family says that I have powers like they do, but unlike them, I'm fully human."

"Are they bestien?" Roderic asked, his smile faltering.

Emma shook her head. "Their powers come from a different world than ours."

"Oh! I've never heard of such magic. But I suppose it was inevitable that another world would find us. Anyway, thank you for sharing that demonstration with me."

Emma returned Roderic's look of gratitude with a smile. The strange owl-man was growing on her.

"Detective, you said you had a few questions?"

Barnaby cleared his throat. "Erm, yes. It was about something Emma saw last night."

"I want to know if you've heard of Frau Perchta?" She asked.

The owl-eyed man's face fell slack, his knuckles turning white as he gripped the corner of his writing desk a bit too hard. "You don't mean the Hexenfrau von Weihnachten?"

She nodded, and the shopkeeper *tsked* several times. The

room fell silent. Suddenly Roderic stood and rushed over to a stack of boxes resting on the floor near his desk. He tapped his fingers on his lips, scanning them in search of just the right one.

Emma fidgeted with a loose string of her dress.

"And what is… this Christmas spirit thing you said?" Barnaby asked.

"You caught that, did you?" The shopkeeper gave a nervous chuckle. "Die Hexenfrau, or the witch woman of Christmas, is the worst sort of Hexengeist there is. The evilest bestien there ever was. Aside from Krampus, of course. Now that's a nasty Hexenmann."

Emma looked to Barnaby, whose colourless expression mirrored the horror she felt.

"So, what you're saying is that this Frau Perchta fable that Emma's circus-mum grew up with is *true*?"

"Indeed, all tales are rooted in some sort of truth," Roderic said over his shoulder. He peeked inside one of the stacked boxes but shook his head and muttered something under his breath before he moved on to the next. "I would show you more if only we had your book on hand. It is really quite useful in such circumstances as these, that compendium—Aha!"

The petite man shivered, his head cocked to one side, and he blinked rapidly until his eyes grew twice in size and his irises flashed yellow. Emma gasped. It was almost like her own eyes when she used her powers, but this was different. More animalistic than human.

Roderic's bulbous-tipped nose jetted out and sharpened into point now resembling a beak more than a nose, and a pair of wings shot out from his shoulder blades in a puff of feathers.

"Good heavens, he's a bird!" Barnaby coughed as the smoke went down the wrong pipe.

The shopkeeper flapped his calico-feathered wings,

which lifted him off the ground. He flew up to the ceiling, where he reached for the box at the very top with three-taloned claws for hands.

"A *bird*?" Roderic laughed. "I'm no bird."

"Then what are you?" Emma asked, eyes wide as he floated back down to stand before them.

"That, my friend"—he shrugged his shoulders and how wings, talons, and beak retracted with a shimmer — "is a very long story. One we don't have time for. Not if Frau Perchta is on the loose here in Halifax. Did you happen to see who this bestien possessed?"

Emma shook her head.

Roderic sighed. "Well, we'll just have to work on your sense of smell then, won't we?"

"Wouldn't you be able to track down the witch?" Barnaby asked. "I mean, you can smell magic."

"Oh no, she would smell me and my magic from a mile away, but you, dear Emma, she won't expect." He placed the box on the counter of the giant apothecary case. "Now, where is that Hexenspiegel?"

"Spiegel," Emma repeated under her breath. Hadn't she heard this before? Her heart skipped a beat, and she leapt up. "I heard the cloaked figure say that. I mean, something like it, anyway. There was a bit more to the spell I can't remember."

"I'm sure you did," Roderic said as he pulled out a silver and black hand mirror from the box. "Spiegel means mirror. It is the opening into our world for the witch spirits to travel. It allows them to prey on those who seek them.

A Hexenspiegel or witch mirror, like this one when, allows one to trap a witch into a single mirror through a spell, though only for a short time. But"—he lifted a knobby finger — "once you trap this Frau Perchta, it is imperative that you bring it back to me here so that it may be sealed. For only through an enchantment can this mirror be transformed into a Spiegelgrab."

Emma and Barnaby both frowned.

"A mirror grave," Roderic translated and handed the small hand mirror to Emma. "I must warn you, be very careful when approaching this Hexengeist."

"I will," Emma replied.

She admired the Fleur de Lis motives that swirled around the mirror's handle. It looped up in glittering silver along the back of the mirror, which portrayed a wide-eyed cat with a pendant between its ears. The design continued on the front of the mirror and wrapped around the oval glass, ending in two points at the top where the ears were.

"I'd suggest that you, Sir Barnaby, be with her while she hunts."

"I will," Barnaby said mid puff, his fingers trembled a bit.

"So, when this is turned into a grave, she won't be able to come out?" Emma asked.

Roderic nodded. "The enchantment will freeze the witch within the confines of the mirror, which is mostly impenetrable."

"What do you mean 'mostly'?" Barnaby flicked the ash off the tip of his cigarette.

"Bestien can never die. Their spirits can only be banished but can be reconjured using spells like the one Emma witnessed."

"Then what good is trapping it?" The detective asked.

"Why, to keep them from hurting others, of course! And if we can trap her before she's struck the better, but she will kill, and you will know her work, for she leaves hundreds of bowelless corpses in her wake."

Emma glanced up at Barnaby, who wiped a bead of sweat from his brow with a kerchief.

Roderic gasped. "She's already struck, hasn't she?"

"Yes." Barnaby licked his lips nervously.

"Then there's no time to waste." Roderic ushered them towards the exit and unlocked it. "Take the mirror, find the one who is possessed by aiming it towards them. But whatever you do, do not let them see you! For Frau Perchta will shatter the glass making the device useless."

Emma held the mirror gingerly. "But how will I know who to point it at? I can't smell magic."

Barnaby was already through the door, and Emma figured he was bounding towards the shop's front door on wobbly knees. He could be a tad fearful. But she couldn't blame him. He was magicless, surrounded by demons, witches and other bestien spirits. At least she and her circus family had supernatural abilities. She could only imagine how scary it was for the detective.

"There may not be enough time to develop it, but we can try." Roderic paused, a thoughtful look spreading across his ow-like features. "Tell you what, come back tomorrow after closing. There may be something Gertrud and I can teach you that will help speed up the process."

"Thank you." Emma smiled and turned to leave when Roderic patted her arm.

She looked up into his owl-eyes that still glowed yellow.

"Remember, your sense of smell can only help you be more covert, but the mirror is the only way to trap it. Guard it carefully."

"I will," she promised.

With one last wave, she exited the back storeroom and out the front door after Barnaby. The bitter wind stung her cheeks as she pushed her way out onto the sidewalk. The detective stood next to her horse, and a frantic voice shouted at him from someone just out of sigh.

"How could you not tell us she was safe? We were worried sick!"

Emma's heart skipped a beat at the familiar accent.

"And how do you suppose I do that?" Barnaby asked. "Send a letter through the post?"

Emma neared Barnaby to get a better look and spotted Franziska's mass of snow-white hair pinned in curls on top of her head, standing opposite the detective. Passerbys turned a curious eye at the shouting woman, but Emma was certain it was her silver trousers and matching frilled blouse that made them take a second glance.

"I don't know. Send a carrier pigeon or something." Franziska's cheeks were red with heat, and she waved her hands about frantically. "With everything that's going on in this God-forsaken town, I'd expect—Oh!"

She froze when she spotted Emma.

"Emma!" Her eyes watered as she ran to her, pulling her into a desperate embrace.

A pit formed in her stomach, not realizing how much worry she'd brought upon her circus-mum.

"I'm sorry," Emma whispered.

Franziska stepped back, but her hands still clutched Emma's shoulders. "Are you all right?"

Emma nodded. "I didn't mean to worry you. I just had to find someone who would believe me about Frau Perchta. Detective Barnaby helped me, and so did the owners of this shop after they saw what I could do."

Franziska's eyes darted between Barnaby and the book-shop. "You told them about your magic? Do you have any idea how *dangerous* that could've been?"

"They're different. They have magic, too. Not like ours, but it's still wonderful. You have to meet them."

Franziska's expression hardened. "Das ist verboten. I forbid it, now come back to the campsite."

"What? You can't do that!" Emma's breath hitched, and her lip trembled. "You didn't even believe me, but *they* do, and Detective Barnaby already says that Frau Perchta's killed someone."

"All the more reason for you to go back to the campsite, now, come," Franziska replied, turning to drag her back towards the caravan parked across the street.

"No, it's not." Emma yanked her hand away.

Franziska turned and gaped back at the young girl.

Emma flushed. "You used to treat me as an equal, but now I've just become something you need to protect. Well, I don't need your protection. What I need is to find Frau Perchta."

"Frau Perchta's a myth," Franziska replied with an exaggerated sigh.

"Is it so hard to believe that there's other magic out there in the world? That perhaps the myths you grew up with are true?"

Lady Franziska." Barnaby stepped between them, raising his hands up. "I would've been skeptical too if we hadn't found evidence of what Emma saw at the McLeod House. In addition to what the owner of this shop told us."

"Frau Perchta's a spirit," Emma said. "And she's possessing someone in this town. Only I can stop her because she won't be able to smell my magic."

Franziska gave a nervous laugh, but her eyes betrayed her as a sliver of fear flitted across them as if reliving a distant memory. "Even if I did believe this, that would be all the more reason you shouldn't be running around town exposing your magic to strangers. You could've been hurt, and I would never have known!"

Emma bit her lip. "I know. I should've told you where I was going."

"Good," the older woman said and motioned for Emma to fetch the reins of her horse. "Now, no more of this Frau Perchta business, ja?"

"But I have to do this," Emma cried. "I have to try and stop her before she kills anyone else in this town."

"Why?" Franziska shook her head. "This town would kill you if they discovered what you are!"

"Because"—Emma swallowed hard — "there are people in this town I care about."

Franziska softened when Emma shared a glance with Barnaby.

"It's okay, Emma," Barnaby said. "You should listen to Lady Franziska. It is too dangerous."

"But I have the mirror and the book." Emma's eyes widened. "The book! I have to go get it."

"Emma, you should go home with your family and discuss things. I'll fetch the book."

"And what about tomorrow? I have to help you catch the witch," she replied before directing a look of pleading at Franziska. "He needs someone with powers on his side. Besides, isn't this what you and Antoine have taught me? To help others? What sort of person would I be if I just let Barnaby go after this beast on his own?"

Franziska didn't respond, her face torn with indecision as she chewed the corner of her lip. Emma knew she'd hit a nerve. But after several moments, the young girl's confidence waned, and she slumped her shoulders. It was no use. The Beaumonts had only a few rules. The first and foremost one was to stick together, which she'd broken in merely a day. How could she expect Franziska to trust her now?

"Please?" Emma folded her hands in prayer.

Franziska took a steeling breath. "Fine."

"Really?" A flood of hope washed through Emma.

Franziska nodded. "But be careful."

Emma threw her arms around the woman clad head-to-toe in silver glitter.

"But be careful," Franziska said when she stepped back.

"Of course."

"And if you get her hurt"—Franziska turned on Barnaby, her eyes darkened as she jabbed a sharp claw at him — "or if the town gets wind of her power or us in any way, I'll—"

Barnaby raised his hands up in defence, taking a step back as she moved like a snake ready to eat its prey.

"I'll mache dich kalt!"

Emma's mouth fell open. She'd never seen Franziska so… threatening. Of course, she had no idea what Franziska said, but from Barnaby's paled expression, the message had definitely gotten across.

"Come." Franziska grabbed Clement's reins and led the way back to the caravan.

Emma's cheeks burned with a mixture of embarrassment at Franziska's overreaction and excitement at the prospect of helping others.

"I'll see you tomorrow?" She asked Barnaby in a meek voice.

"Yes, until tomorrow." Barnaby gave a reassuring nod and a tip of his hat in salute.

She skipped across the icy roads, undeterred by its slickness. The prospect of learning more magic sent a flutter through her heart, and she hoped she could learn quickly. She needed to use her powers for something good, like performing alongside her circus family or helping others.

Though she desperately wanted the former ever since she'd decided to join the Beaumonts, she knew this wouldn't be a possibility with the town's growing antimagic sentiments. But somehow, this seemed better. It gave her a sense of purpose in an otherwise chaotic world. Maybe this was her true destiny?

9
O HEXENGEIST

BARNABY WAS PRETTY SURE his heart had never beat so fast in his life. He couldn't get the image of Franziska's cold blue eyes freezing over him like a lake in the dead of winter. She didn't even have to say it, though she had. From her sharp and treacherous features, he already knew that she would put him in the ground if he put Emma in harm's way. He also knew she had the power to do it. Clearly, she reacted as a mother hen would when protecting its young, and he respected that. Though it still made him shiver just thinking about it as he walked down Bishop Street.

He eyed the McLeod House with apprehension. The last bit of sunlight cast eerie shadows across the snow-covered shack. He pulled his sack coat closer as he neared the house with its shattered windows that reminded him more of bared teeth.

"Better get this over with," he said to himself and, with a glance both ways, he pushed the iron gate open.

It squealed behind him, and he ambled towards the front steps. A twig snapped, and he jumped.

"Hello?" His voice faltered.

A gust of wind howled past him. It swept his bowler hat clear off his head, and he scrambled to pick it up from the snow-covered weeds.

He cursed the breeze and straightened. The feeling like the house was watching him swept goosebumps across his arms. What a ridiculous thought that an inanimate object could have eyes. Magic or not, it was still just that. A house long since abandoned. Nothing out of the ordinary there.

"Come on, Barnaby." He dusted off his hat, returning it to the top of his head with a flourish, and reminded himself that he'd only be here for a moment.

The rotten stairs groaned with each step up to the front door. The ice crunched under each footfall. His breath billowed in white puffs of smoke, his chest suddenly growing cold, and he wished he'd remembered his cigarette case. Or at least kept the cigarette Roderic the shopkeeper had given him.

A light flickered from somewhere above him, and he froze. He raised his gaze up to the second-story window and blinked. He could've sworn there was movement just then, but only for a moment before the window went dark again.

Could someone be living there? Or was it Frau Perchta, the Christmas witch? His stomach lurched at the thought, but then he shook it off.

"Don't be daft. There's nothing there." He stepped over the rickety threshold with shaky limbs, his heart still racing at the thought of another presence there with him in the dark room.

He held his breath and turned the corner, half expecting the person possessed by the hexengeist to lunge at him. Why hadn't he thought to bring a weapon?

But nothing happened. He sighed with relief when only a dust-covered empty room welcomed him, the compendium still on the floor half-hidden under the dresser. Had he left it there? He was reasonably certain Emma put it on top of the dresser, not below. Perhaps it'd gotten knocked over in the haste of their escape?

Either way, he was just relieved it was still there. He shuffled from the adjoining room to the leatherbound compendium.

A young girl giggled, echoing from somewhere behind him.

"Who's there?" He grabbed the book and whirled around.

Something blue and eerily translucent darted past the doorway.

Barnaby lifted the book over his shoulders like he was wielding a bat. "I'm warning you, I'm armed!"

The hollow laugh came again. It sent chills down his arms. He took careful steps towards the archway into the front hall he'd just entered from, the book still hoisted in preparation to launch at anyone—or anything—that charged him.

"*What are you doing here?*" The hollow voice asked from the darkness.

Barnaby's eyes darted about the room, wide and dilated. "Show yourself!"

Seconds later, a spectral image of a young girl flickered from the foot of the stairs. She hovered just above a rotten step.

Barnaby blinked several times, praying it was only his imagination. But there she remained. He swallowed hard. Could it be that the McLeod House was *truly* haunted? It wasn't an entirely foreign concept, the existence of ghosts, that is. He'd witnessed the spirit of his own nephew, Archie, after his death not long ago. But this was different somehow. Perhaps it was because this little girl wasn't his family or that there was a killer on the loose. Whatever it was, it unhinged him.

"What do you want?" His voice quivered.

The young girl didn't move, save for her golden hair that fluttered in a nonexistent wind. Her eyes suddenly grew wide, and her mouth fell slack as if in pain.

"I-I'm sorry to intrude," he said, taking a step backwards as she neared. "I was only getting my book."

He stumbled as he turned to leave and nearly ran into a uniformed man who stood at the entrance.

"Oh!" He exclaimed, lowering the book. "Excuse me, officer. I was here investigating earlier and just needed to pick up my—"

The officer's eyes slid back into their sockets which made Barnaby stop.

"Are you all right, sir?"

The officer wobbled on his feet, and before Barnaby could grab him, he toppled forward, landing face-first onto Barnaby's shoes.

"Sir?" He knelt by the unconscious man, setting his book down to free his hands.

He reached for the officer's shoulders, giving him a gentle nudge. Nothing. He placed two fingers on the officer's neck. There was no pulse.

Barnaby gasped, unable to comprehend what could've happened to the poor man. A blue light flickered once again and scanned the room for the apparition.

"What happened to him?" He cried to the girl, but she'd already vanished.

A sudden desire to flee washed over him, but he couldn't. Not with a dead body at his feet. He had to alert the police that this man, whoever he was, was dead. But how? And by who?

With one last gulp and a dab of a kerchief to his dripping forehead, he carefully turned the body with a grunt.

The uniformed body flopped over with a thud to expose a

gaping hole where the man's stomach should be. His belted frock coat was torn to shreds, along with his uniform. If he didn't know any better, who would've thought this man was mauled by an animal. Barnaby doubled over, his stomach convulsed as he dry-heaved. If he hadn't skipped lunch, he was sure it'd be all over the floor by now.

"*Are you next, my pet?*" The girl asked, followed by a harsh cackle.

An involuntary whimper escaped Barnaby. He squinted, the girl hovering once more at the stairwell.

"Who are you?" Barnaby asked, but the only answer he received was a flash of bright red light.

It enveloped the room until the girl morphed into a phantom of an old woman—nay—a rotting corpse with black coal eyes just as Emma had described.

"Frau Perchta!" He clutched his chest, fear constricting the airflow.

But how was she here? Hadn't Emma said she'd possessed someone in a black cloak? Where were they? Or, could it be possible that the spirit and the possessed could be in two places at once? The thought of this sent a shiver down his spine.

The spirit witch shot out across the room, up to the ceiling and hovered above his head. Her crown of goat horns curled back, adorning grey flesh that clung to her hollow browns. She glowed as bright as the moon, a grin spread across her face. Her snake-like tongue jetted out, licking her chapped lips.

"Stay away from me!" He stumbled back, his foot smashing through the floorboards, which sent him keeling head over heels onto the floor.

A high-pitched cry sent Barnaby's hands grasping either side of his head. He rolled onto his back just as the ghost witch flung herself at him. Then, he picked himself and the book up without a second glance and leapt over the dead body towards the exit. As he sprinted like his life depended on it, guilt stung at the thought of leaving the dead body. But his desire to live overcame this compulsion. If that was Frau Perchta, he was lucky to even be alive. There was no way he'd be returning tonight. He made himself feel better by telling himself he'd return to report it in the morning.

His heart slowly returned to a normal pace, and he looked down at the large book in his hands. He had to find out more about this witch if they had any chance of finding the one who she possessed. Where were they? And what sort of person could conjure up such a spirit such as the one he'd just witnessed? He also wondered if a witch spirit could roam around without their vessel. If so, the possibilities of murder were endless, which meant the town was in more danger than he'd first thought.

He flipped the book open, but his heart sank when the only relevant page he could find was completely blank. A White residue covered where the text should've been as if it'd been a chalkboard wiped clean.

The detective's flat,
Grafton Street

Wilson woke up with the dawn and stretched his aching back. The couch was becoming unbearable to sleep on night after night. He really did need to find a place of his own if he was going to stay in Halifax much longer. At least until the conclusion of this case. He had many affairs to tend to back in London, but he imagined he'd be back in Halifax. It may even become a second home for him. If he could find suitable accommodations, that is.

A loud snort came from the adjoining room, curtained off for privacy. Barnaby must've still been asleep. He checked the time, and though it was still early, he decided it was prudent not to waste any time to get on with the investigation.

There were so many still to interview. He needed to speak with each of the Talmages individually, Mrs Peaton, the secretary, and the cat lady Mrs Tilcott. Oh! And Lauretta, the fiancée. Getting each one alone would be tricky but necessary to find out the truth of who killed madam Onay and bring justice to this town. But who to interrogate first?

He contemplated various strategies while he put the kettle on. Mr Talmage was the obvious choice, but the handwriting from the killer's note didn't precisely match the one from the laundry list he'd found. It was close, perhaps even a familial match, but with a tiny difference. The calligraphy of the 'f' was written with a backward slope indicating left-handedness, and from his interactions with Mr Talmage, he'd always used his right.

However, just because the handwriting was all wrong didn't absolve the foundryman entirely. There was still the point of him having a secret office under the stairs for some unknown reason which was suspect even if it had nothing to do with the murder. He would just have to folder that mystery for another time as finding the killer was much more pressing.

With a fresh cup of steaming coffee, he returned from the kitchenette to the sitting room. Then he froze. A trail of mud leading from the front door to Barnaby's curtained-off bedroom blocked his path.

He ground his teeth. "Must I always clean up after him?"

Though they were good friends, it was times like these Wilson couldn't help but wonder why. He kept his place in such a mess it was practically unlivable. And it wasn't as if he didn't know Wilson's views on messes. They were habits that made the establishments of the unrefined. But, for better or worse, he couldn't deny Barnaby had always been an admirable ally and one whose companionship he couldn't live without.

The coffee sloshed when he slammed the mug down with a sigh. A droplet spilt out on the tiny dining table. With his hands now free, he dampened a rag under the faucet and, in tandem with some soap, he mopped up as much of the dirt as he could. What sort of rush could Barnaby have been in not to remove his shoes first before going to bed?

Then he saw it. The ridiculous leatherbound compendium. It sat on the floor beside the flat door, but its condition had significantly worsened since he last saw it. Curious.

He took one last swipe of the rag across the floor before he made his way to the book. He scooped it up, eyeing the front cover. Red dots spattered the title. Licking it, his face soured, and he spluttered.

"Blood?"

But whose blood was it? Was it Barnaby's? Had he been attacked? And what sort of business had Barnaby been up to last night that he'd put himself in that kind of danger?

His first instinct was to barge into his room and demand answers. But where would that get him? It would only put his friend on the defensive and less likely to produce the truth. No, he would set the book down exactly where he'd left it and see what Barnaby did.

Would he offer an explanation unprovoked? Or would he avoid it altogether? It wouldn't necessarily make him guilty if the latter but convey to Wilson that he knew something important about the blood. If the former… Well, it would depend on how he reacted.

A knock from the front door made him jump.

"It's Chief Inspector Plundell," an angry voice called, followed by an even louder knock. "Open this door!"

Wilson quickly tossed the book in the corner just out of sight and swung the door open.

"Where is it?" The chief inspector barged in, arms swinging in a boisterous fashion.

"Where's what?"

"'*What*'?" The chief inspector scoffed and pointed his finger at Wilson. The vein in his neck above his collared uniform bulged. "You know bloody well what I'm talking about."

He waved at the organized mess strewn across the desk in neat piles.

"Please mind your volume, inspector," Wilson whispered, bringing an index finger to his lips and motioning that Barnaby was asleep in the next room.

As if on cue, the detective whimpered in his sleep. "*No! Don't take my teacup.*"

Chief Inspector Plundell's face scrunched in confusion.

Wilson shrugged. "He's been like this all night, the poor man. He must've had quite a night, and I'd really hate to wake him."

"Fine." The officer rolled his eyes. "Now, where's the note?"

"What note?"

"Don't be daft!"

"Inspector, please mind your volume," Wilson hissed.

The inspector huffed. "I'm talkin' about the note, the one the killer left. Give it to me, or I'll arrest you."

"On what grounds?"

"Obstruction comes to mind."

Wilson pondered this and sauntered to his desk. "That's

the second time you've threatened to arrest me. If you could, I'm certain you would've done so by now."

The chief inspector reddened. "How dare—why, I should just—I'm warning you, detective! This is your last chance."

"Once again, I must remind you to mind your volume." Wilson shook his head and jabbed a finger towards the next room.

Chief Inspector Plundell folded his lips over his teeth, his red mutton chops puffing as he let out a slow breath.

"Anyway, there's no need for you to go all red in the face," Wilson said, picking up the coveted letter on his desk and handing it to the officer. "I had every intention of returning it."

"Of course, you did," the chief inspector snipped.

He snatched the letter and took a glance at it, probably to ensure it wasn't a trick. Satisfied, he turned and left without so much as a farewell.

"How rude," Wilson muttered as he picked up some documents that fell.

The stool scraped the floor when he pulled it under him. He glanced up at the front door to be sure he was alone before opening the top drawer. A set of pens, a bottle of ink, and extra parchment welcomed him, but it was the scrap of paper that drew his attention. He pulled it out, revealing a perfect match to the killer's note he'd just given the chief inspector.

A sly grin spread across the detective's face as he admired it. The chief inspector would never notice the difference between the forged note he'd run off with and the real one now in his hands. He set the note aside and pulled out his list of suspects to expound upon them.

The top name listed was Mr Dods which he promptly scratched off. He'd recently found out that the old dockmaster had been ill for some time now, and being bed-ridden seemed a perfectly reasonable alibi. One he verified, of course. Perhaps they should send him something?

Mr Kirkham from the *Acadian Recorder* was also a poor suspect, but if all other avenues proved a dead-end, he would interview him as a last resort. He hated speaking to reporters. There was always an angle for them. One simple conversation, and you wound up being front page for being a conspirator to one murder or another. There were very few industries more profitable to a newspaper than murder.

The butler, Victor, from the Halifax Club was also a somewhat murky suspect, but he remained on the list since he would've known Madam Onay's schedule. He also saw her on the day of Irvin Talamge, Jr's murder and could've concluded that she murdered him. There was also that strange way he fawned over the man. Definitely suspicious enough to believe the butler could and probably would avenge such a loss.

He then focused on the final name on the list, '*The Talmages*'. This needed to be expounded upon since he was more familiar with their dynamics. He scratched out the name and proceeded to list out each of the four Talmage's he suspected in detail.

Mr Irvin Talmage, Sr — Relation to the deceased? Father.

Mrs Talmage — Relation? Mother. Though, from her frail disposition, Wilson had a hard time believing someone of her temperament could kill Madam Onay in the manner in which she was found. However, there was always the possibility this was a higher-to-kill situation.

Mrs Peaton — Relation? Secretary and something more?

She was the one he found most curious. How did a secretary make it into the inner circle of such an influential and private family? And the way she spoke about the fiancée with such authority, more than a simple secretary would have.

Perhaps her motives were to protect Irvin from an

unwanted marriage, but the actual target, Madam Onay, got caught in the crossfire? But then, why display Madam Onay's body in such a flamboyant way?

Wilson shook his head. Given the note that was left, this had to be a kill of vengeance, which, considering Mrs Peaton's relationship with the Talmages and commanding presence, still made her a viable candidate.

And finally, he added the final two names on his growing list of suspects.

Lauretta — the fiancée he still had yet to meet.

And, lastly,

Mrs Tilcott — the cat lady.

It was high time he figured out what exactly connected her and Mrs Peaton to this bizarre family tree.

Barnaby burst through the curtained doorway, his night-shirt pulled haphazardly over his clothes from the previous day, and his nightcap hung off-kilter.

"What happened to you?" Wilson arched a brow.

Barnaby snapped his wild eyes away from the book on the floor, meeting Wilson's expectant expression.

"I-I couldn't sleep," he said.

His hands trembled. Something was dreadfully wrong, and it was up to Wilson to figure it out.

"You were out late." Wilson rose from behind the desk. "Get any further with the investigations?"

He took a nonchalant approach in interrogating his friend, figuring this would be the surest way of getting anything out from Barnaby, who was all out of sorts this morning.

Barnaby squeezed his eyes shut, muttering under his breath before he cried, "She killed another last night!"

"Who?"

"The Hexengeist! Frau Perchta, the Christmas witch, has struck again, I'm afraid."

Wilson choked on a sip of coffee. "I beg your pardon?"

"It's a witch, the Christmas witch!"

"Yes, yes, I heard you the first time." Wilson rounded the corner of his desk to gather his things for the long day of work he had ahead of him. "I'm sorry I asked."

He shook his head at the nonsense Barnaby sputtered about.

"But it's true! I can show you." The petite man rushed to retrieve the book and placed it on top of the dining table. It rattled under the considerable weight of it. "You see, Frau Perchta can only be awakened during Yuletide with a spell. Once she's released, she possesses the conjurer who released her from her Spiegelgrab. It's all in here."

"Spiegel-what? Barnaby, you're speaking in riddles." Wilson sighed. "And if I humoured this ridiculous theory of there being a... a Christmas witch, pray tell who might want to be possessed in the first place?"

"Emma said she heard the conjurer's request to 'make things right and"—Barnaby raised his index finger—"according to the legend, she preys on those in mourning over a lost love. It all fits! The objective of whoever killed Madam Onay was clearly revenge. They must've been related to Irvin or close enough to be considered family."

Wilson had to credit him. Aside from his hysterical theory that was unrealistic and quite problematic in the realm of reality, he was on the right line of thinking. Whoever killed Madam Onay had to be close to the Talmage family. Still, he couldn't bring himself to humour him too long.

"Thank you for that wonderful deduction, but I've already determined a list of familial suspects," Wilson smirked, downing the rest of the black coffee. "Which, in case you were wondering, all have viable motives and capability to commit murder without the need for any explanations of witchery."

The colour drained from Barnaby's face.

"Besides," Wilson continued, "I wouldn't expect the Talmages to risk performing any sort of dark art rituals under the current anti-magic sentiments spreading throughout the town."

"You must believe me. She killed another at the McLeod House just last night. I saw it."

"You saw this fictional character kill someone?"

"Well, no." Barnaby wrung his hands. "But when I was there earlier—"

"You were at that house twice yesterday?"

"Yes, once in the afternoon. Emma wanted to show me where she'd seen the witch, but we weren't alone. In our haste, I forgot the compendium, which is why I went back last night. The officer was at the front door, but he was already dead."

Wilson stopped in his tracks as he flung his frock coat over his shoulders.

He turned his hand on the door handle. "An officer? At the McLeod House?"

Barnaby nodded, and Wilson furrowed his brow. Hadn't he sent an officer to go inspect a disturbance at that residence?

"What time were you at that house the first time?"

Barnaby tilted his head to the side. "Sometime in the afternoon, why?"

"And he's dead? You're certain?" Wilson asked, ignoring his question.

"I am."

Wilson took a deep breath. What if it were the same officer he'd sent to check out that disturbance? A tinge of guilt hit the back of his throat at the thought. But then, could it be a mere coincidence? Surely break-ins happened all the time there. The police must've stopped by that house hundreds of times within a day. It could be an officer for all he knew.

"This is why I was out late last night." Barnaby rushed around Wilson to block his way, lifting the compendium up for Wilson to take a closer look. "And then there was a ghost. A young girl appeared, probably one of the McLeod children still haunting the place. She cried out to me!"

Wilson rubbed his temples as he contemplated the horrifying idea that Barnaby was the source of the disturbance he'd sent the officer after.

"The pain in her face was unbearable to witness, but I couldn't look away," Barnaby continued, his voice rising. "She desperately tried to warn me about the murder, and when I turned, there he was! The police officer. He was just... *dead*!"

A chill ran through Wilson at the thought of the killer being at the house at the same time as Barnaby. How could he put himself in such danger? What if he'd been killed, too, along with the officer? But there was something in the timeline that didn't make sense. If this was the same officer he'd sent in to search the house, how could the killer have killed him upon entrance without Barnaby seeing who it was? Perhaps Barnaby's lack of sleep had him hallucinating? It wouldn't be the first time.

"The officer just fell straight at my feet, and when I turned him over, he had a hole where his stomach should be, just like Madam Onay's. It all fits. Frau Perchta—"

"Enough with this Frau-whatever nonsense," Wilson snapped, his patience growing thin.

"I swear to you it's true! I can show you where the body lies." Burnaby turned in a hurry, but Wilson grabbed the book before he could leave with it.

"I will go, but this"—he wiggled the hefty book in one hand—"stays here."

"Yes, yes, good. Wouldn't want to forget it again."

"Yes, of course, because that would be dreadful." Wilson rolled his eyes, yanking the door open. "But by all means, bring the magic book for all the townsfolk to see. Maybe we'll be next up at the gallows?"

"Now who's being dramatic?" Barnaby lifted his chin and marched through the doorway and down the stairs.

Wilson ground his teeth. Barnaby was so insufferable that he had half a mind to shut the door and let him go on his own. But if the stomach stealer had struck again, he needed to be at the scene to investigate if there was any chance of him solving this case.

Besides, the McLeod House was only a block from the Talmage's foundry. So, he could spare a few minutes to investigate with Barnaby before heading over there to speak with Mr Talmage's secretary.

With a sigh, he quickly followed his colleague out into the brisk winter morning in the hopes of finding a dead body and a clue.

10
IT'S BEGINNING TO LOOK LIKE MURDER

THE MCLEOD HOUSE was already swarming with police officers when they arrived at Bishop Street. Dozens of officers stood to create a barrier between the bystanders, all curious to see what had happened, while dozens more entered the home.

Wilson's chest tightened. It was definitely the same house he'd sent the officer into, but how could he have known Madam Onay's killer would be inside? He'd been so focused on getting to Dr Larson's he hadn't even thought twice about it.

He kicked himself for being so foolish. But, of course, their killer would be hiding in the abandoned house no reasonable person would step foot in. He wondered if it had a basement and whether this could be the original location of where Madam Onay was murdered? He would have to get inside to investigate this.

"Oh no." Barnaby slowed his pace. "They'll be searching for me, won't they?"

"Don't be daft, dear Barnaby. Did anyone see you leave the premises yesterday?"

The significantly shorter detective furrowed his brow. "I don't think so."

"And did you commit the murder?"

"Of course not!"

"Then you have nothing to fear." Wilson dodged the last group of spectators that crowded the police blockade.

"Halt, there!"

Barnaby and Wilson nearly ran into the officer who stepped between them and the dilapidated fence surrounding the McLeod House.

Wilson cleared his throat. "There will be no halting unless you wish to halt the investigation of this murder even further?

"Why, I—erm." The baffled officer scratched his head as Wilson stepped around him and darted for the gate.

"I'm Detective Wilson Davies, along with my colleague Detective Barnaby Grey, and we have important information for the chief inspector."

"Now, wait right there!" The officer replied, but Wilson was already through the gate.

"He's inside, yes? We'll show ourselves in," Wilson said with a wave. "No need to bother yourself. We'll announce ourselves."

"Apologies for the intrusion, and many thanks," Barnaby called over his shoulder to the officer, nearly falling on the icy sidewalk as he raced after Wilson.

Once inside, the detectives were welcomed by a cramped foyer crowded with officers who circled like vultures around the crime scene. The room was lit only by the morning sun that shone through the cracks in the walls and broken windows. Tufts of snow and dust reflected in the light as they floated down to the rotten floorboards where the lifeless corpse still laid. His belted frock coat was all in shreds, and his exposed stomach was utterly hollow.

Wilson cringed at the sound of Barnaby holding back vomit.

"Ah, well, isn't this a surprise," the chief inspector greeted them with a scowl. "Twice in one day. Don't suppose you'll leave my crime scene in peace this time?"

"None at all," Wilson replied.

"Twice?" Barnaby arched his brow.

"I'll tell you later." Wilson moved further into the dingy front hall.

The inspector eyed the detectives with a suspicious look. "Well, just stay out of my way, will you? And if I see you steal something again, I *will* arrest you."

Wilson wanted to remind the chief inspector that he never saw him steal anything the first time but refrained. It wouldn't do any good, and he didn't want to jeopardize the case.

"Of course, inspector." He waved to the inspector and walked around the other officers to get a closer look at the dead officer's face.

He knelt by the body, his mouth falling slack in recognition. It was definitely the same officer he'd met on the street yesterday. How could this happen? Why did he have to tell the officer to investigate anything when the noise could've just been Barnaby fleeing from his own imagination just minutes before the killer returned to his hideout? If he'd known, he would never have given this poor officer the recommendation to investigate.

"Inspector, do you know this man?" Wilson asked, but Chief Inspector Plundell had already exited into the adjoining room.

Another constable cleared his throat, his face nearly as white as the corpse in front of him. "That would be Constable Fleming, sir."

The detectives looked up at the uniformed man who approached them.

"And you are?" Wilson asked appraisingly.

"Constable Janson." The officer extended a hand to both of them. "You're the detectives, yes? We're quite happy that you're here. What happened to Fleming, it's... quite impossible, and I've heard that is both of your specialities."

"Have you now?" Wilson frowned and gave a side glance to Barnaby. "Do tell me how—?"

"That's very kind of you to say," Barnaby said, cutting him off.

Wilson narrowed his eyes at the shorter detective, but Barnaby refused to meet his eyes. What was he playing at?

The constable didn't notice their awkward exchange and proceeded to expound on the case. "If this house wasn't haunted, I'd swear we'd be dealing with some kind of occultist."

"Not him, too?" Wilson muttered.

Barnaby sent an elbow into his side to shut him up. "How do you mean?"

"Come, let me show you," the constable motioned for them to follow him into the next room. "But the townsfolk mustn't get word of this. They'll be wanting the heads of anyone and everyone who even walks near this house."

Wilson gaped at the constable but followed. How ridiculous could two people be? Could an occultist have murdered Madam Onay? Certainly. But a ghost? Now, that was out of the question. Apparitions didn't exist. They were merely hallucinations of the mind. What sort of nonsense were they teaching these officers?

"We found this door by chance," the constable said once they entered the empty room, aside from the single dresser and a broken framed painting just large enough to hide the secret door on the far wall. It was currently being investigated by the chief inspector.

"If the door hadn't been disturbed and left ajar, we never would've found it. The chief believes someone was using this place for ritualistic purposes."

Barnaby's eyes widened, and a twitch of his lip gave Wilson the sudden impression that his colleague knew about this secret door. Was there something Barnaby wasn't telling him?

"And what do you believe?" Wilson asked the constable.

"I believe it was the ghost of the McLeod children, of course."

Wilson let out an exasperated sigh. "Of course."

"Have you seen the children before?" Barnaby asked, his voice shook. "What did it look like?"

At that moment, Wilson tuned out the two men's exchange of ghost stories and proceeded to deduce what might've *actually* happened. He backtracked from the room to the front entrance just as the officers pulled out a rug covered in strange symbols—he made a mental note to come back to inspect it before they towed it off to evidence.

He examined the officer's dead body and its position relative to the front door. It was just as Barnaby described. The constable didn't make it very far, but why would he remain here from the afternoon until dusk when Barnaby returned the second time? It didn't make any sense, but Wilson tucked the question into a section of his mind for later reflection.

Wilson eyed the floor, thankful that this room hadn't been dusted. He scanned the many patterns the dust laid out for him, each footprint telling a story of their own. But there were so many that when he thought he was on to the one that belonged to Constable Fleming, it was quickly lost in a sea of other footprints that scattered the evidence into nothingness.

"Bullocks." He ground his teeth. If only he'd gotten to the scene before the stampeding fools in there compromised the dust patterns.

Just as he was about to give up, a sliver of hope spiked when he spotted a tiny discolouration on the floor next to the dead body's left foot. He frowned, wondering how he'd missed this before.

He rushed to the floor and knelt beside it, lowering his head mere inches from the ground to inspect the droplet and sniffed.

Just as he suspected. Iron.

He then rechecked the bottom of the constable's right boot, but it was clean. The left one drew his eye to a large smudge of something dark and gooey he hadn't noticed before. His heart skipped a beat, and he quickly fetched a kerchief. With a quick dab, the cloth returned a smear of deep crimson. The same shade as the droplet on the floor. He licked the smudge, and metallic notes welcomed his taste buds. It was most definitely blood.

But where did it come from?

With a second glance at the shoe, this time, he spotted the source. It nearly blended in with the rest of the blood covering the body, but, thankfully, this blood was significantly darker than the rest. He followed the red trail up the side of the constable's shoe up to his ankle and pushed back the pant leg to reveal a slender gash along the length of his calf.

The blood around the cut had long since dried up, but he noted that the red puffiness that framed it signalled that it must've occurred prior to the disembowelment.

"Marvelous." He grinned and quickly straightened to pursue his theory.

He hadn't noticed it before because he hadn't been looking for it. How could he have been so daft? With newfound vigour, he scoured the front hall for more stains left by the victim's wound. If there was one, there had to be more. Particularly if this man had been injured while still alive.

His frock coat whirled as he danced about the room studying every nook and crevice of that room. He found a few dots near the stairs and some more by the fireplace, if one could call it that, though these were shallower than the rest. Wherever there was a droplet of blood, so was he.

The constable had been quite active. It was almost as if he'd been chasing something. Or someone. He walked nose to floor from the fireplace to the adjacent room where the secret closet was being removed of the occultist's contraband.

Barnaby cleared his throat. "What are you doing?"

Wilson froze at the window, balanced on one leg while the other hovered by the windowsill. A tiny speck of blood splattered the broken glass. "Investigating, of course."

"You look ridiculous."

"There's hardly time to consider one's own appearance when solving a murder." Wilson replaced his foot on the ground and thrust his upper body through the gapping window. "Our victim saw something from the window, but he was here only for a moment before he was startled by something."

"By what?" Constable Janson asked, coming to stand next to Barnaby.

"The assailant, of course." Wilson whirled around, doing his best to imitate the movements of someone in fear for their life. "He turned sharply and…." He swung his arms as he looked around. "Ah, there."

On hands and knees, he lowered to inspect the foot of the dresser, which was painted with an array of dried red dots.

"What is it?" Constable Janson asked, craning his head to see over Wilson's shoulder.

"Blood." Wilson stood and brushed his trousers clean, though there probably was no point. He'd have to burn them anyway. "Probably from the first cut, but before that, he was alerted to someone coming at him from behind."

"Then, right as the killer was upon the poor lad, he—" Wilson backtracked and followed the footing of the killer for his captive audience.

Creak!

"Right on cue." Wilson chuckled. It was all too easy. "The assailant walked right over this bit of warped wood, which warned the officer he wasn't alone. Then the killer… cut his ankle? What would he do that?" Wilson crossed his arms, mostly speaking out loud because it helped him think. He snapped his fingers. "Unless!"

"Cut? Cut what?" Barnaby asked; a quiver in his voice revealed he didn't like the sound of this.

Wilson grimaced as he once again lowered to the floor.

"The cut on the constable's leg. Didn't you see it?" Wilson strained, reaching his arm underneath the tiny space between the floor and the bottom of the dresser.

"I must tell the chief," Constable Janson said and hurried off.

Barnaby moved to Wilson's other side and crouched beside him. "Do you think it could be the source of the blood covering my book? It was sitting right there when I returned, but it wasn't like that before."

"The thought did cross my mind." Wilson groaned and pulled his arm from the dresser's depths. He sat up, brandishing a small knife with a stallion's head at the butt of its handle. "And look what I have here?"

"A letter opener?"

Wilson rolled his eyes. "Yes, that's quite obvious, but more importantly, I believe we have the weapon which inflicted the gash on the dead constable's left ankle."

Wilson lifted the opener and brought the blade to his thumb. The width matched the cut, that was for certain.

"But if they were standing, why would he cut the constable's ankle?"

"Your book, of course."

Barnaby blinked. "My book's the murder weapon?"

"No, of course not. Your book, though still up for question, couldn't have killed that man in there. However, the blood on the cover does make one wonder."

"Then how could it also be the letter opener?"

Wilson examined the letter opener. "Well, we'll have to look at the back of your book to be sure, but I *believe* the book is how the victim thwarted our assailant's attack with the letter opener."

With a swing of the arm, he mimicked the motion he assumed the assailant would take from where he stood.

"Ah!" Barnaby cowered away.

"Stop. I wasn't going to hit you." Wilson spun around, dropping the letter opener as if the compendium had been smashed in his way. "The book blocked the attack. The attacker must've stumbled after his weapon. Ah, yes, see?" He pointed to a crook in the floorboards where the tip of the sharp blade hit. "Then, while on the floor, the killer did the only thing he could do in such a vulnerable position."

Silence followed as he caressed the letter opener.

"And that is what, exactly?" Barnaby prodded.

"He killed the constable with this"—Wilson wiggled the blade in his hands before pocketing it. "On the bright side, we know something about our killer."

"How could you possibly have figured that out just by a little letter opener?"

"Because our constable didn't fight back once the attacker

was on the ground. Isn't it obvious, Barnaby? Why, it's plain as day! He assumed the assailant wouldn't take another stab after being knocked to the ground. Why do you think that is?"

"Find anything?" The inspector asked, joining them by the window.

Wilson quieted, glad he'd already concealed the weapon caked with blood. "Only dust and grime, inspector. However, there was a nasty cut on the left ankle of the victim."

"Yes, one of my men just informed me of that." He stood awkwardly silent between Wilson and Barnaby, giving them a suspicious eye. "Well, if you find any other key pieces of evidence...."

Wilson's lip curled, but he made no attempt at tossing the inspector a bone.

Barnaby cracked. "We'll come straight to you, sir, of course."

The chief inspector grunted with a nod before shouting the order for the men to clean house and regroup at the station.

"Alone at last," Wilson said when the final officer left the abandoned house. He retrieved the letter opener with his kerchief. "Now, let's see who you belong to."

"By the engraving, of course." He waved to the bottom of the silver handle near the stallion's head. "And I believe we now can confirm with a newfound certainty that the Talmages, or someone very close to them, is, in fact, the culprit. But which one?"

Barnaby grabbed the letter opener and lifted it into the light that gleamed through the window to better see the engravement. "Talmage's & Sons! Are you saying that one of them are now walking around possessed by Frau Perchta?"

"Of course not." Wilson snatched the murder weapon back from his colleague and returned it to the kerchief. It would have to suffice until he was able to stow it in a proper container for preservation. "That would be absurd. I'm only saying that one of them killed Madam Onay, and now we can add Constable Fleming to that list."

"But—" Barnaby began, but Wilson didn't wait to find out what he had to say next and darted towards the front hall.

"Did you happen to notice if there was a basement?"

"No, I don't think so." Barnaby quickly caught up to Wilson as he searched the premises in hopes of finding a secret door to a cellar or lower floor.

"Pity. Well, never mind. I shall find it if there is one." Wilson darted down the nearest hallway. "Still plenty of time before the foundry opens. I should have time to scour this place top to bottom."

His adrenaline spiked as each door, or rotten archway presented a possible entrance to a basement. He hoped that there was one. It would prove his theory that Madam Onay was, indeed, below ground-level when she breathed her last. That, and reveal the source of the frankincense and myrrh fragrance she was drenched in. Though he did find it odd that the dead officer didn't share these same woodsy notes. Perhaps it was as simple as one being a planned murder and the other one of impulse? Either way, he had to find this basement.

"You're going to the foundry?" Barnaby asked.

Wilson paused by the door frame which led to the kitchen. "Yes. I need to interview my first suspect, Mrs Peaton."

Barnaby's cheeks turned hot pink. "Mrs Peaton? The poor widow?"

"That's correct, and I assure you she's neither poor nor recently widowed."

"This is outrageous." Barnaby spluttered and looked away,

running a shaky hand through his matted hair. "She's a secretary!"

"Yes, a secretary with a close relationship to the Talmages. One I'd like to understand on a more personal level."

"And what of her disposition?"

"If you're referring to her being the Talmages secretary, her inconspicuous vocation makes her the perfect suspect. However, if you're referring to her disposition of being female, in our profession, I've met quite a number of women fully capable of committing murder."

With that, he spun on his heel to leave but paused to glance over his shoulder. "Are you coming?"

Barnaby shifted from one foot to the other. He finally shook his head. "I should check the book for markings from the letter opener, and I'd like to read more about what we're dealing with."

"A work of fiction won't bring you hardboiled evidence, dear Barnaby, that I'm certain of," Wilson called over his shoulder as he brushed through a wall of cobwebs into the kitchen.

The floorboards groaned from somewhere behind him, and he froze.

"Hello?" He called. "Is that you, Barnaby?"

No one answered. He held his breath for a few moments before he moved on. It was probably nothing.

He continued his search, opening cupboards and tapping walls for any sign of more secret doors, but there was nothing here. No basement, no evidence, and he was getting tired.

A thunk came from behind him, and he jumped. His breath hitched. He was most definitely not alone. He tiptoed to the entrance of the kitchen and pressed his back to the nearby wall.

Footsteps shuffled by. Wilson held his breath and inched

his way to the edge, leaning around just enough to peer down the hallway. Why didn't he think to grab his pistol before leaving the flat?

The floor squeaked again as someone walked about the front hall. He popped his collar and cracked his jaw. He would just have to handle this the old fashion way.

His muscles tensed as he pushed himself off the wall and whirled into the hallway.

"Halt!" He shouted, followed by a snap.

A match illuminated the woman's silhouette who held it threateningly. Wilson stopped in his tracks. What was she doing? The match was dropped before he could ask, and the space between him and the mysterious woman was enveloped in smoke.

He coughed and brought his frock coat to protect his lungs. The flames licked the floor and the walls as the woman ambled away. Her over-feathered purple teardrop hat perched on the top of her head was the last thing he saw before the fire consumed the entire hallway with an unnatural speed. How could a house light up so quickly?

"Balls," he gasped. There was no way to get to the woman this way.

He turned around and spotted the back door, he raced for the handle, but it wouldn't turn. He groaned and tried the window, which somehow still had its glass and used all his might to pry it open. His fingers strained against the wood panel, but it wouldn't budge.

Smoke billowed into the kitchen, and the woosh behind him sent his heart racing. He couldn't die now. Not like this. He ripped off his frock coat. He coughed as the fumes filled his lungs. Without a second thought, he wrapped the coat around his right fist and slammed it against the glass. It cracked but remained intact. The woman was getting away. He didn't have time for this.

He swung again. This time a longer line spidered across the window. He gave it a good kick. It shattered under the pressure, and he hoisted himself through it, the shards tearing at his arms and gangly legs.

A pile of snow broke his fall, but he wasted no time in getting back up. His back cracked, and he let out a moan, but he didn't let this stop him. Instead, he raced for the front gate just as the purple feathered hat vanished around the corner.

"Stop!" He called and broke into a full sprint after her.

He reached the sidewalk; the bright sun forced him to blink several times to adjust to the light. The iron gate closed with a click behind him, and then he spotted her. His breath hitched at the jolt of recognition. Salt and peppered hair spun into a tight bun peeked out from underneath the purple feathered hat. Mrs Peaton weaved through a crowd of work traffic who had yet to notice the fire which lapped up the McLeod House. But why would she be casually strolling if she'd just committed arson? How curious.

"Mrs Peaton!" He shouted after her.

She glanced back with a stern glance before crossing the street.

"Mrs Peaton, wait!"

He would have to play this carefully as ever. Though a simple secretary, her connections with the Talmages would make it difficult to accuse her if he didn't have sound evidence. Unfortunately, he didn't think Constable Plundell would be very accepting of his witness statement even though he *did* see her with her very distinct teardrop hat set fire to the McCleod house. He would just have to keep an eye on her until he could catch her in another unsavoury act. In the meantime, perhaps a little pressure might make her more inclined to a misstep?

"There you are," he greeted as he jogged up beside her, his lengthy frame easily matching her quick pace.

"Oh!" She jumped as if he surprised her. Tufts of purple feathers flew off her overstuffed hat. Her eyes widened when she met his gaze. "Why, Mr Davies, what do you mean by sneaking up on a woman so early in the morning?"

He narrowed his eyes at her, but she kept the mask of shock and innocence plastered upon her face. Excellent. The hard way was always more fun than when arsonists confessed straight out.

"My apologies, Mrs Peaton, I merely meant to say hello. In fact, it's a wonderful coincidence that I should run into you as I was just about to call on you at the foundry."

"Why? And be quick about it as I'm running late." She pursed her thin lips.

"Of course. I shall escort you."

She gave a short scowl before a jerky nod, her posture stiffening before continuing her path up Granville towards the foundry. Wilson noted her eyes flitted about as if she were looking for someone. Another accomplice, perhaps?

"I won't take too much of your time," Wilson said, folding his hands behind his back as he matched her pace. "Do you frequent the McLeod house often?"

"What?" She chirped, avoiding eye contact. "I was in no such place."

"Really? I could've sworn I saw you just now."

All the signs of guilt were present on Mrs Peaton today, from her averted gaze to her unnaturally high-pitched intonation. A lie never smelled so sweet.

"Well, I wasn't." She lifted her nose to the most upturned position.

"Ah, my mistake." He pocketed this for now, though he would revisit reasons a secretary to a foundry-owner would set fire to an abandoned building if not to hide evidence.

"Is there something specific that you wanted? Or was it simply to pester me?"

"Oh yes, of course. I was curious to know how long you've known the Talmage's? You do seem very close."

She frowned, but then her features softened infinitesimally. "Many years. They're a good family."

"One of the best in all of Nova Scotia, I imagine."

She harrumphed, but from the affection in her eyes, he knew she agreed.

"And how long have you worked for Mr Talmage?"

"It's been… fifteen? Maybe twenty years?" She gazed off into the distance. "But I knew them long before that."

"My, a very long time to be sure. It's a shame that the Talmages never made you anything more than a secretary. I mean, after all, you've been through. Why, Irvin Talmage, Jr must've just been a wee babe then."

A warm smile lifted her ordinarily stern features at the mention of Irvin junior as a small child. "That he was. Such a sweet child, that one. He'd run about my garden determined to pick me the best flowers."

"Really? I'm quite surprised at the thought of you being his nanny."

"I was no such thing!" The woman's face shrivelled back into a look of disdain as soon as she said it.

Wilson arched a brow. "It sounds as though you and the Talmages have always been close."

He observed Mrs Peaton's features, intrigued by the significance of her outburst after such an uncharacteristically tender moment. She remained stoic as ever.

"I'm so very sorry for your loss. I'm certain these memories have made the events of yesterday all the more painful."

She cleared her throat, blinking away the sudden moisture. "Yesterday was a horrible disgrace. How dare such a thing delay my godson's funeral?"

"Ah, so you were his godmother?" The bells went off in

Wilson's head. It definitely explained her unusually close relationship with the family.

Mrs Peaton bit her cheek but made no response.

"Did you and the family have any trouble getting to the church?"

"Not that I can think of." She tilted her head. "Why do you ask?"

"Oh, no reason. It's just something Constable Plundell said."

Her eyes snapped to his, taking the bait. "And what might that be?"

"I'm not certain I should say." He paused for dramatic effect. "But between you and me, he did mention that it's looking more and more like the killer may be a member of the family or someone quite close to the Talmage's."

"You don't mean me, do you?"

"Of course not, Mrs Peaton," Wilson said, reassuring her. "I wouldn't be here if I did. All I want to know is if anything out of the ordinary occurred?"

Her shoulders visibly relaxed at that as she paused, probably pondering how best to respond to his question. If she reacted too quickly or in great detail, he would know for sure that she was lying. Of course, this wouldn't be definitive evidence, but if he could make Mrs Peaton think he was on her side, then perhaps she would be comfortable to continue with whatever heinous plan she had up her sleeve next.

"Not that I can think of. Though Hazel Tilcott did have trouble finding her gloves that morning."

"Did she? And were they ever found?"

The older woman shook her head. "It's the strangest thing, too. They were the same ones she wore when we arrived the night before, and she didn't even notice they went missing until the next morning when Victor arrived to escort us to the church."

"Victor, the butler from the Halifax Club?" Mrs Peaton nodded. His gut said that she was lying, but he would have to pay Victor a visit later to be sure. A good detective always double-checked their suspect's stories. "And you stayed with the Talmages all night on the eve of the service?"

"Indeed. Mr Talmage thought it cruel for us to be alone and that Mrs Talmage could use the company. I quite agreed. The poor thing hasn't slept for days. Weeks, even."

Wilson's heart sank. If Mrs Peaton stayed with the Talmages all night until they left for the church, then this would give her an alibi for Madam Onay's time of death. But was it possible he was missing something? He would have to talk to the others in order to find out.

"And did anything else out of the ordinary occur that morning?"

She paused, presumably to think of her answer, but her facial features remained unnaturally still, vacant of emotion. "There was one thing...."

His lungs expanded as she trailed, the well-rehearsed tone of her voice sounding alarms in every corner of his being.

"Well, shortly after breakfast that... *fiancée* of late Irvin's, Miss Lauretta? Well, she barged in unannounced all in a fit."

Wilson studied her reactions carefully. Her eye gave just the slightest twitch at odd intervals as she described her lie.

"She begged me to let her see Mr Talmage, though he'd gone off to his study and requested to be left undisturbed until time to go to church. Can you imagine?"

"Hardly."

She shook her head. "If I were you, I'd be looking more closely at her."

Wilson held back a grin. Of course, she'd accuse the fiancée. Who else besides the parents of the deceased would have such great motives to commit a revenge murder? The fiancée, of course, and if the idea had come from anyone else besides the woman who'd just set ablaze a house to cover her own tracks, he might've considered it.

"The nerve of her." Mrs Peaton's pace increased with the speed at which she spoke. "It took me a great deal to get rid of the girl and all by myself, too, what with Mr Talmage indisposed and Mrs Talmage was nowhere to be found. You know, she really should make an appointment with Dr Larson."

"Who?"

Mrs Peaton scoffed. "Ms Lauretta, the ex-fiancée, of course. Anyway, Mrs Talmage turned up just in time, and we were on our way."

Intriguing that both the Talmages went missing the morning before the funeral. Was this true? Or was it just part of Mrs Peaton's tall tale? What would the arrest of Mr Talmage's secretary, their son's godmother, do to the family? Then another thought occurred even more unsettling than the last. Had the Talmages put Mrs Peaton up to it?

He wanted to prod Mrs Peaton on the subject, but they were now at the entrance to the foundry, and he thought it best to wait and see if her alibi checked out.

She turned to stand between him and the door, her scowl letting him know that he wasn't welcome inside. "Now, is that all?"

"Not quite. I just have one last question," Wilson replied. He took a closer step and lowered his voice so passerby couldn't overhear. "Did the foundry supply you with the tools to sent the McLeod House up in flames?"

"Now you listen here, *detective*"—Mrs Peaton's glare turned ice-cold, and Wilson didn't think it possible for her jaw to be clenched any tighter — "I don't know what you're talking about, and I've had quite enough of you harassing me as if I had anything to do with that Madam lady's murder. I was just as shocked as the rest of the Talmage's."

Wilson narrowed his eyes. Was that a clue? If the Talmages were behind it all along, they wouldn't be surprised one bit. But why disturb their own son's murder in such a grotesque manner?

"You've no right accusing me of anything." She jabbed an index finger at them. "But mark my words, she deserved what she got after murdering this city's sharpest minds and one of the greatest family's only son. I wish I had done it, but I didn't, and if you bother me again, I will report you to the chief inspector. Do you understand?"

She didn't wait for a response and stormed into the foundry. The door locked behind her with a click bringing a sense of finality to their conversation. Wilson smiled to himself. He'd hit a nerve and, though she denied it, she knew more than she was letting on. Even if she didn't have the knowledge to disembowel her victims to avoid identification, the look in her eyes when she'd admitted to 'wanting to' meant something. Now he just needed to find a hole in her plot, so he was off to compare stories with Mrs Tilcott, Victor the butler, and the fiancée.

11
NO SMALL WONDER

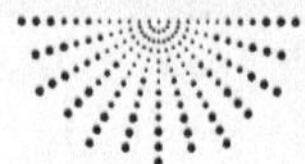

Engel's Emporium,
Albemarle Street

"Is this necessary?" Emma asked. She shifted in her seat next to Antoine on the driver's box.

He merely gave her a stern nod as he prodded the horses who pulled the caravan onward. Their hooves clapped down Albemarle Street towards the bookshop.

"You shouldn't be alone on these streets, not with the murders and threats against those with power."

A wheel hit a pothole and jostled them.

"Careful!" Artus protested from within the caravan.

"Oh, quit your whining, brother," Antoine hollered back.

Emma groaned. "But I won't be alone. Barnaby will be with me. And so will the Engel siblings. Besides, I think my powers have proven that I'm perfectly capable of defending myself."

"Whoa!" He pulled back on the reins, and the horse's clopped to a trot until they were directly in front of the brick and mortar shop. He turned in his seat to face Emma. "Listen, we must be careful. You especially. Your magic is still unpredictable, and with the town out for the blood of all thos with magical abilities, it's not safe."

Emma slumped her shoulders, knowing in her heart that Antoine was right but not liking it one bit. She didn't want or need a babysitter.

"Do you really think Kizmet would ever leave your side now that a killer is once again on the loose?"

Emma bit her cheek. She knew that he wouldn't. The panther had grown fond of her, which was sweet, but he could be a bit overprotective. "What about Absinthe? Wouldn't he rather stay with her?"

"She'll be with Artus and us investigating the Halifax Jail." Antoine hopped out of the driver's box and extended his hand to assist her.

She climbed over the railing, ignoring Antoine's hand. "But doesn't having a panther escort me into that shop make me even more of a target for the intolerant?"

"It's better than nothing," he replied. "And since the shop is closing soon, there shouldn't be a large crowd. Kizmet should be able to stay out of sight until then."

She sighed, following him down the snowy path. How was she going to explain this to Barnaby? Or, better yet, the shopkeepers? Kizmet was massive, and in that little shop, she had no idea how anyone could miss him. But there was no use in arguing. When the ringleader decided, it was final, just like Antoine's decision to uproot them once again in search of a safer town. At least if she could eliminate the danger of Frau Perchta, then maybe they'd be able to perform again so that she could finally be on stage alongside them. They'd promised her they'd include her and her light show act, which she so desperately wanted, but what she desired more now was to ensure the safety of everyone she could leave behind. Particularly Barnaby.

The caravan door swung open, and Franziska flew off the vehicle's threshold, pulling Emma into her arms. "Please be careful, ja?"

"I will." Emma smiled as she hugged her circus-mum back.

"And we'll pick you up here just before sundown." Franziska pulled away and studied her reaction.

"Of course."

Kizmet hopped from the caravan and stretched his legs with a yawn before he trotted to Emma's side.

"Oh hush, Absinthe. Your complaining won't help." Artus scolded from within, followed by a loud hiss. Artus popped his head out of the caravan, a mass of black hair tangled around his face. "Are you quite finished? We're getting restless here, and I think Timur is about to suck my blood dry."

Emma giggled.

"Yes, yes, let's go." Antoine ushered Franziska back into the vehicle.

The older woman gave Emma one last glance, and her eyes watered.

"Go. I'll be fine."

Franziska nodded and finally joined the rest of the circus in the caravan, and they drove off in a hurry.

"Oh, good, you're here." A voice behind her made her jump.

She spun around just as the front door of the bookshop closed behind Barnaby. He walked across the small sidewalk to her but froze when his gaze fell upon the giant black panther seated calmly at Emma's side.

His mouth fell open and closed as if to speak, but no words came.

"Barnaby, you remember Kizmet, don't you?" Emma gave

a nervous laugh and patted the top of the panther's head that nearly reached her shoulder.

"Ye—erm—yes?" He brought his fist up to his mouth and cleared his throat. "Forgive me, it's just…."

He looked over his shoulder at the bookshop. The door swung open as the last customer left the shop before Mr Engel flipped the wooden sign over to read 'closed'.

Emma's heart skipped a beat when the woman locked eyes on Kizmet.

"Oh!" The woman exclaimed, her eyes wide. She quickly picked up her skirts and raced off.

So much for keeping Kizmet out of sight. Emma held her breath, praying the woman would forget what she'd seen. Or remembered Kizmet as a rather large house cat.

Barnaby turned back to Emma, and his face turned ashen. "What's she—?"

He pointed to Kizmet, who let out a low rumble.

"He," Emma corrected.

"My apologies, but what is *he* doing here?"

Emma bit her cheek. "Antoine and the others found out about the murders. They didn't want me to be alone. Especially not with the town wanting all of our heads for having magic."

Barnaby nodded his approval. "Rightly so. There's too much violence and unrest in these parts, I'm afraid. Not to mention the fires."

Emma frowned. "The fires?"

"Yes, the McLeod House was burnt to a crisp this morning. Wilson said he saw it himself. Believes it to be at the hand of Mrs Peaton, but I doubt she's the witch we're looking for."

"Who's Mrs Peaton?" Emma asked.

"Oh, she's a secretary." Barnaby waved it off. "Come, let's get you both inside and out of sight."

Kizmet grunted in agreement which awarded him a nervous side-glance from the detective.

"Will he behave himself?" Barnaby's voice shook.

"Of course, why wouldn't he?" Emma asked, following the detective into the warmth of the shop. Kizmet narrowed his eyes up at Barnaby as if to take offence. "He understands what you're saying, you know."

Barnaby's face turned stark white, and he quickly shut the door behind them. "Mr Engel will see us at the tea counter."

With that, they marched down the aisle of books.

"Do you have the mirror?" Barnaby asked over his shoulder, taking care not to look in Kizmet's direction.

Kizmet didn't seem to mind, though. He was too preoccupied glancing side to side for any danger.

"It's right here." Emma taped her leather satchel Franziska made for her out of a smooth, beige hide.

"Good, good."

They rounded the last row of shelves, and white smoke that smelled of cool spice welcomed them. It billowed from a black cauldron placed in the centre of a table so short it required sitting on the floor.

"Ah, perfect timing!" The owl-eyed shopkeeper waved Emma in to sit on a small pillow at the table opposite him.

Emma moved to the cushion just as Kizmet stepped out from behind her and let out a loud roar.

"Whoa, Kizmet!" Emma scolded, pulling Kizmet back from the wide-eyed shopkeeper. "Stop that."

"Well, what do we have here?" Mr Engel replaced his half-moon spectacles on the bridge of his nose. "A *Kenntnishreiches Tier*? Gertrud! Come quick!"

Emma frowned. That wasn't the terrified reaction she expected. Instead, Mr Engel acted more intrigued than scared.

"What's all this shouting about?" Gertrud flung the door

to the storeroom open, and instantly her nose curled up, and she let out a loud sneeze. "Roderic, you didn't get another cat, did you? You know I'm allergic."

She wiped her nose but froze when three humans and a panther stared back at her.

"Oh!" the shopkeeper's sister exclaimed.

"Yes." Mr Engel rounded the table and carefully approached the large, black coloured feline.

Kizmet huffed and shifted away.

"It's alright. They're friends." Emma reached to scratch behind his ears, but his hackles stood upright, and he lout out a low rumble in warning.

"My apologies," Mr Engel said and raised his hands. "It's just I've never had the honour to meet a panther with such a unique power in person. Where did he come from?"

Emma's cheeks burned. "He's with me. My family wouldn't let me go without him. Dangerous times, and all."

"Of course, my dear. Well, a special welcome to you is due." Mr Engel bowed to the black panther whose emerald eyes carefully appraised the shopkeeper.

"Forgive me, I-I—*hachoo!*" Gertrude let out a loud sneeze.

"My sister will have to keep her distance. Her gift makes her a tad sensitive to the feline species."

Barnaby leaned his head to the side. "How do you know about this panther's ability to understand?"

"Oh, I've read much about them," Mr Engel replied. "This panther is an extraordinary creature. It's rare to come across an animal who's communicated with someone with a very particular type of magic. Someone with a telepathic ability must've triggered this panther's talent of understanding."

"That'd be Artus," Emma said, glancing between Barnaby and Kizmet. "He's the younger brother of our ringleader who can communicate with animals. Not everyone, just those who are open to it, I guess."

"Ah." Mr Engel nodded. "Well, as long as he's friendly, he's welcome here."

Kizmet crossed one paw over the other and gave a short bow.

"Come on, then. We've much work to do before you go witch-hunting."

"Roderic, don't call it that! Not all witches are like Frau Perchta." Gertrud scolded him before sneezing once again.

"Forgive me. It was merely a joke. Now, best be off with you, Gertrud, before you topple over from hyperpnea."

Gertrud rolled her eyes and tossed her snowy hair over her shoulder. "Oh, all right. But if anything interesting happens here, you'll call for me?"

"Yes, of course." Mr Engel waved his sister off.

With a sigh, she waltzed back into the dark storeroom, the keys jingling at her waist.

"Now, let us test your senses." Mr Engel returned to the table once the storeroom's door snapped shut.

Emma glanced down at Kizmet for approval. He grunted and nudged her with his nose. Then, satisfied he wouldn't make another outburst if she tried to approach the table, she tucked her skirt underneath her and sat cross-legged on the pillow.

She breathed in the steam that billowed up from the cauldron. "It smells like fresh mint."

"Very good." Mr Engel took the seat across from her. "What else?"

She narrowed her eyes and took another sniff. "Something sweet like… cinnamon? But more spicy, I think."

Mr Engel nodded, stirring the brew. "Close. You're gathering the notes of pimento or, as it's more commonly known, allspice. It brings good luck. Which, to get you ready to hunt the likes of Frau Perchta, we'll need a lot of."

Emma grimaced. It was true, but it still hurt. Why was

everyone underestimating her? The thrill of proving everyone wrong hummed through her limbs. She couldn't wait. But no sooner had the thought entered her mind than the gaunt face of Frau Perchta wiped out all of her confidence. Perhaps a bit of luck couldn't hurt?

With a sigh, she leaned over the cauldron and breathed in as much as she could. Smokey mint filled her lungs which forced a shiver.

"Now, again, but this time when you breathe in, I want you to keep your mouth open." Mr Engel sprinkled something blue into the mixture, and it popped.

She wasn't sure what keeping her mouth open could possibly do, but she did as he instructed. The fumes from the bubbling mixture tickled her cheek as she drew in another long draw.

This time there was no mint or cinnamon, and she gasped. "I can't smell anything."

"Really? Hmm." He paused and furrowed his wildly long eyebrows. "Why don't you try once more?"

Though Emma doubted trying again would change the results, she humoured the old shopkeeper and leaned into the mist.

She shook her head. "There's nothing there."

"May I try?" Barnaby asked, stepping up behind her.

"Of course, though it rarely can be smelled by anyone non-magical."

"Why not?" Emma asked just as Barnaby knelt beside her and took several long whiffs of the blue smoke.

"Simply put? This is the aura extracted from the *Normales Vefumarin*."

Emma glanced at Barnaby, but his expression mirrored her confusion.

"It's what we call the scent that all non-magical exudes," Mr Engel clarified. "It's so subtle that even the magical can miss it. In the beginning, we all thought humans didn't have an aroma at all until the infamous French scientist Jean-Michel Vasseur discovered it. It's all in the book. Barnaby, do you have it with you this time?"

"Yes, of course." Barnaby fetched the compendium from his things and handed it to the shopkeeper, its spine broken and spattered with blood.

Emma frowned. What happened to it? Had Frau Pertcha struck again? Her stomach twisted. She hoped she'd be able to learn to smell the difference between non-magic and the magical in time.

"Here we are," Mr Engel said after flipping through several pages. He turned the book so that they both could read for themselves. "There's no other scent in the world like those without magic."

"And all with magic can smell it?" Emma asked, brushing a hand across the intricate drawing of a medieval village depicting a knight and a magical person sniffing the air.

"Most can once they've developed their senses. You see, the magical auras are much more… aromatic that they can often overwhelm the senses. But"—Mr Engel lifted his index finger, a twinkle in his owl-like eyes — "once you can smell the *Normales Vefumarin,* you can pick out the scent of anything."

Emma bit back a laugh at how excited the old man was. He sounded like a boy setting out on an adventure.

Barnaby cleared his throat. "Wait a minute. You *extracted* someone's aura? From a non-magical?"

"Exactly."

"But… how?"

"There are ways." The shopkeeper chuckled. "Now, Detective Grey, did you get anything when you smelled the cauldron?"

"No. Nothing at all." Then Barnaby paled. "You don't

mean that whoever is possessed by this witch will be able to smell that I'm non-magical?"

"Yes, but that really isn't a concern as they smell humans everywhere, but"—Mr Engel turned to Emma — "*you* have a rare magic, and I believe if you can develop your magical senses a bit more, you might just succeed in finding this bestien spirit and vanquish it. Or at least contain it."

Emma straightened. A lightness rose within her chest at his confidence in her. But then her excitement faltered. "But won't she smell me coming for her? As you say, the scent of magic is powerful."

Mr Engel shook his head. "She won't recognize your particular aroma. That I'm confident of. It's not like most scents, so you've got the element of surprise."

"And what if I can't develop my senses?" She swallowed hard.

"Impossible. I'm certain you should be able to." Mr Engel paused, chewing a corner of his lip. "But perhaps your power works a little bit different than mine. Yes, that would make sense, especially since your power comes from a different world. Shall we try something else?"

Barnaby and Emma shared a questioning glance as Mr Engel dug into a drawstring bag next to the cauldron.

"Eat this." Mr Engel handed them each a small yellow square. "It's ginger to cleanse the pallet."

Emma took a bit of the stringy, soft yet chewy square. She'd never had straight ginger before. Especially not in this consistency. At first, it was sweet like candy, but then a burning spice hit the back of her throat, and she coughed.

"Careful, it's rather potent." Mr Engel placed a tray filled with glass vials of all sizes next to the cauldron and uncorked the first with a pop.

He tapped a bit of the light yellow powder out into his palm and tossed a pinch into the brew. Sparks shot up in all directions, and out of curiosity, Emma slowly leaned over the cauldron's edge to take a peek.

"It just needs one last ingredient." Mr Engel opened another vial, this one larger than the last, and sprinkled globs of brown clumps that looked like mud.

The mixture hissed and snapped. The once blue smoke vanished in a mist of angry yellows and browns.

Mr Engel gave it one final stir. "All right, now tell me what you smell."

Emma shifted onto her knees, her hands bracing herself on the edge of the table and peered over the cauldron. The thick smoke enveloped her until it vanished, and all she could see was the muddy concoction. It snapped, and she jumped back with a gasp.

"It's all right. Just breathe."

She didn't know who it was that spoke, her ears were full of steam, and her eyes stung. But she couldn't close them no matter how hard she tried. It was as if her eyes were glued wide open, unable to peel away from the thick mixture that churned as thick as molasses within the pot.

With a deep breath, she filled her lungs with the rising steam. Notes of wood and sweet spice assaulted her senses. It reminded her of what she smelled at the McLeod House, although more potent.

Suddenly, A cackle echoed in the distance, and her heart clenched.

"Did you hear that?" She asked throatily, nearly choking on the smoke.

"Hear what?" Someone asked, but the voice was too muffled for her to tell who it was.

The harsh laugh returned, and the hair on her arms rose.

"You're late, you whore...." A woman sneered.

Chills swept through her. She knew that voice.

"You'd do well to do as you're told, you ungrateful child." Emma's late mother's hiss swept through her.

A terrifying cold hit her square in the chest as she relived her mother's last words, and then the voice changed. It twisted into the deep growl of her father. The bookshop disappeared, and in its place was a small, shabby room with a single window.

"I've been waiting for you...." A burly, red-bearded man lunged at her.

Emma tried to run and break free from whatever spell this potion had put on her, but there was no use. A full moon glistened down through the open window illuminating the dark room just as thick hands gripped her. Her father shoved her against the dresser. A perfume bottle toppled over and shattered onto the floor. An ear-splitting scream resonated from somewhere, and it took Emma a minute to realize it was hers.

"No!" She sobbed. "I won't let you do this. I won't!"

She writhed against the fists that held her hostage, but it was no use. The iron grip on her shoulders wouldn't budge. She slumped against the wall. Where was Detective Barnaby? Or even Mr Engel? Surely that hadn't sent her into the past to be tormented. Why didn't they *do* something?

The world around her darkened, and her hope faltered. Then it happened. At first, it was a mere whisper in her fingertips, but it grew until her entire body hummed with magic. A smile spread across her face at the familiar sensation of power consumed her.

Her spine twisted in a pleasant agony, dark veins slithered up her arms, and the darkness she tried so hard to stifle took hold of her. But she couldn't remember why. Hadn't it been her power that had saved her all those years ago?

Sharp slivers pierced through her cuticles and replaced her fingernails with black claws. She let out a scream that melted into laughter when her bones cracked and slid through her shoulder blades. Her wings slid through and extended out from her body.

She locked eyes with the red-bearded man she once called father and snatched the drunk's neck. She didn't know if it was a vision or just a memory, but she welcomed the darkness of her magic like a glove.

The bearded man wheezed against her grip and finally let go of her shoulders. His face turned pinker as she clenched against an artery. She nearly finished the job when suddenly her throat locked up, and she couldn't breathe either. Her father vanished in a puff of smoke, and suddenly she was falling.

Her heart jumped into her throat as she fell. She lashed her arms out, trying desperately to find something to break her fall, but there was nothing but the smoke around her. She gagged against whatever stifled her, fighting with all of her might to survive.

"What's wrong with her?" The voices returned, and then a blinding light enveloped her.

She gasped as her throat finally relaxed and her lungs filled with fresh air.

"Get her away from this dark magic!" She recognized Detective Barnaby's worried voice.

Hands gripped her shoulders, and her body lifted from the surface of the table. She blinked back the smoke in her eyes. Kizmet's emerald eyes were the first to come into focus, followed by Mr Engel pocketing some smelling salts and Detective Barnaby's pinched expression. She rubbed her nose, and Kizmet nudged her arm.

"I'm fine," she reassured the panther.

"Here, drink some water." Mr Engel handed her a cup.

She drank the cool liquid without hesitation and sighed.

The water cleansed her burning throat and washed the itchy fumes away, and she sighed.

"What did you smell?" Mr Engel asked, taking the cup when she was finished.

"That's what you ask?" Barnaby cried. "After this poor girl just suffered a fit of a spell? At least ensure that she's alright first."

"I know what I'm doing. Besides, Emma already said that she was fine." The shopkeeper scowled back at the detective.

"That's not the point."

"I did smell something," Emma said, ignoring Barnaby's outburst.

"Yes? What was it?" Mr Engel leaned in

"It..." she paused, looking off to the side as she tried to put the scent into words.

It was more than just a scent. More than a memory, even. She'd been transported back to London the night she first received her powers. A night she tried to erase from her memory. She swatted the tears that sprung out of nowhere.

"It was earthy like musty pine, but with a hint of something sweet. It smelled... nice." She licked her lips. "Then it did something no ordinary scent could do. It forced me to relive when I first experienced magic. I... I used it for revenge."

"Yes, I imagine this scent would do that. That's what calls her forth."

"What calls who?" Barnaby asked.

Emma rubbed her face, swaying on the pillow she sat on at the shock of realization. It was like a gate that had been shut since she'd first experienced magic burst wide open.

"It's her," she gasped, her fingertips tingling as the scent that still hung in the air called on her magic. "It's the scent of Frau Perchta. It's what we smelled at the McLeod House."

A smile spread across Mr Engel's owl-like features. "That it is. You've got the nose for this."

She took a long breath of air and laughed in disbelief. Never in her life would she have ever imagined it possible to identify someone simply by breathing in their aroma, but there it was.

"How can you be so sure?" Barnaby gaped between the shopkeeper and Emma.

"It's all in the compendium, of course." Mr Engel flipped through the pages until he landed on the page with a woman with two faces.

Emma studied it, recognizing the fair maiden on one side and the hag on the other. It was the spirit in the mirror, both how the witch first appeared and what she turned into after the cloaked figure started the incantation.

"Frau Perchta emits the aroma of Frankincense and Myrrh. See?"

Barnaby glanced at the page and shrugged. "I still don't see how one could identify this smell out of thin air."

"Well, let's hope Emma can," Mr Engel replied. "It's the only thing that will save us."

"I can," Emma said, her eyes still affixed to the horns poking out of the hag's wrinkled forehead. "After what that aroma made me relive, I'd know it anywhere."

"Good." Mr Engel clapped his hands together. "And now, my dear, you are ready to go hunting."

Emma snapped her gaze up to meet Mr Engel's. "What? Tonight?"

"You must be joking." Barnaby rubbed his face. "We're up against a violent witch, and now after smelling some herbs and spices, you think Emma's ready to go up against her? She fainted not a few minutes ago. Clearly, she's not in a state to go hunting."

Mr Engel shrugged. "I believe her power and determined nature are quite strong. Perhaps stronger than you think?"

Barnaby's mouth fell open, unable to produce a response, but Emma's heart leapt with excitement at the possibility. Now that she could identify the scent of Frau Perchta, could she do it? Could she go out into the town and recognize it as well? Her fingers tingled with electricity, her power itching to be let loose. Mr Engel believed in her power, but did she?

Mr Engel rested both hands on her shoulders and peered into her eyes. "How do you feel?"

Emma took another deep breath. Yes, she'd once lost herself to the darkness. But that didn't mean she should be afraid to use her power in the face of the dark. Her circus family had helped her gain control of her power, but she knew it would take more to defeat the witch. Perhaps it would ignite the voice of darkness she'd been controlled by that first night she received her power. But wasn't saving her family, friends, and the town from the Christmas witch worth the risk?

A calm washed over her as the static energy of power hummed within her stronger than it ever had before. She was powerful. She knew that. Was she more powerful than Frau Perchta? Her heart jumped. She had no idea, but with a renowned sense of purpose, she was ready to find out.

With one final breath, she lifted her chin. "Let's go hunting."

12
THE TILCOTT TROT

Mrs Tilcott's House
Salter Street

WILSON KNOCKED on the panelled front door of Mrs Tilcott's home. Its coiled iron bars protected a sheet of obscured glass that showed no sign of movement. The neoclassical style house had a pitched gable roof and symmetrical windows that faced towards the harbour several streets down. Ship sails peeked over the tops of the houses across the street.

A chill swept through the buildings, which carried notes of sea salt and fish rank. Wilson pulled his scarf tighter and pounded against the door once more.

"Mrs Tilcott! Are you home?"

Finally, movement reflected against the glass, and the lock was turned open.

"Detective Davies? What a surprise." The older woman gave a polite yet guarded smile. She still donned the same pearled hairnet she wore when Mr Davies met her at the Talmage's.

"My apologies for dropping by unannounced like this, but I was hoping you might spare a moment to assist with the ongoing investigations?"

"Oh, of course." She waved him in and out of the cold.

The foyer was a modest hall that parted on either side into various rooms. He followed the elderly woman into one of the drawing rooms. She motioned for him to sit in one of the two velvet wingback chairs angled towards the fire that crackled.

"Thank you." Wilson sighed and eased his aching back into the seat.

They sat in silence for a few moments while the fire melted his icy bones.

"I'll fetch us some fresh tea," Mrs Tilcott hoisted herself out of her seat to pick up the tray on the end table next to her. "My tenant usually helps me in the evenings after her work, so I'm all on my own."

"Your tenant?" Wilson asked.

"Yes." She cleared her throat. "Since Mr Tilcott passed, I've rented a room in the lower level. An old lady like myself can't manage stairs these days. Best to leave that sort of exertion to our young ones, yes?"

It was, of course, a rhetorical question, and she disappeared through the side door. Wilson sat alone with his thoughts and the fireplace that snapped and sizzled in rhythmic intervals. He narrowed his eyes. Why would Mrs Tilcott be so bothered by him asking about her tenant? Of course, he could be entirely wrong on the matter, but the way in which she babbled on while finishing were all the telltale signs of someone avoiding further questions on the subject. Of course, he wouldn't forget and would inquire further, but, much like asking Mrs Peaton about the McLeod House incident, Wilson knew that tact was his best option forward.

If he pushed her too hard, it was unlikely that she'd answer any of his more important questions, and he couldn't take that chance. Not with the next kill looming on the horizon. So far, there'd been two murders. One each day since the funeral, and he was beginning to think it was a pattern. If so, then there would soon be another dead body on their hands, and what were the chances of him catching the killer before then? The odds were slim, he knew that, but he had to try.

Tea rattled on a tray signalling Mrs Tilcott's return.

"Ah, allow me." Wilson stood and took the tray.

She smiled her thanks and lowered into her chair. That's when Wilson noticed the notepaper and ink next to the tray had been on the end table. It glinted in the light, and he had to take a second glance to ensure he'd seen it correct.

"Scribing a letter, I see." He carefully replaced the tea and poured two steaming cups. "Is that gold-lined parchment?

"It is. Good eye, detective." Mrs Tilcott's eyes lit up. "My mother swore to only write with paper lined in gold, and I guess I, too, have adopted this practice."

She lifted her chin as if that were something to be proud of. Plain, unlined notepaper was the trend for personal correspondence nowadays, but he didn't expect a woman in advanced years as Mrs Tilcott to know this.

"I'm writing to my daughter, you see," she continued before Wilson could get a word in edgewise. "Oh, and she'll be paying me a visit in the Spring. Isn't that wonderful? It's been ages since I've seen her. She lives so far away."

Wilson suddenly wished he hadn't asked. The paper itself was in bad taste enough as it was without the exclamations of an adoring mother.

"Ah, yes. Quite lovely." He smiled, taking his seat. "Now, I'm much obliged that you'd see me so impromptu, but as you know, there was yet another murder, and I daresay time is not on our side."

Mrs Tilcott tsked. "Yes, I heard about that. What a tragedy, losing such a young officer."

"Indeed," Wilson said as she poured two cups of steaming tea. "Could you tell me about the events leading up to that horrible display of Madam Onay's body found at St Paul's?"

"Events? Why, other than the… well, you know"—she mouthed 'the body' — "nothing happened—Oh!" her hand shook, either from nerves or old age he couldn't tell, but it sent the porcelain lid flying off the teapot. It clattered onto the tray.

"Here, allow me." Wilson stood, taking the pot from her trembling hands.

"You're too kind." She smiled, her crow's feet at the corners of her eyes crinkled.

He waited until the frail woman was safely tucked herself into the armchair with a fresh cup of tea before continuing. A whiff of warm cinnamon met his nostrils, and he savoured its warmth.

"Mrs Peaton mentioned something about having a rough time getting to the church that morning. Something about a glove?"

"Oh, that." She chuckled and took a sip of her tea.

"Did you ever find it?"

"Sadly, no. They were my Sunday best, too."

"Did anything else go amiss?" He prodded. "Mrs Peaton didn't have much time for questions this morning."

"No, I don't suppose she did. Always running about. A working woman since her husband passed. And a godmother, too!"

"Yes, I did hear about that."

"Such a tragedy." She turned and fixed her eyes on the fire.

"I wonder," Wilson began, setting his tea aside and leaning forward. "If you might be willing to go over what happened that morning? In your own words, if you please."

"Well, there's not much to tell, I'm afraid. We stayed the night at the Talmages, though I suppose you already know that from Mrs Peaton." She rested her cup on its saucer. "What a welcoming family they are. For the most part, anyway, and the food was magnificent. It always is at the manor."

Wilson drew his eyebrows together. "What do you mean 'for the most part?"

She grimaced. "I would never speak ill of the family, but the way they treated the late Irvin's fiancée! Oh, it would make anyone question their civility. She came to the house that morning just before breakfast."

"Did she?"

"Yes. She desperately wanted to attend the funeral, but the Talmages banned her from the whole event. How very sad."

"Yes, indeed. I actually met her that morning. She was outside the church and quite distraught."

Mrs Tilcott gaped. "Did she? Oh, well, I'm not surprised she made a second attempt. She loved our dear Irvin, the poor girl."

"I gather the Talmages didn't approve of her impending nuptials to their late son?"

"Definitely not. It was never said, but we all knew why." She took a sip of tea. "Her father was a simple brightsmith. He died this past year, you know. I felt sorry for her. Here she was all on her own with not a penny to her name."

For reasons unknown, the mention of a brightsmith triggered a sense of familiarity. As if his mind stored some memory he'd forgotten. Why did this sound so familiar to him?

He failed miserably at retrieving any recollection of it and decided it best to press on. "Not the sort of woman a wealthy heir might marry."

"I'm afraid not."

He tilted his head at the way her eyes watered. "But you approved?"

"Only because Irvin was so very much in love, and I'm quite the romantic." She beamed, but the sparkle in her eye soon dimmed. "Then it all went wrong. I can't say why, but just the morning before his murder, Irvin broke it off without any explanation as to why. It was quite uncharacteristic of him. Can you imagine?"

She didn't give him a moment to reply, and he let her vent since he imagined Mrs Peaton rarely gave her the opportunity. He wondered why no one had ever mentioned that Miss Lauretta was no longer engaged to Irvin prior to his murder. It would explain why Mrs Peaton referred to her as the ex-fiancée. What could have happened? He would have to ask someone with a little more memory to spare than the elderly Mrs Tilcott and more forthcoming than Mrs Peaton. Perhaps Miss Lauretta herself?

The woman said something of red winter berries from her window at the Talmages that tore him from his musings. "Sorry, what was that?"

"I said my room had the best view of the Talmage's front garden," Mrs Tilcott shouted.

"Ah, that's right. So, you would've seen the comings and goings of anyone who stopped by that morning?" Wilson held his breath and observed her reaction with care.

Her eyes fluttered repeatedly, but that could've been caused by a bit of dust or the spice from her tea.

"I suppose so, yes. At least until breakfast when I went down at seven."

Approximately around the time, Madam Onay was

murdered, Wilson mused. "It's wonderful that you all were able to share a meal together."

She drew her mouth into a straight line, tapping her fingernails on the wooden engraving on the armrest of her chair. "That would've been lovely, but only Mrs Peaton was able to join me. Mrs Talmage was still on her walk, and Mr Talmage refused to leave his office."

His heart sank. Unless Mrs Tilcott was covering for Mrs Peaton, which was highly unlikely, this gave Mrs Peaton an alibi for the murder of Madam Onay. But she still had to have some involvement, right? She had, after all, set fire to the McLeod House to cover something up. But if she wasn't the killer, then who was? He had to get his hands on more handwriting to compare.

Then there was the fact that Mrs Talmage left that morning, to who knows where at the exact time Madam Onay was murdered. Chills swept down his arms. Could it have been her? The seemingly feeble wife and heartbroken mother who avenged her son's murder?

Wilson cleared his throat. "You saw Mrs Talmage leave that morning?"

"I did."

"Strange. Mrs Peaton made it sound like she'd vanished into thin air."

"Oh, that old gossip would say something like that." Mrs Tilcott huffed. "I told Mrs Peaton that I'd seen Mrs Talmage leave from my bedroom window that morning. She returned in time for us to leave, though I did think it strange that Mrs Talmage denied ever leaving the house."

"Very." Why would someone innocent deny something so trivial?

Mrs Tilcott shrugged. "I'm certain it's nothing to worry about. The poor woman must've been all out of sorts that morning, and I don't blame her for being a bit scattered. But Mrs Peaton! She was relentless."

"Oh?" Wilson arched a brow.

"She kept prodding her about where she'd been and how it was unsafe for her to go out on her own." Mrs Tilcott took a sip of her tea.

"And how did the Talmages take it?"

"Not well, I'm afraid. I told Mrs Peaton not to shout at Mrs Talmage, but she wouldn't listen. It took me a great deal to persuade Mrs Talmage to even go to the funeral."

"You're quite the caring friend, I see."

She smiled and rested her teacup on its saucer. "We've known each other for a long time. The three of us grew up as if sisters."

"And Mr Talmage never emerged from his study that morning?"

"Not until close to ten, or so. After Victor arrived."

It was curious that out of all those closest to Irvin, Jr invited to stay at the Talmages the night before the funeral, Victor wasn't among them. He knew the butler was close to the deceased and would have personal knowledge of Madam Onay since they both worked at the Halifax Club. He needed to find out the butler's whereabouts that morning before he arrived at the Talmage's. Perhaps he would unveil another piece of the puzzle?

"Ah, I see. Well, I best be off, but I do have one last question." Wilson set his tea aside and leaned forward. "Was there anything else you noticed from your room's window? Anything at all that was out of the ordinary that morning."

"I… I don't think so." She frowned as she tried to recall, then suddenly jerked her eyes to meet Wilson's gaze. "There was one thing. I didn't think of it until now, but I did hear something odd, not a few moments after Mrs Talmage left."

Wilson waited on the edge of his seat while Mrs Tilcott thumbed the handle of her teacup.

"It was like a rustling in the bushes just out of sight. Almost as if a dog or some other large animal was wrestling with something."

"Did you ever see what it was?"

She shook her head. "I vaguely remember a large black shape out of the furthest corner of the property, but it all happened so quickly it could've been merely an old woman's imagination."

She chuckled but stopped. "Goodness, you don't think it could've been a bear, do you?"

"I can't imagine it would make it to the Talmage's without causing a scene."

"No, I suppose not."

"Thank you for your help and for the tea. You've been quite helpful." He rose, and Mrs Tilcott followed. "Oh, no need to get up for me. I can see myself out."

He bowed low, and she flashed him a pleased smile.

"Do come back, detective. I don't get many visitors these days." She called on his way out.

"That I will," he replied just as he turned the corner into the hall. "I definitely will."

He swung his frock coat over his shoulders and reached for the door handle when the oak door swung open in a hurry. The bitter wind howled as it swept into the small foyer and the petite Miss Lauretta marched in over the threshold.

"Oh!" She froze mid-unlacing her winter bonnet when her doe-eyes caught his gaze.

"Detective Davies? Is everything all right?" Mrs Tilcott called, her voice nearing as she came into the foyer. "Oh, you're back early, my dear."

Wilson's focus flitted back and forth between the old

woman and Miss Lauretta. "You don't mean she's your tenant, now, do you?"

"Yes, yes, I do." Mrs Tilcott flew by him to shut the door. "Quick, don't let the cold in."

"Of course, Mrs Tilcott." Miss Lauretta flushed, patting her head of brown ringlets when she removed her bonnet. "So sorry. I was just startled. I didn't know you had company."

Miss Lauretta placed her bonnet on a hook near the door as if she knew the place, and then it clicked. She was the tenant. Could this explain the older woman's guilty behaviour during tea?

"Detective Davies was just leaving." Mrs Tilcott gave him a wide-eyed look as she rushed Miss Lauretta off. "Go feed Mr Whiskers. He's in the kitchen."

"I'd best be off." Wilson gave a short bow once again and made for the door, then turned back with a frown. "Sorry, did you say Mr Whiskers? Isn't he—?"

Wilson stopped when Miss Lauretta gave a subtle shake of her head. Mrs Tilcott tilted her head to the side and glanced between the two women.

"Sorry, never mind." He smiled.

Strange. Was Mrs Tilcott losing her mind? Hadn't Mr Whiskers died long before? Perhaps she had a new cat with the same name, but from Miss Lauretta's reaction, it seemed there might be more going on than what he perceived.

Miss Lauretta's shoulders relaxed. "Lovely to see you, Detective Davies. I'll just be off to tend the cat."

"Yes, go on then," Mrs Tilcott waved her off before turning back to Wilson. "Please don't tell anyone about this."

"About what?"

"About Miss Lauretta," she hissed, gripping Wilson's arm. "Of her living with me. If the Talmages or Mrs Peaton ever found out, they would… well, I'm not certain what they would do, but they wouldn't be happy about it."

He furrowed his brow, uncertain why Mrs Tilcott was so worried about the Talmages finding out that Miss Lauretta was living with her. It was a nice thing and, if Mrs Tilcott was indeed losing her mind, it seemed best that she had someone there to watch over her.

He gave Mrs Tilcott a reassuring pat on the hand. "Your secret's safe with me."

With that, he replaced his top hat and took his leave. Though he still had yet to match the note's handwriting, this meeting had proved fruitful after all. And now he was off to see a butler about a murder.

13
CAROL OF THE HEXENGEIST

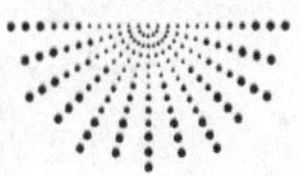

GOVERNOR'S MANSION
Barrington & Bishop St

EMMA DARTED ACROSS BISHOP STREET, away from the charred remains of the abandoned house and toward the Governor's mansion. Figuring that her best chance at catching Frau Perchta would be while the scent was still fresh in her mind, she didn't want to waste any time to begin the hunt.

It had taken some doing, but she'd finally convinced Barnaby to go. That is, of course, after she agreed that Kizmet would remain at the bookshop with Mr Engel. Kizmet wasn't happy about it, but luckily he listened to her after pointing out that it was safer for all involved. Especially from the suspicious townsfolk who might think a large panther walking the streets had something to do with magic.

With that, she'd dragged Barnaby out to catch Frau Perchta before the sunset. Her mission was simple. Find the witch and use the mirror to trap her before rushing back to Mr Engel for him to enchant it. She fiddled with a loose string that hung from the rose-pink pantaloons she donned. Perhaps the plan was too easy. Would it work? Was she capable of capturing the spirit without hurting anyone, including the one it possessed? Her ribs tightened. Perhaps this was a job better suited for someone else.

"Are you certain the witch is *here*?" Barnaby hissed, close on her heels as she paced the length of the fence for an entry point.

"Yes," Emma replied, swallowing her doubt. "That gust of wind carried notes similar to Frankincense. I think."

"Well, that sounds promising."

She glanced back at Barnaby, whose pale complexion sent another tinge of uncertainty racing through her mind. Could she have gotten it wrong? She shook her head. Now was not the time. It was too late for doubt.

Her chin lifted as she summoned all of her confidence and turned to the mansion before her. Its large windows glittered purple and gold in the reflection of the evening sky.

"What could the witch be doing here?" Barnaby's breath was so loud Emma was sure he could be heard by anyone inside the Georgian styled mansion. "She couldn't be visiting the Governor!"

He chuckled but then stopped. "Could she?"

"Stop worrying. I've come prepared." She brushed a hand over the silver mirror secured in a belt at her waist.

"Yes, I see that, but what if Frau Perchta isn't here?"

"She's here." Emma walked along the side of the fence for an entry point. The wrought iron fence was dotted with stone pillars that surrounded the mansion.

She appraised the height of them. With a boost from Barnaby, she'd probably be able to leap over. Or, if the full moon were out, she could shift and, with her wings, just fly over. Her heart raced. But then the voice of darkness would return, and she couldn't risk that. No, she would have to do this the old-fashioned way. Then she spotted it, a metal latch a few steps away.

"Come on, this way." She sniffed the air. The faint notes of must and something sweet fluttered through the breeze that rushed between the iron fence.

"Wait." The detective's hand pulled her to a halt.

She frowned up at him. He crouched near the hedges that framed the sidewalk and the fence, eyeing something down the street.

"What is it?"

"Isn't that?" He pointed. "Yes, I believe it is!"

She peered around him and stopped. Her heart fell at the site of the familiar wooden caravan parked diagonally opposite of the Governor's mansion. It still had Franziska's garland draped around the top of it.

"What is your family doing here?"

Her jaw dropped as all words fled her. She glanced between the caravan and the mansion. What *were* they doing here? Weren't they supposed to be at the Halifax jail?

"Unless..." she gasped, marching to the gate.

Barnaby's voice hitched. "Unless what?"

But she couldn't comprehend his words over her racing pulse. She yanked at the latch and slipped into the garden surrounding the mansion. Sombre shadows blanketed the soft grass. She dashed towards the side of the house, pressing her back against the stone. The sun hadn't quite set, and she didn't want to risk being spotted.

"What—?" Barnaby wheezed, finally catching up to her. He folded at the waist and tried to catch his breath. "What's this all about?"

"I think I was right," she whispered, scanning for some way in. "I believe Antoine is actually sensing whoever conjured Frau Perchta. They must have power, right? A human witch, as you described, and that's why they're here instead of the jail. I'm sure of it."

A loud crash from a room above them drew their attention.

Emma's ears hummed. "I must get in there. They're all in danger!"

Barnaby called after her once again, but she was too focused on getting inside to hear him. She raced for the small door near the front and tugged on the handle. It thudded to a stop against the lock. Sweat dripped from her brow, her ears ringing. What could she do now?

Suddenly glass shattered from the window overhead. She ducked. A harsh cackle echoed above, and she glanced up, shielding her eyes from the falling shards.

A bright blue spectral in the form of a woman in a flowing gown flew from within the mansion out across the front garden. But where was the human who she possessed? Could a spirit act without its puppet? The thought sent chills down her spine. She had to do something. But what?

"Stop!" Emma shouted.

The ghost glanced over her flickering shoulder. Her thin hair lapped around her goat horns. Frau Perchta's eyes flickered black, a sneer spreading across her face as she let out a harsh cackle before she disappeared over the treetops.

Without even thinking, she raced after the spirit, bounding around tree trunks and leaping over their gnarled roots. Her heart protested against her chest, but she barely noticed it over the adrenaline that coursed through her veins.

"Emma!" Barnaby's desperate voice called from somewhere behind her, but she didn't stop.

Frau Perchta's form was fading into the distance. Her heart skipped a beat in panic. The witch was getting away!

The wrought iron fence drew closer, and she pushed her legs even faster.

She hurled herself up into the air towards the top of the fence that towered above her. She wasn't going to make it. A breath escaped her, and she squeezed her eyes shut. Then, energy sparked inside of her, and suddenly her hands latched onto the top of the fence. She gasped, eyes wide as she dangled from the top of the gate. She couldn't believe it! Glancing over her shoulder for a second, she swung herself over and landed with barely a thud on the other side.

Straightening, she scanned the perimeter for the ghost. The sun had dipped behind the horizon, casting the street in darkness. Her heart skipped a beat. Had she lost Frau Perchta already? She peered out towards the cemetery across the street. A faint bluish glow flickered, but she had no idea how far away it was in the sudden darkness.

"Do you even have a plan?"

Emma jumped at Barnaby's breathy voice from behind her. She turned just as he reached the fence.

"Shh," she hissed. "She's in there."

"In the cemetery? You can't be serious." Barnaby gagged.

"Stay here. I know what I'm doing."

"Wait!" Barnaby rattled the fence for a way out, but she didn't have time to waste.

A lamp down the street flickered to her right, and she allowed her instincts to take over, focusing on the light's energy. She forced her skyrocketing breath to slow and stretched her hand out towards the lamp. It snapped dark, and suddenly her fingertips tingled with warmth. She rubbed them together, and flames rose up, lighting her path.

She marched across the street towards the cemetery with catlike stealth. Her hand glowed brighter against the dark fog that rolled between the tombstones and mausoleums.

"I know you're out there," Emma called, stepping off the street and onto fresh-cut grass.

A low cackle echoed in the fog. The hair on her arms stood up. The mist whipped around her until she was surrounded. The musty sweet aroma of Frau Perchta assaulted her senses, and before she could snap her finger and send the fire to break through the fog, blue lightning flashed around her.

"AH!" She cried. A corner of the blue energy sliced through the sleeve of her blouse and nicked her shoulder.

She grabbed her arm, extinguishing the fire in her palm as she massaged the pain that coursed bone-deep. Her jaw clenched, realizing she now had no means of defending herself without the energy. Where would she find more?

"So you're the little rat who traced me to my secret hiding place," a deep voice sang from behind her.

Spinning around, she smacked into someone in a black cloak, the hood pulled low to obscure their face. Her eyes bulged, and she backed away, but the hooded figure moved towards her with each step backwards.

"Let's *play a game, little rat."* The bluish spectral of the old hag lunged out from the hooded figure.

She backed away from the witch's razor-sharp fangs, up against the side of a mausoleum and her breath caught in her throat. The hooded figure didn't budge, but the ghost of Frau Perchta flickered, and her semi-translucent claws stretched out to caress Emma's cheek. She pressed herself as far back against the cold concrete. A shiver ran down her spine as she realized she was trapped.

My child... a voice that wasn't her own whispered in her mind, one she hadn't heard since first receiving her power. *You've forgotten who you are... You need me...*

"No!" She cried, squeezing her eyes shut as she tried to

remember Antoine's lessons on control over the darkness they all carried.

But the instructions were muffled in her memory as if her inner darkness wanted her to forget.

Open your eyes! Look at what you're facing... The darkness within Emma sent her eyes flying open, and she met the cold stare of Frau Perchta, who hovered over her.

"I can't!" She sobbed, clenching her fists together as she tried to fight off the darkness that crawled up from the pit of her stomach.

Frau Perchta's cold grip wrapped around her throat, and the ghost tilted her translucent head to the side. *"Who does the little rat speak to?"*

Emma gazed upward, eyes watering. A full moon peeked out between the treetops. She kicked herself for not remembering the date. The darkness always came for her during the full moon, and it made her lose control if she didn't drink blood. Did she have any with her tea that morning? She couldn't remember, but if she had, it definitely wasn't enough.

"Soon, the little rat will speak no more." Saliva dripped from between Frau Perchta's rotten teeth. *"Then my plan of revenge will be restored."*

Hot tears welled up as Frau Perchta's grip tightened. She gasped, her air running out. Then a thought occurred to her. Maybe she didn't have to surrender to darkness to defeat Frau Perchta.

Stop resisting me... The darkness whispered as agony twisted within her like snakes inching up to pierce through her shoulder blades.

Her whole body shook. Her eyes flashed with light as she lost control. Then she remembered the mirror secured at her waist. If she could just get to it, she'd be able to trap Frau

Perchta's spirit and get away from the conjurer as fast as possible.

With a trembling hand, she searched her belt for the mirror.

"Brechteram," the cloaked conjurer whispered and suddenly, the bones in her fingers snapped.

Emma's mouth fell open and let out an ear-splitting scream that hardly triggered as her own. Pain swelled from her broken hands, unable to grip the mirror.

Was this her end? Had she overestimated herself? Perhaps the darkness was her only option. It could heal her, couldn't it?

Yes... let me in... together, we will do great things...

Tears welled up in her eyes as her broken body grew limp. Frau Perchta's glowing spirit hovered in front of her, the skull-like face twisting in a heinous grin at her pain.

She was about to let herself go when a thought made her stop. If she gave into the darkness, wouldn't that make her into something as ugly as Frau Perchta? It was hard enough to gain the control that she had. Would she be able to face Antoine and the rest of her family if she did this?

But how could she get out of this? The conjurer's powers broke her hands, and she was trapped by Frau Perchta.

"Kill her. Now!" The conjurer cried, and Frau Perchta's grin widened.

"There's *nowhere to run to now, little rat."* She cackled and squeezed Emma neck until her vision speckled with black dots.

Without even thinking, she rested her broken hand on Frau Perchta's grip. Suddenly the pain in her fingers subsided as she drew on the spirit's light energy. Of course! How could she have forgotten? Spirits were nothing but left-over bits of energy. She pressed harder against the glowing witch.

"What's *the little rat doing?*" Frau Perchta cried, tinged with fear.

The witch's spectral form flickered, the glowing blue light fading just a little as Emma absorbed her aura. Then finally, Frau Perchta's grip loosened around Emma's neck, and she fell to the ground in a heap.

"I"—Emma coughed, drawing in a massive gulp of air — "am not a rat!"

She rose up onto trembling feet, her fingers still broken, but the pain was dulled by the electricity that pulsed through them. The darkness within her screamed to be set free, but she swallowed it back. She wouldn't succumb to it. Not this time. In one swift movement, she stretched her hands out towards the spirit, unleashing the energy.

Sparks flew out from her bruised hands, and she tried to direct them at Frau Perchta, but instead, they remained hovered next to her. They spun faster and faster until it created a black hole in the world. She widened her eyes but was unable to move before the whole of energy wrapped itself around her, yanking her into it. Her body twisted in excruciating pain, worse than the darkness that cursed her.

Time stopped as she flew through the air. Her stomach jumped into her throat. Along with Frau Perchta and the cloaked conjurer, the graveyard vanished into a sea of energy, and she spun out of control. There was nothing she could hold onto as she fell through space. She screamed, shutting her eyes as she fell into a deep hole in the world filled with light.

Then it stopped. She landed on wobbly feet on something solid. She stretched her hands out to catch her balance and blinked. The light was gone, replaced with a dimly lit street facing the cemetery. What had happened? And how was she back across the street?

By the time Barnaby found a way out of the garden surrounding the Governor's mansion, Emma had already vanished across the street between the rows of tombstones and mausoleums of St Paul's Cemetery.

What was she thinking going after a Hexengeist like that all by herself? He shook his head, glancing back at the fence he'd witnessed Emma leap over and wondered how she had scaled such a great feat.

Movement from between the bars of the fence caught his attention, and he squinted. A black panther padded across the garden towards him. It must've been Kizmet's mate, Absinthe. Franziska soon followed; her crown of white ringlets were impossible to miss. She glided towards him from the mansion with the Beaumont brothers not far behind. He scanned the parameter for the vampire they called Timur, but he was probably hiding in the shadows, which didn't bode well in Barnaby's opinion.

"What are you doing here? Where's Emma?" Franziska asked when she reached the gate, her brow wrinkled her porcelain face.

"She didn't want to waste any time." He gestured towards the cemetery with reluctance. "After discovering she could use her senses to track Frau Perchta, she led us here."

Franziska's eyes widened. "And where is Emma now?"

She shoved her leg between the narrow, wrought iron bars of the fence. Bones crunched under the pressure, and Barnaby winced as she forced herself through. Once she reached the sidewalk beside him, her body bent and cracked back into place.

"What did he say, Franziska?" Antoine asked once he and Artus reached the gate.

"Emma is in the cemetery." A deep voice came from

behind him, making him jump. "And she's struggling with the darkness. I can sense it."

"Then why don't you go help her?" Barnaby turned and came nose to nose with the giant vampire. His sorrel brown eyes glared down at him, and for a moment, he thought he saw them flash blood red.

The vampire parted his lips to reveal sharp fangs, and Barnaby gulped, taking a step away from him.

"Sorry, I didn't mean any disrespect." Baranaby raised his hands up. "What are you doing here, anyway? I thought you were going to the city jail."

Timur narrowed his eyes at him but moved to stand next to Artus near the fence, which was a much healthier distance. The vampire always made the hair at the back of Barnaby's neck stand upright.

"John Walsh was moved here to a cell below the mansion," Antoine replied, speaking more to the circus than to him. He glanced at Franziska with concern. "But he didn't take our offer. Something about it not being time? I don't know what he meant by that."

Franziska shrugged. "Perhaps he has other plans."

Heat rushed to Barnaby's cheeks. "You mean you've offered your magical protection to the monster who murdered my poor nephew? How could you?"

The entire circus crew froze.

"Sorry?" Antoine tilted his head.

Barnaby glared back. "He's in prison for a reason. He's a monster."

"We're all monsters in one way or another," Antoine replied. "But if I'd known, I wouldn't—"

Emma's scream came from somewhere in the fog beyond, forcing everyone to forget their bickering.

The entire band of circus misfits raced across the street and were halfway into the cemetery before Barnaby could even move. Sweat beaded his forehead as he pushed himself to follow. What if she was hurt? Or worse? The thought of it made it hard to breathe.

He barely noticed Artus and his panther as they flew by him into the dark garden filled with tombstones.

"Wait," Antoine ordered.

They all came to a halt to stare at the ringleader.

"What is it now?" Artus glared at his brother from the cemetery's edge.

Antoine motioned for them to listen. He didn't have to ask Barnaby twice. After witnessing the ghost of Frau Perchta first-hand, part of him wouldn't step into that cemetery even if his life depended on it. But guilt struck the other part of him. Here was Emma risking her life to save the city, a city that would do no favours for her sacrifice, and he knew he had to protect Emma and help somehow. But why was Antoine ordering off their rescue?

Suddenly, the bluish silhouette of Frau Perchta hovered once again above the tombstones. Barnaby glanced between Franziska and the rest of the circus members. Their mouths fell open at the sight. He smirked to himself, his shoulders straightening. If Emma's family hadn't believed her before, they did now. Hopefully, it taught them to trust her instincts. They hadn't led her astray yet.

The air around them tightened, and light flashed from somewhere in the graveyard. A loud pop came from Barnaby's right, and there she was. Emma appeared out of nowhere next to him on the sidewalk.

"Emma?" They all gasped.

Her feat wobbled unsteadily, and she blinked several times, her eyes still sparkled with gold magic.

"How are you here when you were just over there?" Barnaby scratched his head.

"I can't believe it." Antoine slowly released a breath in

awe, joining them on the sidewalk. "Your power… it must've created a light portal."

A sound that resembled the equivalent of a panther clearing its throat caught Barnaby's attention. Absinthe nudged Artus with her head.

"Yes, Absinthe," Artus replied to the panther's telepathic message. "It means she can teleport."

Barnaby shook his head, unable to fathom what it would be like to understand what animals were thinking.

A loud plop drew their attention back to Emma. She now lay on the cold concrete, and her eyes rolled back into their sockets.

Franziska screamed and ran to her, gripping the young girl's motionless shoulders. "Please, Emma, please wake up!"

Barnaby raced to their side and knelt beside them. He checked for a pulse. A sigh of relief escaped him when the vein in Emma's neck thumped against his index finger. "She's still breathing."

"I'm so sorry," Franziska sobbed as she placed a kiss on the young girl's forehead. "I should've believed you sooner. Please, let it not be too late."

Barnaby's eyes watered at the thought of losing the poor girl. He thought of her as a daughter, and his heart ached at what terrible thing happened to her in that cemetery.

"We're in danger. Something's happened at the mansion," Timur hissed and sniffed the air. "There's blood. We need to leave. Now."

Shouts in the distance and the echoes of police on horseback punctuated the vampire's warning.

Barnaby's stomach loosened at the thought of smelling blood and wondering what could've drawn the police here so quickly, but he pushed through the nauseating sensation. He had to get Emma to safety.

"We should take her to the bookshop," Barnaby offered. "I know the owners. They'll be able to help her."

"Then we'll go there," Antoine said with a nod. "Come, we'll take our caravan."

Barnaby bent at the waist to pick Emma up, but a hand on his shoulder stopped him. He looked up and met the crimson-eyed vampire. Then, without a word, he scooped the girl up in one broad arm as if she weighed nothing.

He nodded his thanks and offered Franziska his arm instead. Together they raced down the dark sidewalk to where the circus's caravan was parked, ensuring to avoid being spotted by the stampede of police on horseback and in various carriages flooding the Governor's premises.

Barnaby hadn't the slightest idea of what could've happened. Perhaps it had something to do with the witch when she flew out of that window? What had the spirit been doing in there anyway? And where was her conjurer? The idea that Frau Perchta could move around on her own sent chills down his spine. There were so many questions that plagued Barnaby's mind in between bouts of nausea as they returned to the little bookshop, but there was one that made him sicker than he'd ever felt before. Would Emma survive?

14
A PARTRIDGE IN A PEAR TREE

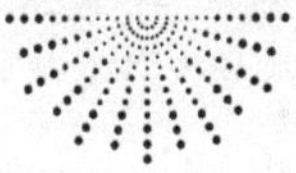

The Halifax Club
Hollis St and Prince St

WILSON STORMED out of the club, irritated that the butler had been less than helpful and, as it turned out, had a solid alibi for his time spent during the morning of the murder. Victor had worked a shift that morning, so there were several witnesses to confirm this, plus Mrs Talmage, who he'd run into on his way out of the Halifax Club.

He'd spotted her leaving Langdon's, a jewellery shop opposite of the club.

They'd shared a few pleasantries, and Mrs Talmage explained she was looking for a gift to commemorate her son. Other than that, there was very little to take note of, aside from the butler mentioning that Mrs Talmage was in a hurry to leave the shop. But who wouldn't be in her position? After all, it was the morning of her son's funeral, and for the mother to be late would be improper.

Wilson had hoped to glean more information than what

Victor had to give, but at least meeting him wasn't a total waste. He'd gotten to enjoy a well-deserved meal at the club before taking his leave. It brightened up his spirit, knowing he wouldn't have to endure another rancid meal cooked in the kitchens of Barnaby's landlady. That was no slur on Mrs Mable's part; the grouchy old crone did try. But he didn't trust her kitchen to be any cleaner than the cobwebs that grew in all corners of that flat building.

"Mr Davies!"

A familiar voice jolted him from his musings, and his eyes flitted up in time to witness the young constable from the other morning dash across the street.

"I've been searching for you everywhere."

"Constable Janson? Why, what is it?"

A deep line creased the constable's otherwise youthful face, and his eyes darted about wildly. Something was definitely amiss.

"I'm not supposed to say, but"—he leaned inward, glancing over his shoulder to ensure no passerby could overhear — "I fear the chief inspector is making a grave mistake."

"Naturally," Wilson replied. "But how, exactly?"

Constable Janson tapped his foot impatiently. "Well, Mr Davies—"

"Detective."

"Yes, of course, Detective Davies, well we think there might've been a murder."

"You think?"

The constable swiped a bit of sweat off his brow. "Yes, at the Governor's house, and what's more is that the chief inspector has arrested Mr Talmage for the doing of it."

"The Governor's dead?"

"Careful! Not so loudly, please." The constable raised his hands. "Yes—I mean no—well, we believe so, but we can't be certain."

Wilson frowned. "You can't be certain if there's been a murder? Why, how can you even call yourselves a police force if you can't tell a dead body from a live one?"

"That's the thing, there isn't one. Not exactly. Just, would you please come to the scene and have a look? I don't think the chief inspector is in his right mind. He's arresting Mr Talmage!"

"Why would he do that? Oh, never mind, just lead the way," Wilson replied, figuring it couldn't hurt to check out the scene if only to prove himself superior to the chief inspector.

He motioned for Constable Janson to head back down Hollis Street but then stopped. Out of the corner of his eye, an angry shopkeeper shoved Mrs Talmage out of Langdon's Jewelry. Quite unnecessary, in his opinion.

The poor woman, what could she have done for this shopkeeper to treat her in such an unseemly manner? His frown deepened. And wasn't that exactly where the butler said she'd visited the morning of her son's murder? Was it a coincidence that she returned or something far more nefarious? Then, deeming this much more pertinent to his current case, he dashed across the street.

"Wait a moment," Wilson called over before the constable could protest.

He neared the storefront, where the shopkeeper bickered with the frail middle-aged woman.

"—Why, I would never!" Mrs Talmage huffed, her right hand, still clutching her purse, flailed wildly mimicking the pink feather on top of her winter bonnet that whipped about in the wind. It distracted from her other hand, which was angled behind her back.

Wilson had never witnessed Mrs Talmage so lively, but then he caught a glimpse of her other hand tucking something gold being between a fold of her skirt at the waist. He raised his eyebrows. It was all an act, a ploy to distract the shopkeeper from noticing her hide the stolen trinket.

"Don't deny it. I know what I saw," the shopkeeper spat, sending dots of moisture to collect in his handlebar moustache.

"You can't speak to me this way. I'm Mrs Talmage, I'll have you know."

"Yes, and do you really want everyone to know that you're a thief, too? Look"—the shopkeeper waved in Wilson's direction — "the authorities are here. Will you lie to them, too?"

The detective furrowed a brow and glanced over his shoulder. He rolled his eyes at Constable Janson, who marched up to them. Were there any officers in this town who would listen to him?

"Officer, detective," the shopkeeper addressed them both, but Wilson's attention was solely on Mrs Talmage, who pinked in their presence. "Mrs Talmage took something from my shop, she has. It's there in her purse."

"It most certainly isn't!" she huffed, her mask of shock and horror broke only for a second when she caught Wilson's knowing stare.

"Sir, would you please stop shouting," Constable Janson said as he came to stand next to Wilson. "What is it that you claim she stole?"

"A gold brooch, good officer, and I daresay it's quite valuable."

"And what does it look like?" the officer prodded.

The shopkeeper huffed as if this was the hundredth time he'd answered this question.

"It's oval-shaped, studded with emerald leaves"—annoyance soon vanished from the shopkeeper's demeanour as he described the brooch with longing— "and golden pears all attached to a winding branch at its centre. Why the craftsmanship is remarkable, and there's even a partridge perched on its nest at the centre of it. And now it's there in her purse! The woman should be arrested on the spot."

Mrs Talmage clutched her purse tighter.

"Now, there will be none of that, sir." Constable Janson sighed and muttered something about not having time for this before turning to Mrs Talmage. "I do apologize about this, Mrs Talmage. However, would it be such an imposition if I search your purse? If only to appease the shopkeeper that you didn't do this?"

"Of course, officer. I know you're only doing your job." Mrs Talmage hung her head and handed her purse over to Constable Janson, careful to avoid Wilson's stare.

He smirked as Constable Janson searched in vain for the missing brooch. The woman was an extraordinary thief, which contradicted his first impression of her. This both surprised and delighted him. Particularly that neither the constable nor the shopkeeper had noticed her slip the ornamental pin into her skirt, and none of them would ever assume a woman of Mrs Talmage's rank and mild disposition to be so devious.

But why would she stoop to stealing when she could probably buy the brooch outright? Was this why she'd denied ever leaving the manor the morning of the funeral? Not anything to do with the murder, but still a reason to have guilt?

"There's nothing here," the constable said, showing proof to the shopkeeper.

"I told you I didn't do it." Mrs Talmage snatched her purse back and tucked it under her elbow.

"But I saw it. I know I did. She—" The shopkeeper stopped, eyes wide as he wrung his hands. "But then who…?"

"Perhaps it was that younger lad who came up beside me?" Mrs Talmage offered. "Whom you let get away while you wasted your time interrogating me. Now, if you'll excuse me, I must be going."

"I'm so sorry, madam," the shopkeeper said, offering continued apologies as Mrs Talmage trotted down the sidewalk as fast as her heeled boots and layers of maroon skirts would allow.

"Now that *that's* settled"—Constable Janson turned to Wilson — "can we be going? The chief inspector will want to clean up the scene soon, and you must see it before that."

"Yes, yes, I'll meet you there, all right?" Wilson assured the officer as he pursued Mrs Talmage. "But do give me a few moments with Mrs Talmage, will you?"

To Wilson's relief, Officer Janson didn't attempt to follow this time. He wouldn't be long, but he desperately needed to speak with Mrs Talmage alone. He'd spoken to all the Talmages and those within their inner circles save her, and this was the opportune moment. She didn't know that he'd witnessed her theft, and he could use this to his advantage. Besides, he found solving an *actual* murder was more important than one where there wasn't even a dead body. It probably wasn't even a case at all.

"Enjoying your plunder, are we?" He whispered under his breath when he strolled up beside her.

She was caressing the glittering partridge at the brooch's centre.

"Oh!" She jumped, and her winter bonnet nearly flew off her head. "Detective Davies, I didn't see you."

She hid the hand that held the brooch behind her back.

"No need to hide it. I spotted you slip it into your secret pocket in your skirt before the constable asked to search your purse. You're quite a sneaky one, aren't you?"

She flushed. "I-I didn't…."

"You shouldn't lie about it, Mrs Talmage, not to me, anyway. Not while you're on my short list of suspects for the murder of Madam Onay. And who would want to avenge Mr Talmage junior's death more than the one who birthed him?"

He didn't actually think she did it, but he found this was an excellent strategy to garner information. And perhaps she had seen something while out stealing from the local jewellery house? Any little clue could lead him to the actual killer, and if a little lie could help him get there, then so be it.

She gasped. "I wouldn't… I *couldn't*!"

"You could," he pressed, stepping closer to tower over the middle-aged woman. "On the morning of your son's funeral, you were missing during the precise hours the murder was committed. Not only that, but that same morning you denied ever leaving the manor even though you were explicitly seen leaving it."

"I—" she looked away, blinking repeatedly. "I didn't mean to lie, but you see, I couldn't explain where I'd been because…."

"Because the wife of one of the richest gentlemen in all of Halifax has become quite the little thief?"

She met his gaze with wide eyes and swallowed visibly. "Uh… well, yes."

It was barely a whisper, but he heard her loud and clear. She slowly brought her hand out from behind her back, producing the brooch. The copper glint of the pears caught sunlight just right and sparkled.

"But, you see, I had to." She cupped the brooch. Her fingers lingered on the partridge's golden feather embellished with tiny diamonds. "That man was selling what was rightfully mine."

Her eyes welled up with tears which made Wilson pause.

"What do you mean?"

"This brooch went missing from my jewellery box some time ago. It was a gift from—" Mrs Talmage choked back a sob, and her shoulders slumped.

For a moment, she resembled the Mrs Talmage that he first met, a woman in mourning at a great loss, and suddenly he understood why this woman was so distressed.

"It was from your son, Irvin, wasn't it?"

She nodded and took the handkerchief he offered to her. "I went there weeks ago and saw it. I told him it was mine, but he wanted proof which I didn't have, and my husband said it must've been lost. So then I asked the shopkeeper how much and that... that horrible man said he wouldn't sell it to me."

"And what about the morning of the funeral?"

Her lower lip trembled. ""I went to take what was rightfully mine. But I was followed."

Wilson tilted his head. "By whom?"

"I can't say for sure, I just heard this... scratching noise and heavy footsteps all the way from the manor to the shop. I went in, but I left immediately in case someone from the manor had followed me. I didn't want anyone to see what I was about to do."

"But someone did see you."

She nodded. "I ran into Victor, but I knew it couldn't have been him who followed me since he'd been working all that morning."

"But then who at the manor would follow you?" Wilson wondered aloud.

"Why, Mrs Peaton would. That I'm certain of." She blew her nose.

"Ah, yes. She is quite the nosy one, isn't she?"

A harsh laugh escaped the tear-stricken woman. "To say the least. She was always so forceful, especially matters involving my son."

"Took the duties of godmother a bit too seriously, did she?"

She paused, her lips parting for a mere moment before

nodding. "She and Mr Talmage would speak on matters regarding him as if I wasn't even there! I warned Miss Lauretta when they got engaged, but—"

"And you approved of your son's engagement?"

"I did. But my husband and Mrs Peaton were beside themselves when they found out."

Wilson tapped his chiselled chin with his index finger thoughtfully. Mrs Peaton was becoming ever more intriguing. Her as well as Mr Talmage.

"Well, thank you for your time, Mrs Talmage," Wilson said, bidding her a good day before heading off to the Governor's mansion.

It was obvious Mrs Talmage had no idea what was going on or the gravity of what she'd heard. Both Mrs Tilcott and Mrs Talmage had listened to a strange scratching noise, and he was certain this was no coincidence. The murder had taken place at another location not a few hours before the funeral. That would mean someone would've had to transport the dead body from whichever basement the murder had been committed to the church during broad daylight.

What were the chances of the murderer doing so without being seen or heard? The odds were slim, and he was beginning to think these two women heard just that. It would reveal part of the path the murderer took that morning and, potentially, point them in the direction of where the murder happened.

His stomach fluttered at the possibility. He couldn't wait to complete his errand at the Governor's mansion and get back to the flat to pin this new information to the map.

It took Wilson no time at all to walk the three blocks to the Governor's grounds, and a huge crowd surrounded the property by then. Protestors lined the sidewalk, spilling out onto the street alongside St Paul's Cemetery.

Wilson frowned, not knowing what was stranger; the number of people shouting with signs calling for the head of the devil or the alarming number of officers for a case without a dead body.

"Do you not see what has happened?" A workman shouted to the crowd as he took a stand atop a park bench. "Dark magic is at work here. Mark my words!"

A slew of 'yes's' and 'here, here's' followed.

"Witches are among us, and who will protect you and your children?" He paused, his wild eyes taking in the growing procession. "The chief inspector? The constables?"

"Boo!" Hollered the crowd.

"Yes, boo to them!" The workman on the park bench motioned towards the constables surrounding the mansion. "They can hardly see the magic when it's right before their very own eyes."

Wilson shook his head, pushing his way towards the gate. It was preposterous how many spectators appeared to be listening to this hogwash. For the life of him, he didn't understand why the officers didn't arrest him before they had a riot on their hands. Seriously. Had the sensibilities of the townspeople *and* the constables all been thrown out like some ship's jetsam?

"Apologies for my delay," Wilson called to Constable Janson, who waited by the mansion's front entrance. "I must say, this is far more of an ordeal than you let on at the club."

Constable Janson clenched and unclenched his jaw before responding, obviously irritated at Wilson for keeping him waiting.

"It seems the word got out."

"About what?" Wilson asked. "I honestly don't think the absence of a dead body at the Governor's mansion deserves this much protest. And why blame their self-proclaimed 'devil'?"

He suddenly stopped and turned on the constable. "Don't tell me John Walsh escaped the secret cell?"

"How do you know about the Governor's cell?"

"I'm a detective."

The constable scratched his head. "Well, last I heard, they were moving him out, but it all seems suspicious if you ask me. The Governor's been missing all night, and it appears his stomach was left behind."

Wilson blinked. "His stomach? That's wonderful news. Perhaps Dr Larson can test it for poison."

"Really? The Governor's dead, and all you can think about is that bloody test? You're not the least bit concerned as to where the rest of him might be?"

"Well, of course, I am," Wilson replied. "But the results of the test could aid in that regard, not to mention in solving this case."

"I doubt the doctor will get much from that. It's in terrible shape." The constable shook his head but motioned for Wilson to follow him into the mansion.

His mind raced as the constable led the way in. Thus far, there had only been two murders, but the pattern was clear. All of them involved missing stomachs, not the absence of the whole body. Could the killer be changing his strategy? If so, why now and why the Governor?

"Right this way," the constable said once they reached the second-floor landing and motioned to the heavily guarded double-oaked doors directly in front of them.

Wilson straightened his frock coat and strutted past the guards into the spacious office. His confidence faltered upon entering, and he gasped. If Barnaby had been with him, he would have certainly been ill upon witnessing such a crime scene.

A breeze blew in from the broken window opposite them, sending the sweet metallic notes of blood to tickle his nostrils. Blood painted the walls of bookshelves and spilt into pools onto the marble floor, which was surprisingly clean for the amount of blood in the room.

"Not the books," he moaned, noting the precious cloth bindings of volumes even he didn't own.

He scanned the room for the source of this horrible infliction, but there was only a stomach perched on top of a stack of papers strewn across the noble desk at the centre of the room. Definitely not enough to do this amount of damage. Wilson rarely witnessed this amount of blood at once in his life, save for that one incident in a bar in London, but that crime scene had included endless dead bodies. Here there were none. So, where did it come from?

"Constable Janson!" Chief Inspector Plundell barked, and Wilson turned. "I told you to fetch the doctor, not *him*, you imbecile!"

The chief inspector glared at them and marched from the doorway into the room, probably with every intention of kicking them out.

Wilson smirked. He'd like to see the chief inspector try. He towered over Plundell's stocky build, and he was confident he'd not only be able to outrun but also outwit him.

"Sir, I did fetch the doctor," Constable Janson replied, stepping between the chief inspector and Wilson. "But I thought that since you arrested Mr Talmage—"

"You're not paid to think. You're paid to obey." The chief inspector jabbed a finger at them. "Now, you're interrupting my murder investigation, so I suggest you both leave at once."

"I must ask, do you really think Mr Talmage had anything to do with this?" Wilson asked, waving his hand at the blood-splattered books. "How would assaulting the Governor aid him in building his business empire or whatever it is he's into these days? I think it's much more likely this had something to do with your prisoner downstairs."

"Which is exactly why I had John Walsh moved." It was the chief inspector's turn to smirk, and he crossed his arms proudly. But then his face twisted in confusion, turning on Constable Janson. "Wait, how does *he* know about that?"

Constable Janson opened and closed his mouth without being able to form words.

"Pardon, but have you or haven't you arrested Mr Talmage for all this?" Wilson arched a brow as he took a closer look at the blood splatter on the bookshelves.

It was curious how meticulous of a pattern it was. There were no blood trails or markings on the floor other than what dripped from the bookshelves themselves. Surely if the murder had been committed here, there would be a lot more blood on the floors? Unless whoever did this took the time to mop it all up, but even that would've left some soap residue behind, which there was none. No, whoever did this took care in painting every inch of the room except for the floors and the desk.

"Yes, but only overnight for his own protection. The man was trembling with fear like he'd seen a ghost when we found him, talking madness and gripping a piece of paper similar to the one left in the first victim's mouth.

It must be the same killer, particularly since the Governor's stomach is left right there for all to see." Plundell stopped, his face turning pinked and scowled at his own obvious overshare. "Not that it's any of your business."

"Of course not," Wilson replied, moving to stand behind the desk. He tilted his head at the toppled chair and disturbed rug. "There was definitely a struggle, but no blood spilt, so that's good, at least."

"Would you *please* leave my crime scene? Your services were never asked for."

"And yet here I am. You're welcome." Wilson grinned, but the smile quickly faded when something dawned on him.

If whoever did this was here to assist John Walsh, that would mean that his partner in crime was still at large. Had he been wrong about Madam Onay all along? Was her death his fault? He swallowed back the guilt and forced the thought from his mind. It wouldn't help to solve the case at hand to be so preoccupied with the past.

Then he frowned, spotting something else that was entirely wrong. "That's odd."

"What is?" The chief inspector and the constable asked in unison.

Wilson glanced up, forgetting he wasn't alone for a moment and returned his attention to the unusual paperwork on the desk.

"Did you have an officer analyze these documents?" Wilson asked.

"No, I didn't think it was relevant, seeing as how there's been a murder.."

"Oh, really?" Wilson blinked repeatedly. "Honestly, inspector, I'm quite embarrassed for you that you didn't notice how orderly arranged these letters and documents are. It's almost as if they were put on display for us, and I can assure you that no governor would leave sensitive bills lying around on their desk for all to see."

The chief inspector was speechless.

"You think it was left for us by whoever killed the Governor?" Constable Janson asked meekly.

"Indeed, along with this"—he waved at the mutilated stomach, the pale flesh sticking to the corner of one of the letters — "which is clearly not of the human variety which leads me to believe the Governor might still be alive. For now, as long as we can catch our murderer in time."

Plundell cleared his throat. "H-how do you know that it's not human?"

"Why, it's clearly two sizes too large."

"He is correct." A voice from the doorway gained their attention. Dr Larson stood with his top hat in the crook of one arm while his other gripped his medical bag.

Wilson gave the doctor an appreciative smile. "Dr Larson, your timing is impeccable."

"Thank you for coming so quickly, doctor." The chief inspector shook the doctor's hand while giving Wilson a stern glare. "Davies here was just on the way out. Now, if this isn't a human stomach, then what does it belong to?"

The doctor shrugged. "I couldn't say for certain, but at first glance, I would say swine? I'd have to take it for analysis back at my office."

"Marvellous," Wilson replied, scooping up all the documents from the desk. "In the meantime, I shall take these for further examination. Now, let's find the Governor alive, shall we? If our murderer hasn't killed him yet, we've quite a small window to find him."

With that, he marched awkwardly for the office door with all the letters and bills. Even the ones that were under the swine stomach. He was only mildly surprised that Plundell didn't try to stop him, but the chief inspector must've realized he was right. Perhaps he finally came to his senses about how out of his depth he truly was? Whatever it was, it gave Wilson a rush of satisfaction that invigorated his awkward trek back through the mob, which appeared to be moving on to pester someone else.

Good riddance, he thought. Nothing could deter him from getting to Barnaby's flat. Not even the protestors could, and he took care not to drop a single document from the stack that towered up to his chin. He was so close to solving this case, he could feel it. Though it would take some time, he was certain there was a reason the intruder left these documents so neatly arranged and whatever it was, he was determined to discover it and bring down the killer once and for all.

15
WE WISH YOU A MERRY DEMISE

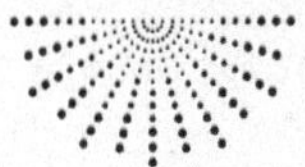

Engel's Emporium
Albemarle Street

BARNABY PACED BACK and forth within the space allowed between the aisle of bookcases and the tall counter near the back of the bookshop. He eyed the storeroom door for any sign of movement.

Roderic, his sister, Gertrud, and Antoine, the ringleader, had been in there with Emma all night trying to remedy whatever shock her magic had put her in. It was now past dawn, and she still had yet to regain consciousness which caused Barnaby's stomach to knot. If anything happened to her, he knew it would be his fault.

How could he let her go after Frau Perchta alone? He should've been there despite not having powers, and he kicked himself for being so reckless. But, from the permanent glare Franziska gave him from the counter she was perched on, he knew she agreed.

In contrast, Artus and his panthers took on much more

passive demeanours. He sat on the floor with them on the opposite side of the room, studying a chessboard. It appeared the panthers were playing a game of chess with him, which astounded Barnaby. How human-like were these creatures? The question was a good distraction as he waited for what felt like an eternity for any news on Emma's wellbeing.

For the hundredth time, Barnaby trotted past the last row of bookcases. An encyclopedia the size of a footstool plopped off the shelf. It landed on his foot with a thud.

"Ow!" He gripped his smarting foot.

Timur poked his head around the bookcase. "Sorry."

Barnaby glared through watery eyes, but then the door to the storeroom swung open, making him forget all about his foot.

Roderic emerged from the storeroom. Franziska leapt off the counter, her white curls falling from her updo, and all of them came to congregate around the tea counter in anticipation.

"She's not—?" Barnaby choked, unable to finish his question without tears welling up.

"She's all right," Roderic said, and they all sighed with relief.

"Is she awake?" Franziska asked.

Roderic nodded and dabbed his forehead with a kerchief. "But she's a bit dazed, I'm afraid. The, uh, mixture"—the shopkeeper grimaced, and Barnaby instantly knew he was speaking about a concoction involving blood — "Antoine prescribed helped stabilize the darkness within her. Still, the amount of raw energy she produced took a toll on her."

Artus furrowed his brow. "What does that mean?"

"It means that she's weakened, though I did provide a potion that will help her to heal."

Franziska shook her head. "But she's able to cure any

wound. That's part of her power over the light. I've witnessed it."

"We both have," Artus agreed.

"She may be able to heal others, but it seems not herself. Or at least not from this particular wound." The shopkeeper shoved the kerchief into a pocket and cleared his throat. "I've never heard of this amount of power in a fully human species, and I fear... I fear that if her powers continue to grow in this manner, her body may deteriorate."

"Lies!" Franziska lunged at the tiny shopkeeper, but Artus stopped her. "Let go so I can strangle this little owl with his own waistcoat."

The panthers growled from behind Barnaby, making him jump.

"Franziska, it's okay," Artus said, barely above a whisper. "He doesn't know how strong she is."

The slender woman blinked back the tears that jumped to the brim, threatening to spill over before finally backing down.

"She's asking for you, Detective Grey," Roderic offered quietly, pushing himself as far away from the angry woman that towered over him as the tea counter would allow.

Barnaby barely comprehended the shopkeeper's words and pushed through the open door leading to the storeroom within. He was faintly aware of being followed, but his focus was on getting to Emma.

His eyes adjusted to the dim room. A lamp flickered from Roderic's desk. Antoine and Gertrud were bent over some book that must've been the compendium from the size of it, while Emma lay on a small cot pushed up next to the solid oak apothecary case. Her arms were connected to various tubes that wounded up to a glass container hooked at the ceiling. It dispensed something that bubbled green directly into her veins, and his heart clenched.

"What have you done to her?" He ran to her side, falling to his knees.

Her ruby red hair caught the light from the lamp, and for a second, he could've sworn the girl sparkled with light.

"She's all right, detective." Roderic came to stand next to the bed, removing the needle from a vein in her arm. "It's a potion that works as a sedative targeting her supernatural abilities to subdue them. If I hadn't injected her with it, she would've been overpowered by her own magic."

Barnaby glared at the owl-eyed shopkeeper. "How do you know so much about her power?"

Roderic shrugged. "I don't, but even though her power is of another world, the mechanics of magic are all the same."

The detective could hardly wrap his head around what the short owl-man said, but then Emma stirred, and he forgot all about the mysterious potion.

"Detective Barnaby?" She pulled herself up onto her elbows.

His shoulders slumped in relief. "You're alive!"

"Of course." She furrowed her ruby red eyebrows. "What happened?"

"You don't remember?"

"I..." She trailed, looking into the distance, and for a second, her eyes glowed with speckles of gold. Then, as quickly as it appeared, she blinked the light away and refocused on the detective. "I remember being in the cemetery with Frau Perchta. She was right in front of me!"

Her eyes watered. She looked down at her hands splotched with deep purple bruises that were already beginning to fade. "When I tried to get the mirror she... she broke my hands. How are they healing so quickly?"

Barnaby looked to Roderic for answers, and the short man shrugged. "I have a device that speeds up the reparative stages of bone injuries."

"Of course, you do." Barnaby shook his head and returned his attention to Emma.

"Thank you," she said; a half-smile touched her face for a moment before returning to a frown. "I was so close to capturing her, but then I tried to use my power, and suddenly I was somewhere else entirely. I'm so sorry."

"For what?" Barnaby asked.

"I let everyone down. I should've been able to catch the spirit, but I couldn't. It doesn't make any sense."

She shivered, and he draped a nearby quilt around her shoulders.

"Don't even think to blame yourself, Emma," Barnaby replied, his voice thick with emotion. "This was my fault. I shouldn't have let you go into that cemetery alone."

"None of us should have," Franziska added, stepping up to stand beside the detective.

"You… you believe me?" Emma's eyes grew wide as she looked past Barnaby at the rest of her circus family and the shopkeepers congregating in the crowded storeroom.

It was so packed that if anyone made any sudden movements, Barnaby was confident the endless stacks of boxes would topple over and drown them.

"We do," Antoine replied from the desk, his voice tinged with regret.

Franziska patted Emma's shoulder. "They're working on a strategy to catch Frau Perchta's spirit as we speak."

Emma's mouth fell open in disbelief, glancing between her and Antoine. "You mean it? We'll do it together? No keeping me behind 'for my own protection'?"

Antoine shook his head. "That is, once you're fully recovered, and you promise to follow the plan?"

"I promise!" Emma leapt up from the cot, cringing slightly at her aching limbs, and threw herself into Antoine's arms.

"No, no, no!" Barnaby jerked to his feet. "Not but a few

hours ago, the poor girl just had her hands broken, and you expect her to join in some suicide mission against the very witch and conjurer who did this?"

"It's not a suicide mission. We have a plan," Antoine replied, raising a hand for the detective to calm down, but he wouldn't. It was all balderdash to him.

"A plan that will put Emma in harm's way? Again?" Barnaby flitted his gaze between the ringleader, his brother Artus, who sat on an overturned box along with his two panthers, and Franziska. Surely one of them had to agree with him. He shook his head when no one piped up. "You must be mad if you think I'll stand by and watch that."

"Roderic found the ingredients for a spell that should temporarily disguise our scents," Gertrude interjected, gaining Barnaby's attention. "That is, once Emma locates the witch again. It's quite a good plan with low risk. You should hear it."

Emma leaned on the desk for support and turned to Gertrud. "I'd like to."

Barnaby raised a hand to his temple and shook his head. "Have you all gone mad? She's just a child!"

Emma's eyes watered, and he instantly regretted saying it, but not for voicing his disapproval of putting her in danger again.

"I mean, can't you see that she's still injured? She can barely stand," he added.

"I can stand, see?" Emma stepped away from the desk but let out an involuntary gasp. "Besides, Mr Engel has that healing device."

"It's too dangerous," a deep voice said from the back of the storeroom.

They all looked over at the dark olived-toned vampire who stood next to a stack of boxes that towered near the exit. Timur returned their stares with a decisive gaze that

Barnaby respected. Perhaps there was more to him than just a blood-thirsty vampire?

Barnaby's eyebrows rose. "I'm glad you agree."

"I don't care." Emma lifted her chin in determination. "It's dangerous either way. If we leave without stopping Frau Perchta, then whoever dies next will be my fault."

He softened his gaze at the young, brave girl he came to cherish as if she were his own daughter. Much like he had his nephew, God rest him. Which made it all the more difficult to bear the thought of her going after Frau Perchta again, even if it wouldn't be alone this time.

He let out a heavy sigh. "What makes you all so certain this plan will work?"

"Because, this time, we'll *all* be working together," Antoine replied. "As a family."

A smile swept across Emma's face.

"In addition, I've seen bits and pieces of what is to come." Antoine glanced down at the compendium opened to the entry on the Christmas witch. "I believe this is the best path forward."

"You've said this before!" Timur snapped. "What's to say this doesn't turn out like it did the last time? Or perhaps your foresight has gotten worse than what you've let on?"

His brown eyes flashed crimson, and Barnaby's stomach quivered, rethinking there being more to him. Maybe his initial assessment of the vampire was correct.

Antoine shook his head. "Timur, I would advise you not to let the past prevent us from moving forward."

The vampire hissed in response, fangs sliding over his teeth.

"I'm beginning to agree with the liability." Artus nodded his head towards Timur, who chuckled, a response Barnaby didn't quite understand. It must've been some inside joke.

Antoine took a step towards Artus, and the panthers growled. "Please, brother, you haven't even heard our plan."

Barnaby backed as far away from the glaring felines as the cramped storeroom allowed. Then a crash sent the hairs on his neck upright. He glanced around to ensure he hadn't toppled anything over, but it didn't appear that he ran into anything but the cot.

"What was that?" Emma asked, eyes wide.

Another loud bang echoed from beyond the storeroom, followed by a horse naying.

"Clement!" Artus cried, dashing for the door. The two panthers wasted no time and leapt after him.

How Artus knew that was Clement naying was beyond Barnaby, but now wasn't the time to prod him on the subject.

"Get the book and wait for my signal!" Antoine called over his shoulder to the women as he, the detective, and the owl-eyed shopkeeper all followed after the youngest of the Beaumont brothers.

Once out of the storeroom, Barnaby blinked several times to adjust to the brightly lit shop. Shouts and screams came from the bookshop's front, and they raced down the aisle between the rows of books. When Barnaby spotted what caused the commotion, he felt his legs go weak.

A mass of people with hateful signs lined the outside of the shop. Some even surrounded the Beaumont's horse and caravan. Angry men shoved their shoulders against the vehicle to topple it while more tried to pry the bookshop's door open.

"What are they doing?" Roderic cried.

Barnaby didn't think the shopkeeper's owl eyes could get any wider.

"We've got to do something." Artus reached for the door handle.

"No!" Roderic lunged himself against the front door,

which rattled against the efforts of the angry group outside. "They'll destroy everything! *Please*!"

"And leave the horses out there to die? They're innocent." Artus leaned over the short, white-haired man whose half-moon glasses slipped to the end of his bulbous tipped nose. "Move. Or I'll have them make you."

Kizmet and Absinthe growled, their emerald eyes locked on the shopkeeper. The poor man swallowed hard but complied.

"Brother." Antoine clasped a hand on Artus's shoulder, his eyes misting over for a moment before clearing. "Go to the left. It is the safest path."

Artus gave his brother a nod, and with one last breath, he yanked the front door open. A jug of a dark, brown substance was tossed at Artus as soon as the door opened. Mush sloshed down his porcelain face, but to Barnaby's surprise, he didn't let this stop him from rushing out into the band of rioters. Was he mad? How could one man get through a crowd like that unscathed? The screams grew louder, and he squeezed his eyes shut, unable to stomach to watch them trample him.

Before he knew what was happening, an arm grabbed him and yanked him forward. His eyes flew open to meet a man with a grizzly beard and a scowl etched across his face.

"What are you doing? Let go of me?" He tried to tug against the stranger, but he was much stronger than the detective.

"Quiet, traitor." The man shoved him out of the bookshop and into the cold.

Barnaby's squinted against the bright sunlight. The crowded street echoed with the hatred of the mob, sending shivers down his spine. He lost track of Antoine and the others but prayed they were safe. A crash came from behind him, and he ducked. He looked over his shoulder at the bookshop in time to see the bay windows shatter into a million little glass pieces. Some threw rocks while others pried their way inside, shredding priceless books and toppling bookcases.

It made Barnaby's skin crawl to see all this hatred, the destruction. Why would anyone do this?

"Stop this!" He cried, but his request was met with a blow to the side of his head.

His ears rang as he slipped on the ice, barely keeping himself upright. Dots speckled his vision, but before he lost consciousness, he saw someone toss a lantern into the bookshop.

The man with the grizzly beard shouted something he couldn't discern before something hard slammed against his leg. He collapsed to his knees and gasped, blinking back the tears of pain as the building in front of him quickly erupted into flames.

His heart clenched. Through the dots that speckled his vision, he remembered Emma and the others were still inside, but there was nothing he could do. Another blow to the back of his neck sent him flopping against the cold sidewalk, and everything went dark.

EMMA LED the way as the women barged out from the storeroom armed to fight, only to come to a skidding halt. Fire blocked the length of the shop between them and the exit, lapping up the toppled bookcases and precious books like they were mere kindling. But Emma hardly noticed this as her eyes locked on what was going on out in the street beyond the fire.

The townsfolk held Antoine and Mr Roderic at gunpoint while a burly man punched Barnaby to the ground.

"NO!" Heat rushed through her body that had nothing to do with the fire.

She had to get to them and fast, but the flames licked at every turn.

"Quick! This way!" Franziska shouted, motioning to the opposite side of the shop with a narrow opening that had yet to ignite.

"But the books and my potions!" Gertrud cried and stomped at a burning book to try and quench it.

Franziska grabbed Gertrud's arms and pulled her away. "Leave them."

The fire moved fast and soon engulfed the tea counter behind them. There was no turning back now. Gertrud repeatedly coughed as smoke filled the room. Fire wooshed up the wall beside them. Emma shielded her eyes to keep sight of the exit. How could it still be so far away?

A massive pile of splintered wood still impeded their path that would be impossible to climb without injury. But did they have any other choice? They had to get out of there before the whole thing burned down.

Emma hiked up her skirts and climbed over the first overturned bookcase. She turned back to help Franziska and Gertrud when her feet slipped. Her hands shot out to catch her fall, but they were still too weak, and she hit her head on a jagged piece of wood.

She rubbed her brow, dazed and completely turned around. She was faintly aware of someone shouting for her in the distance, but these cries were drowned by the groans of the wooden planks above her. She looked up to find the main support beam hung on by a thread, and her stomach flipped over. They weren't going to make it.

You need me... the voice she'd tried so hard to stifle crept inside her mind, and this time she listened.

It was their only option. They would die if she didn't

unleash her full powers. If she lost herself to the darkness, then so be it.

That's right... let me out...

She closed her eyes, searching her mind for the place where she'd been taught to contain her more unstable abilities. Antoine warned her never to open it, but it would seep out on its own during the full moon and threaten to control her. Only blood kept it at bay, and only then did she have the power to use it with her own free will. This was also discouraged since it was unpredictable.

The unknown of its full potential made it dangerous, but she would have to risk it. Her loved ones were in danger, and her powers were the only way she knew for sure she could save them.

The box inside her mind quivered in anticipation when she finally found it. *Yes... set me free...*

She sucked in a deep breath of air, reminding herself that her family depended on it, and she yanked the constraints around the mental box free.

Static energy swept through her, snug and familiar like her favourite pair of wool stockings. It rushed from her chest and spidered out to the rest of her. A pain she knew all too well tore through her as a sensation like bugs crawling under her skin ran up her spine.

It feels good to finally be free, doesn't it? Her power whispered to her.

"Only until I save my family," she gasped, shivering as spasms of pain assaulted her.

Seems a pity... we could do great things together...

She opened her mouth to protest, but instead, an ear-splitting scream escaped her as two black limbs stabbed through the delicate skin below each shoulder blade. They crawled out, expanding into two giant wings with black silk feathers. Her body went numb from the shock. Then something changed. Her hazel eyes flickered with a light brighter than the sun, and the smoke that once stung them vanished.

The orange and blue flames that sizzled around her shifted into strings of curling light as if it were energy itself. A sly grin pulled at the corner of her lips. This was it, the power she'd been searching for. It was all around her, just waiting to be manipulated.

It lapped greedily at the walls and floors without order, but it whispered to her, begging to be under her command.

She pushed herself up from the rubble, shaking off the soot from her feathers and stretched her hands out towards the flame. It snapped in response, but slowly the heat obeyed. The fire leapt off the half-charred wood and swirlled into her waiting grasp. It tingled her fingertips as it clung to her like honey.

A loud crash yanked her from her reverie, and she looked up as one of the support beams fell to the ground, just missing Franziska's head. Gertrud leaned against her as if she were about to faint. Together they stumbled over the last of the rubble to the exit, but not before another groan from above sent Emma into motion. Adrenaline pumped through her veins as she allowed her instincts to take control. She raced towards the two women, her feet barely touching the ground.

The final beam snapped loose, and she flew up, gripping the plank before it could smash down onto them.

"Go!" Emma grimaced, flapping her wings as she strained against the weight of the ceiling. Too bad Timur's vampire strength wasn't one of her abilities.

"Not without you!" Franziska cried.

Gertrud swayed beside her, the smoke taking its toll on the poor woman.

"Just go!" Emma cried through clenched teeth. "Get her to safety!"

Franziska paused, her singed white eyebrows drawing in. "Fine, but wait there. I'll be back for you."

"No rush." Emma gave a nervous laugh, sweat beading across her forehead.

Why aren't you letting go? The voice that wasn't her own cooed. *I thought you wanted me...*

Emma chewed her lip as she struggled against both the forces within her and the growing fire. Heat flared around her. She glanced down. The fire licked at her heels. There was no way she would survive this.

Her arms quivered against the weight of the ceiling. Perhaps this was how it was meant to be? Her life for the safety of her family and friends? Whoever was responsible for setting the fire would be no match for the Beaumonts. Especially Franziska. They didn't need her.

Let go... You'll feel better...

She sniffed. Tears threatened to spill over at the thought of everyone she would leave behind and all the things she had yet to do. But her muscles ached, and the fire was too great. She pushed against the beam one last time. Her wings brimmed the fire as they flapped once more before her muscles gave out, and she tumbled into the arms of the fire.

Everything spun and flashed bright gold before darkness speckled her vision. The monster within her laughed, a booming sound of victory before she vanished into the scorching flames.

16
I SAW TWO FACES

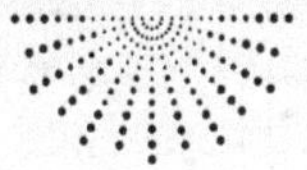

POLICE WHISTLES ECHOED, and weapons clashed against bone. Barnaby jolted upright. All around him, Albemarle Street had turned into a war zone. Constables worked to contain the burning shop while others fought to control the mob who'd armed themselves with anything they could get their hands on. Some waved mallets around like swords while others wielded more deadly armament.

A gun blasted next to him, and he jumped. His ears rang, and he looked up in time as a man with a rifle pulled the trigger on Antoine, who knelt beside the bookshop owner. The ringleader ducked just before it grazed his cheek. He moved with grace towards the shooter and grabbed the gun before the man could shoot Roderic, whose limbs were tied to a rope and his head bowed. As impressive as Antoine's manoeuvre was, Barnaby couldn't help but wonder how he could foresee the bullet but not the destruction of the Engel sibling's shop. Perhaps all of this could've been avoided?

He didn't have time to contemplate this further as one of the protestors sent a hard kick to Antoine's abdomen that knocked the breath out of him and sent him staggering back to the ground.

"Let's see how your magic does against being drawn," one of the burly men sneered, lunging towards the ringleader to tie him up with the same rope that bound Roderic.

Barnaby gasped. The rope on the other end was connected to a horse-drawn carriage. His whole body went ice cold when he realized they planned to drag these poor men through the streets. They would never survive.

Without hesitation, the detective leapt to his feet to help but winced when he put too much pressure on his right leg. It throbbed, and he was confident he wouldn't be able to walk normally on it for a while. Where were Artus and his panthers? Surely they could help, but to find them in the midst of the crowd as they destroyed shops was an impossible feat. He probably was too preoccupied with saving their horse and caravan anyway.

Antoine grabbed the collar of one of the men tying up his ankle and smashed his forehead against him. The man staggered back in shock. Then, while he still had the upper hand, Antoine tucked his toe under the rope and, with a single kick, launched the line up into the air. Like a noose, it latched around the neck of the man. Antoine tugged on the rope, warning the man who pulled at the rope not to move.

Antoine looked over his shoulder at Barnaby. "Stay back! Save the book!"

What did he mean by that? He furrowed his brow, pondering this while Antoine helped Roderic out of his constraints. As soon as he got the shopkeeper's foot out, even more, men fought against them, and soon the two were lost to the crowd.

The detective prepared to stagger after them but then remembered Emma was still inside the burning shop. Turning around, he limped towards the entrance. He covered his nose with his free hand while the other remained extended out for balance. It didn't matter that he could barely walk; all that did was that he got to her in time.

Suddenly, a mass of smoke puffed out from the door. Seconds later, Franziska emerged, her white hair spilling with ash, and her arm slung under Gertrud stumbled and lost her grip on the compendium. It tumbled into a pile of snow. Barnaby grimaced against the pain as he rushed to pick it up before the moisture could damage the pages.

"Quick, stay with her!" Franziska shouted, guiding Gertrud to sit on the sidewalk.

Barnaby gave Franziska a nod before she turned to enter the shop once more, but just then, the ground rumbled, and suddenly the roof caved in. Bricks crumbled, and dust billowed. Barnaby shielded his eyes. A sudden gust of wind whooshed everything into the centre of the ruined bookshop, dragging several unsuspecting protestors up with it. Their screams would haunt him for years to come.

It took all of Barnaby's strength to keep a grip on the compendium, and suddenly he understood Antoine's warning. The debris whirled around the heart of the fire until a figure emerged from the flames.

Barnaby gasped. "Emma?"

A fiery winged version of the girl he thought he knew hovered over the burning rubble. But whatever this was couldn't be here, could it? Or was this the transitioned form she'd once told him about? Either way, it made even Franziska take pause.

Emma's giant black wings sparked with fire and licked at her skin without burning. Black flames spiralled up above her and formed into a dragon with two horns and embers for eyes. He'd never seen anything like it in his whole life.

Everyone who stood in the street froze as she flapped her wings, sending sparks of fire shooting out in every direction.

Her golden eyes locked on the mob that surrounded Antoine and the shopkeeper for a moment before she lunged for them.

"Wait!" Franziska cried, running after Emma, but she was no match for the girl's half-dragon speed.

She flew through the air like a hawk about to snatch up its prey before plunging down amidst the armed crowd. Screams and shouts followed, and Barnaby looked around for a better vantage point. He spotted a crate nearby and hobbled to it. Hoisting himself up, he gasped when he spotted Emma.

Her fiery wings were arched above her like weapons aimed at a burly man who gripped Antoine by the collar. He was confident the ringleader could've gotten out of that hold, but it appeared he was too busy trying to calm Emma down.

Death reflected in her eyes, and her face twisted in anger until it was no longer her own but half-burned to reveal a skull. She drew in a deep breath of air and let out an ear-splitting scream that sent a flood of fire rushing from her mouth. It twisted and twirled around them, forcing the protestors to take a step back from her family. The man gripping Antoine faltered but still wouldn't let go, and Emma snarled at him.

"Emma, don't!" Antoine shouted loud enough for Barnaby to hear.

The girl paused for a moment, the light in her eyes dulling once before she sucked in another gasp of air. Another bout of fire launched from her mouth. It flew through the air at the burly man holding Antoine, but at the last minute, the ringleader shoved the man aside. The torrent of fire merely grazed the man's arm instead of consuming him entirely. The man yelped and ran off in fear, clinging to his wound.

Fear gripped the townsfolk, and like a disturbed ant's

nest, the mob shot out in every direction, desperate to get away from the fire-breathing beast. Men and women tumbled over each other and scuffled in the snow-filled streets. It would be a tale Barnaby was sure the entirety of Halifax would tell for quite some time until it became an old legend.

"Emma!" Franziska pushed past a desperate man and nearly slipped on a piece of ice. "It's okay, just breathe!"

Half-girl half dragon with flaming red hair glanced between Franziska and Antoine, her brow crinkling in confusion. It was as if she didn't recognize them. She crouched, prepared to launch another spewing stream of lava.

"Remember who you are!" Franziska halted a few steps from her. "You're not this darkness. You're the light."

The words made Emma pause, cocking her head to the side as if there was a special meaning behind them. Antoine rose to his feet and mirrored Franziska's cautious stance. Emma's wild eyes darted about, evaluating the threat. Flames still lapped all about her, and her wings snapped, threatening to take flight. The beast hovered above her like a guardian, whispering to her to kill them all. Barnaby's brow tickled with sweat from the heat emanating from the flames that engulfed her.

Emma's head jerked towards a nearby constable who glanced between her and the water cart he pushed. She hissed, sending sparks flying at him. He let the cart topple over and scuttled down an alleyway. Her wings thrashed to take flight and chase after him, but someone shouted from down the street, gaining Emma's attention.

Barnaby followed the sound, startled by the abrupt clop of hooves. There Artus was, guiding the caravan with two black panthers and a vampire atop the roof. It ambled towards them, teetering as if on the brink of collapse.

"Brother! Look what I saved!" Artus called from the driver's box.

The hinges securing the wheels squealed unnervingly as it came to a stop beside them, and Barnaby winced at the sound.

"Artus! Can't you see we're in the middle of something?" Antoine scolded his brother, who went completely still at the sight of the girl with the fiery wings and dragon-like ghost hovering above her.

Clearly, this wasn't her usual form.

Roderic coughed, yanking Emma's attention to the shopkeeper, slowly picking himself up from the snow-filled street.

"Emma, look at me!" Antoine cried when her half skull face glowed with fire. "Listen. Everyone who wanted to harm us is now gone. We're not in danger anymore."

There they stood, the once vibrant street now bleak and deserted of all life save for them. The only thing left of the fire were the flames that snapped around Emma and the Engel's Emporium's charred remains.

"Remember what we practised?" Antoine moved another step away, hands up in defense as if approaching a lion about to pounce. "Take a deep breath and let the power ease from you like a waterfall. Let it return to its rightful place within your mind."

With one last growl from the dragon, the fire around Emma suddenly faded and whooshed into a sea of smoke. Her body shivered as her wings slithered back into her shoulder blades, the poor girl falling to her knees from the impact. Tears brimmed her eyelids, and she wept. Franziska and Antoine both pulled her into an embrace. The toll her powers took made evident as she slumped against them for support.

Barnaby's heart throbbed at the sight. To think of all the

pain, she must've been in and all that she had to go through to get to this point. Was this the price of magic? He hadn't contemplated having supernatural abilities of his own until this case. Of course, when facing such a foreboding nemesis as Frau Perchta was, it did make it tempting. But if this was what it took, he didn't think it was worth it.

The thought of the killer possessed by Frau Perchta still being out there sent chills down his spine. Who would she kill next? And how would they capture her in the mirror now? Roderic had said to bring the mirror back to the shop once the spirit was trapped inside so he could transform it into a tomb of some sort. But, with all the ingredients left behind in the shop now burned to its cinders, Barnaby feared their only hope had gone up in smoke. What would they do now?

17
DING DONG ALL IS TERRIBLY AWRY

Barnaby Grey's Flat,
Grafton Street

WILSON RUBBED HIS WEARY EYES, nearly going cross-eyed from having been up all night poring over the paperwork from the Governor's desk. He was certain the break-in at the mansion had something to do with John Walsh seeing as how he was a prisoner in the basement below. But all the documents the intruder had displayed were either legislation involving closures of properties or personal correspondence between the Governor and Mr Talmage, which planted a tiny seed of doubt within him.

Was it possible that the chief inspector was right? Was the fact that John Walsh was being held there completely unrelated and that the killer of Madam Onay was, in fact, the most obvious choice? There was a part of him that was beginning to think so.

"Such balderdash," he exclaimed to himself, remembering that they were searching for a left-handed killer. Still, why was Mr Talmage at the Governor's mansion in the first place?

He opened his mouth to call for Barnaby when he remembered that his colleague had yet to return from wherever he was gallivanting around these days. The silence was most helpful, but he did wish he had someone to bounce ideas off of.

With a sigh, he pushed himself up from the desk and stretched his aching limbs. More coffee would have to do. He picked up his cup to refresh it for the hundredth time. He'd started the evening prior with gin, moving on to port near dawn after reaching a dead-end. And finally switched to black coffee sometime in the morning to fight the onset of his sleep deprivation.

Though the bills hadn't produced any answers as to why they were displayed for them so meticulously, the letters had proven far more intriguing. Apparently, Mr Talmage had taken it upon himself to reach out to the Governor in regard to safety measures in his foundry and requested funding for the project.

Mr Talmage wrote to the Governor many times in increasing urgency about one of his brightsmiths by the name of Mr McNab—a name Wilson found familiar but couldn't place which particularly vexed him—and experienced ailments due to the harsh conditions of the foundry. Why this was an issue for the Governor to solve was beyond him.

Further correspondence revealed that Dr Larson had treated the brightsmith repeatedly for headaches and stomach pains. As a result, Mr Talmage's petitions for funds grew more demanding. It made Wilson wonder why such a man of importance would pester the Governor so much over a single worker. Didn't Mr Talmage have the means to implement such modifications on his own?

Unless there was another reason for involving the Governor.

He blew on his newly refreshed cup of coffee and returned to his desk, resolving to find these answers within the stack of correspondence he still had yet to sift through. Picking up the following letter, he read it aloud in the hopes of gleaning a new perspective.

"Dear Mr Talmage... blah, blah, blah." He skimmed over the brief pleasantries and skipped to the meat of the letter dated the week Wilson first arrived in Halifax. *"I am quite astounded by your last communication and have brought it upon myself to call on Dr Larson on behalf of your brightsmith."*

It included a signed medical record from the doctor where he evaluated Mr McNab and concluded that his headaches and stomach pains were the result of too much exertion. Dr Larson prescribed the brightsmith more rest for the headaches and coca wine for his nausea.

Wilson's lip twitched upon reading this suggested remedy. He did miss a good glass of cocaine laced wine in the evening. If only his own doctor back in London hadn't been so adamant on him taking a holiday. But alas, the past could not be changed, only analysed for its data.

There was something about the intensity in which Mr Talmage described the headaches and stomach pains that caught his attention. It was almost as if the businessman were experiencing them himself. Which, of course, there was not the slightest evidence of.

Still, for whatever reason, the foundry owner was close to this particular brightsmith whose severity of symptoms made Wilson so inclined to believe that it was beyond the cure of simple rest and coca wine. He was confident that if Dr Larson had read Thackrah's publication on plumbism, then he would have known that Mr McNab's condition and overexposure to the foundry's harsh metals could only mean one thing—lead poisoning. Unfortunately, this old concept was still in its infancy as it related to one's health in work environments.

Mr Talmage agreed. In his next letter to the Governor, he took great offence to the Governor's cavalier attitude regarding his most skilled brightsmith. This one was several pages long, and from the tight loops and smudges strewn about in cursive, Wilson inferred that Mr Talmage had to halt his writing many times to cool off. The handwriting looked slightly off at one point, but perhaps it was merely from his hand cramping after such a long-winded letter.

It rambled on in much the same manner until the last page when Mr Talmage stooped to a myriad of threats. One involved a change of heart in his fondness of a proposed bill being voted on, which percolated Wilson's curiosity. It went on to insinuate the results would not be in the Governor's favour.

Obviously, the Governor and Mr Talmage had some long-standing agreement that would explain their connection. Still, it was on this last page where Mr Talmage was particularly distraught that Wilson noticed something irregular about his calligraphy. The meticulous nature of the script was far less so as Mr Talmage's anger took over and expected occurrence when one corresponded in hostility. But what wasn't was the fact that his slopes and loops became much more hesitant. Unnatural, even, until a particular part of it was entirely struck out in black ink. It made Wilson take pause. What was Mr Talmage hiding?

His chest fluttered at the prospect of unveiling its secrets. He was certain whatever it was that was struck out could be the key to solving the case. He just needed to find a sharp knife.

Wilson stood from his desk once again just as the door to the flat swung open, and Barnaby entered.

"Oh good, you're here. I was just in search of a knife, preferably one recently sharpened." Wilson dashed towards the kitchen but paused when he noticed Barnaby limp as he removed his filthy sack coat as if he'd been drug through the mud. "Good heavens, what happened to you? And what's wrong with your leg?"

Barnaby winced, lowering himself into a chair at their tiny table. "Had to see the doctor. Got trampled by a mob this morning."

"A mob? How on earth—? Oh, never mind, you'll have to explain later. I'm just about to make a break in the case if only I could find a knife."

"What for?"

Wilson opened and slammed drawers as he searched the tiny kitchen. "To reveal Mr Talmage's secrets, of course."

"That makes no sense." Barnaby leaned back with a sigh of relief, resting his eyes for a moment.

"Ah ha!" Wilson brandished the blade he pulled from the last drawer and marched back to the desk. "There was a kidnapping at the governor's mansion, and at first I thought it was an attempt to free John Walsh as he was being held in the basement below, but—"

"Wait, who's been kidnapped?"

"The governor," Wilson replied, ignoring Barnaby's gasps of alarm. "As I was saying, it all pointed to John Walsh, but after analysis of the Governor's desk, I found correspondence between Mr Talmage and the Governor about his brightsmith, Mr McNab, and the poor man's declining health. In these letters, there's an inconsistency with his handwriting, and I must find out what he's hiding."

"Wait, did you say Mr McNab?" Barnaby brushed his wavy umber hair out of his eyes and furrowed his brow.

"Yes, now keep up, will you?" Wilson placed the letter with the inked-out message on a clean surface of the desk along with the knife. "In all of Mr Talmage's letters, his calligraphy is light and careful but then changes as he becomes more agitated. Now, the smudges are consistent with this reaction, but if one is writing angrily, you would expect more pressure to be applied to the page, correct?"

"I suppose."

"But in Mr Talmage's case, the pressure remained consistent despite his handwriting becoming worse until he had to scratch out an entire section."

Barnaby shrugged. "Why is that strange?"

"Because, dear Barnaby"—he waved the knife as he spoke — "it doesn't follow Mr Talmage's usual pattern, which means he's hiding something, and we're about to find out what."

"And what do you plan on doing with *that*?" Barnaby gestured to the knife.

"I plan on slicing the secrets out of the letter, of course."

"That is utter nonsense, Wilson, now where's my cigarette case?"

He picked up Barnaby's case from the desk and tossed it in his direction without even looking.

"Much obliged." Barnaby caught it in one hand and promptly lit one to ease his evident nerves.

"Now that's taken care of, you can sit back, relax, and watch my brilliance at work," Wilson smirked as he took a seat at the desk and pulled out a fountain pen to use as a wedge.

He took a deep breath before turning the page sideways so that the portion of the writing covered in ink was vertical. Then, with smooth precision, he took the sharpened knife and cut a parallel line on either side of the ink so that he could lift it away from the rest of the page.

"What on earth are you doing? Is this the new thing

women call 'scrapbooking'?" Barnaby chuckled but groaned and rubbed his bruised forehead.

"Laugh as you may, but I'm about to show you that no matter how much you try to hide the truth, there's always a way to reveal it."

Now that the cuts were made, he lifted the roughly two-centimetre section of the paper up and inserted the fountain pen to keep the area upright. He then took the knife and lightly carved at the parchment, slowly removing the top inked-out section.

The room quieted, the only sound coming from Barnaby puffing his cigarette. Wilson held his breath as he expertly split the paper into two halves.

"See?" Wilson said once the top ink was thoroughly removed.

Barnaby arched his brow. "Yes, incredible. You've proven it is possible to split a piece of paper into two halves, but what now? I don't see anything below the ink."

"Ah, but you see, it is still there." Wilson picked up the bottom half of the paper and brought it to the window. "I noticed that the strokes used to strike out what was written below were much lighter than the impression on the backside of the letter. So, my theory was that the impression made by whatever was originally written might still be legible and look!"

He waved his hand at the paper. The sun glistened through the glass of the window and illuminated the barely visible impression that remained on the sheet.

"There it is, the shadow of what Mr Talmage wrote before and—" Wilson stopped when he noticed the unusual sloping of the letters. "Well, what do we have here?"

"What is it?" Barnaby asked, but Wilson ignored the question as he rushed to fetch his fountain pen off the desk.

Wilson's breath hitched, returning to the window and

pressed the letter up to illuminate the text once again. He bit down on the pen's lid and pried it off with his teeth. Then, with light strokes, he traced the impression of what Mr Talmage had tried to cover up.

Wilson spat the lid out, letting it fall to the ground without even noticing. An action he would never have done under normal circumstances.

"I can't believe it." He gasped as he studied the backward slopes of the letters.

The short strokes in the calligraphy in the sentence above the etched-out sentence suggested Mr Talmage stopped, presumably out of anger and to get fresh air. When he returned to finish his letter, he must've picked up the fountain pen with his left only to realise what he'd done mid-sentence and inked it out with his right.

"What does it say?"

"It's not about what it says, but how it's written." He rushed to the desk drawer, yanking it open as he searched for the killer's note.

A sudden chill swept through him when he placed the two notes side by side.

"They're a match." Wilson blinked without seeing. It had been Mr Talmage the whole time.

What an act the businessman had put on at the funeral and what must've been his best performance yet at the Governor's house. At least according to Chief Inspector Plundell's retelling of Mr Talmage's 'trembling in fear. Wilson balled his hands into fists as he realised it was all to distract from the man's plot of revenge for murdering his only son. How long had he been planning it? Weeks? Months?

Wilson froze when the sunlight hit the edge of the paper, and a corner of it glinted with gold. Not the whole thing, of course, only a tiny sliver. He studied it closer and realised the edges had been cut perfectly to look like the original page, but the smallest portion remained. He brought the letter closer to his eye to confirm, but there it was as plain as day.

"Gold-lined parchment." Wilson tilted his head, remembering Mrs Tilcott was the only person he knew who would ever use such unbecoming paper, and for the first time in a long while, he felt genuine anger rise within him. "Yes, it all makes sense now."

Wilson paced the length of the desk, the letters still in hand.

Barnaby scratched his head. "I can't make any sense of what you're saying."

"This paper Mr Talmage used is from Mrs Tilcott." Wilson's mind raced as all the pieces fell into place. "He tried to hide it, but there's always the tiniest of clues that remain."

"And what does Mrs Tilcott have to do with this?"

"Nothing… and everything." Wilson's eyes widened. "Her home is the perfect distance from the Talmage's manor as well as the church. And I know for a fact that she has a basement."

"Yes, what of it?"

"The scent on Madam Onay's body hinted at the original location of the crime being a basement and"—Wilson waved his index finger — "Mr Talmage would've known it was empty because he invited everyone to stay at the manor on the eve of the funeral. But did he know about her tenant?"

Wilson paused before waving this off. "It wouldn't have mattered as she was witnessed at the manor at the time the murder was committed, which was the precise time that Mr Talmage vanished, not to return until they left for the funeral."

"Wilson, are you saying that Mr Talmage and Mrs Tilcott not only killed Madam Onay but have also kidnapped the governor and are holding him in her basement?"

"Of course not. Mrs Tilcott has no idea whatsoever that her house is being used to commit such heinous deeds."

"But why would he kill Madam Onay only to make a spectacle at his own son's funeral?"

"To ensure he wouldn't be suspected, of course."

"And what about the constable? And the Governor?"

"Isn't it obvious?" Wilson arched an impeccably trimmed brow. "Mr Talmage must've gone to the Governor to demand that he concede to his demands which he was refused again hence the kidnapping. As for the constable, perhaps this was a mere accident? Or maybe perfecting his craft? Either way, I must get to Mrs Tilcott's before he does."

Barnaby slammed his hand on the table. "Wilson, would you *please* stop for a moment and tell me exactly what's going on? I'm hurt and tired, and my patience is waning."

"I believe that"—Wilson's nostrils flared and tossed the letters on the table in front of Barnaby — "Mr Talmage will want to tie up loose ends, which means both Mrs Tilcott and her tenant are in grave danger."

"You still have no proof that Mr Talmage is the killer, and if he is, then he's possessed with the spirit of Frau Perchta, which means you can't go there alone. Not without me and most certainly not without magic to defend yourself."

"Would you please stop with this foolishness, Barnaby? This has nothing to do with your delusions of the supernatural." Wilson shoved his arms into his frock coat. "And I do have proof. He's left-handed, after all, and the calligraphy fits. Not to mention he's also a medicine man and would know to remove the stomachs of his victims in order to hide the true cause of death."

"How do you know that? I thought he was just a businessman."

"Must I explain everything?" Wilson rolled his eyes, popping his collar. "I came across his diploma of medicine after running into a hidden office under his stairs. As for the calligraphy, look at the letters. The handwriting on the note found in Madam Onay's mouth matches exactly with the ink-out portion in Mr Talmage's letter to the Governor. He's ambidextrous, and to obscure himself, he used his less dominant hand. That is until he made that one small mistake which I just unveiled."

Barnaby studied the letters as Wilson marched for the door.

"And while I'm gone, if you read those correspondences" —Wilson turned back to his colleague — "you'll find Mr Talmage openly threatened to kill the Governor if he didn't provide him with the funds for his foundry and aid for Mr McNab, his most prized brightsmith. If he hasn't already, I'm certain he intends to do so now, and if I don't get to Mrs Tilcott's before he does, then I'm certain both she and her tenant, Miss Lauretta, will both be dead, too."

Barnaby paled. "Miss Lauretta is Mrs Tilcott's tenant?"

"Yes, and would you stop repeating everything I say?"

"Wilson, wait. I don't think—"

"Must go, Barnaby! And get some rest, will you?" Wilson swung the door to the flat open just as Chief Inspector Plundell raised his fist to knock.

"Oh, Mr—er—Detective Davies, just the person I wanted to speak to."

"Me?" Wilson arched a brow at the chief inspector's use of his actual title. It was quite uncharacteristic, along with his flushed cheeks and visible sweating.

The chief inspector cleared his throat and nodded.

Wilson sighed, grabbing his scarf and top hat. "Fine, but as it happens, I'm on my way out and in quite a hurry. Feel free to tag along if you must."

"Wilson, wait!" Barnaby shouted after him. "You're running right into Frau Perchta's trap!"

But Wilson was already out the door and down the stairs with the chief inspector at his heels.

BARNABY GRIPPED the door frame for stability, shouting for Wilson to wait, but he wouldn't listen.

"Stubborn old ratbag," he muttered as he fetched his sack coat and something he could use as a sturdy cane.

Wilson's theory was correct, but his conclusion was so deranged and forcibly concocted that he'd missed the obvious truth altogether. The killer would be at Mrs Tilcott's home, but it wasn't Mr Talmage. Or, at least, not entirely due to the supernatural elements of the case that Wilson refused to believe. But Barnaby knew that the murders were committed by someone possessed by Frau Perchta, and, according to the compendium, she only preyed on those mourning over a lost love.

Yes, Mr Talmage was in mourning, but he hardly seemed the loving type. Not only that, but during Wilson's incoherent ramblings, a name struck a nerve within Barnaby.

The surname McNab was familiar, and rightfully so. It was the exact name of the brightsmith they'd found murdered and left in the city well during their last case. It was also the name of Dr Larson's new assistant who the doctor had called out for while treating Barnaby's leg earlier today, only to remember she was at home. And if he was right, then Wilson was in grave danger.

Barnaby found a tall fire poker with a hooked handle that would do the trick and hobbled out to fetch a carriage. First, he had to get to Deadman's Island to tell the circus he knew where Frau Perchta would be. Perhaps they could concoct a new plan since the other one burned down with the bookshop.

Though he hoped for Emma's safety, they could come up with something that didn't involve her. But, they had to at least try. His colleague's life depended on it. He hadn't the slightest idea how they would destroy the spirit once they trapped her in the mirror without the spells and ingredients in the bookshop, but that was the least of his concerns. Right now, he had to get to the island in time to tell them before the true killer struck again.

18
KILLERS IN THIS HALL

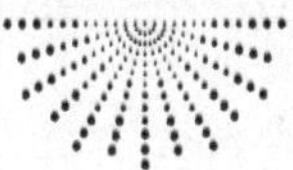

WILSON COULDN'T GET out of the flat fast enough, taking the stairs two at once. He was in a rush against time to beat Mr Talmage to Mrs Tilcott's home, but also to put as much space between Barnaby and himself as he could. What would he say next, that the tooth fairy existed and was poisoning the town?

No, for both their sakes, he wouldn't give Barnaby any chance to say anything senile in front of Chief Inspector Plundell. Not that he cared what the inspector thought, but he didn't want to give him any reason to commit the poor chap.

"Detective Davies, this isn't easy for me to say," the chief inspector called after Wilson, who strutted down the narrow hallway of the main floor towards the exit. "But, detective, I believe we got off on the wrong foot at the funeral."

Wilson frowned, glancing over his shoulder at the chief inspector. "Are you ill, inspector?"

"No, I'm not ill," Chief Inspector Plundell said as he followed Wilson out into the wintry chill that swept through

Grafton Street from the harbour. "I'm tryin' to tell you that I think you're right."

"Well, of course, I'm right." The detective slid to a halt, his sapphire winter shoes kicking up snow. "Wait a minute, what precisely do you think I'm right about?"

He turned to face the sturdily built inspector whose police issued custodian helmet he donned barely reached Wilson's shoulders.

Plundell cleared his throat, glancing down at his muddy boots. "I was told many things about you, most of them dreadful, and I'm sorry to say that I believed them."

Wilson's mouth fell open, unable to believe what he was hearing.

"And I'm afraid that I was wrong." Plundell lifted his chin and looked Wilson straight in the eye.

This admission stirred something within the detective. Was it pride? Respect? He wasn't quite certain, but for the first time ever, he wasn't at all annoyed at being in Plundell's mere presence.

"Not that I'm not enjoying this; it's quite the contrary, actually, but what is this about?"

"It's about your theory, of course," Plundell replied. "I came to say that you were right about the disgrace at the governor's mansion. It did have somethin' to do with John Walsh."

"Oh, that." Wilson sighed, returning to his speedy trek towards Mrs Tilcott's.

Footsteps padded against the snow-covered sidewalk, and the detective rolled his eyes, wishing the chief inspector would go back to shooing him away instead of chasing after him.

"I've come to ask for your help."

Wilson cringed, knowing that if this conversation continued, he would have to admit that, in fact, it was he who was wrong. "You've made it very clear you don't need my help, inspector. What's changed?"

The detective took a brisk jog across Sackville Street and down Barrington towards the cat lady's house. He realized then just how convenient her home was to both the Talmages and the governor's mansion. Chills swept down his shoulders at the thought of the foundryman's devilish deeds.

"Well, for starters...."

Wilson heard the hesitation in the chief inspector's voice, another unusual reaction, but he hardly had the time to deduce what blunder had gotten the better of Plundell.

"John Walsh has escaped."

"What did you say?" Wilson's lip twitched as he turned on the chief inspector once again.

"Yes, I know how terrible this is, but he's gone. Last seen on the docks near a ship headed for London. They think he found a way to sneak passage."

Wilson's nostrils flared and grabbed Plundell by the collar. "How the bloody hell could you let this happen? You imbecile!"

"There—there was a riot." Plundell shook his head, scrambling for words. "It required the attention of all of my men just to put out the fire they caused and make the arrests. Some still got away."

"Well, isn't that quite your forte, letting people just get away?" Wilson spat, shoving the chief inspector back and adjusting his coat's collar.

Plundell stumbled but managed to keep himself upright. "That's why I'm here asking—nay—*beggin'* for your understanding and assistance. If you please."

It took some time for the detective to calm his speeding heartbeat, but once he'd gotten ahold of his breath, he realized it might be more advantageous to work with Plundell than against him. Now that he came to his senses and acknowledged Wilson's detective skills, of course.

With a killer as connected as Mr Talmage was, it would be useful to have the city's chief inspector on his side for a change.

"Fine, you have my assistance." Wilson took a deep, calming breath and continued his march down Salter Street. "There's just one thing I must ask, first."

"Yes, anything."

Wilson glanced down his nose at the stocky inspector, who rushed to match his pace. "That you help me find the governor and stop Mr Talmage from killing Mrs Tilcott and her tenant."

"Before he does *what*?" Chief Inspector Plundell stopped in his tracks.

"I'll explain later. Right now, we have a killer to catch. Come on, keep up."

The chief inspector scratched his head but followed the detective up the steps to Mrs Tilcott's front door.

Wilson was about to knock when he heard voices within, and a pit formed in his stomach. "We may be too late."

"What—?" Plundell began but was soon hushed by the detective who motioned for him to follow.

The frozen grass crunched beneath their feet. Wilson's heart pounded in his ears as he crept around the side of the neoclassical style home, wondering all the while what he would find. Would Mr Talmage have already killed Mrs Tilcott and her tenant along with the governor? Or would he find him in the middle of the act?

Either way, his adrenaline spiked as they inched up to the first window. He held his breath and peeked through the glass. The drawing-room was dark, but he could just make out the wingback chairs he'd sat on when he first visited Mrs Tilcott. Two shadows danced across the floor. The sounds of a moan sent chills down his spine. Then, Mr Talmage and Miss Lauretta finally tumbled from the small entryway into the drawing-room in a familiar embrace.

Wilson gasped. Did his eyes deceive him, or was Miss Lauretta kissing Mr Talmage? And where was Mrs Tilcott in all of this? Surely if her own tenant was having an affair with the town's most wealthy and prominent gentleman, she would've told him about it. Or did she even know?

The chief inspector cleared his throat. "Er, perhaps he's here for other reasons than to kill?"

Wilson jumped at the closeness of the inspector's voice and glared down at him. He stood a mere inch from his shoulder, which made the detective take a pointed step away.

"Maybe, maybe not." Wilson grimaced. "Something still doesn't seem right about this."

The couple stumbled past the window and through a door on the right, still in the throes of passion. Wilson darted off to the next window, shielding his eyes as he peered into a dimly lit dining room. Miss Lauretta pulled Mr Talmage towards the table, her cheeks flushed and eyes full of desire.

"Not the fresh linens!" Wilson groaned when the two knocked into the table, knocking over a stemmed glass full of red wine.

It trickled towards the window staining the white tablecloth with a streak of merlot.

"Shouldn't we be givin' them a bit of privacy?" The chief inspector shifted uncomfortably.

"Shh," he scolded the inspector but then quickly ducked when Miss Lauretta turned in their direction.

Wilson pressed his back against the cold stone. His blood pulsed within his ears as he tried to get control of his breath. Had he been wrong this whole time? What if instead of catching a killer, he was merely prying on a man's personal love affair? A pit formed in his stomach at the thought of all the time he'd wasted investigating the Talmages.

He clenched his jaw. No, he wouldn't allow himself to fall into the trap of doubt. Despite this strange turn of events, the evidence still pointed to Mr Talmage being the killer, and he would not be deterred until he'd thoroughly investigated the situation.

Seconds passed. Minutes, even, but to Wilson, they might as well have been hours. When no one came to the window, and he was confident they hadn't caught sight of him, he slowly inched closer to sneak another look into the dining room.

His muscles tightened when he spotted Mr Talmage holding a shard of glass pressed against Miss Lauretta's neck. Her arms flailed in desperation as she tried to free herself from his grip, but he yanked her back through yet another door and disappeared. Chills swept through him, and he dashed towards the back of the house.

"Was that—Did he?" Chief Inspector Plundell huffed as he followed around the corner.

"Yes, inspector. Your eyes did not deceive you." Wilson paused at the back door and rummaged through a secret compartment within his frock coat. "Mr Talmage is our culprit, and he's about to kill again. Who knows what he's done to the governor and poor Mrs Tilcott."

The chief inspector scratched his reddish-grey mutton chops. "I just can't believe it!"

"Well, you'd better or else that poor girl is going to die in there—aha!" Wilson brandished a makeshift leather mask along with a pair of metal goggles he'd stowed away for this very occasion.

"What in the bloody hell is that?"

"It's my insurance." Wilson pulled the thick leather contraption over his mouth and nose followed by the eyewear and secured it all with a flourish. "Last time I chased a killer in this town, I was drugged and hallucinated all sorts of horrible things. I won't make that mistake again."

This time he would only see what truly existed. He smirked to himself, half wishing Barnaby was with him. Not just to help, but to witness the truth for himself.

The detective took a few careful, even breaths to get used to the gas mask before reaching for his pistol. He paused at the door and glanced down at the stocky officer. "Can I count on you?"

Chief Inspector Plundell gave a reluctant sigh but unsheathed his own pistol from its holster. "There's no denying what I saw. Mr Talmage must be stopped, so you have my full support."

"Excellent." Wilson yanked the door open. "Now, do cover your nose with something and follow closely."

The two snuck in through the back door entering a narrow passageway. Shadows danced down the hallway before them. A strange energy hung in the air, one that sent Wilson's senses into overdrive. The protective eyewear did impede his sight just a little, and his breath was hot on his cheek, but he wasn't about to succumb to any contaminate that might be circulating in there.

Footsteps shuffled from the first door to their right. Wilson gestured for Plundell to follow, and they crept in, pistol pointed at the ready. A full moon glistened through an open window, the wind kicking up a curtain.

Plundell bumped into the detective. The floorboard squealed beneath him. They both froze.

Plundell grimaced. "Sorry."

Wilson lifted his finger to his lips for total silence. His ears perked at the distant thud as if someone was being dragged down below them.

"HELP!" A muffled woman's scream came from somewhere in the next room, followed by the slam of a door.

The two armed men scrambled down the hallway and through the next set of doors, entering what appeared to be a small prep room for the kitchens. Spotting a lantern on a nearby counter, Wilson felt his coat pockets for a match. He prayed he hadn't tossed his case out to make room for his protective apparatus. A sigh of relief escaped him when he found one and struck the edge against something solid.

With the lantern-lit, a warm glow revealed a door near the back of the room. Wilson neared it, eyeing the rug and noticed the corner was kicked up.

"Is that the door we heard?" Plundell hissed.

"Shh! We don't want to alert him to our presence yet, now do we? And yes. That's it."

Together they tiptoed their way up next to it. Wilson placed the lantern at the foot of the rug, ensuring it wouldn't be seen when they opened the door. He reached for the handle. The detective steeled himself before twisting the knob and carefully swinging the door open.

Creeeaaaaak!

Chills swept through him. The two paused at the head of the stairs leading down into the dark abyss, only slightly illuminated by a flickering light somewhere far below them. When no one lunged from the dark depths, the two proceeded with caution.

"Deck the halls with bowels and entrails, fa la la la la!" A sing-songy voice reverberated around them as if coming from the very walls of the house.

"Did you hear that?" Plundell's voice was hushed, but the rise in octave exposed his fear.

Wilson took a quick breath, wishing he could say he hadn't, but the eerie hum still echoed in his ears. His free hand flitted up to his mask and gave it a tug. The straps were still snug which meant he wasn't hearing things he shouldn't. Perhaps they'd misheard whoever it was who was singing?

"Come on." Wilson shook off the desire to race back out of the house to call for backup.

He had Plundell for that, after all. With a sigh, he descended the remainder of the steps into the main kitchen, barely visible. A strange haze cast the room in ominous blues.

Plundell gulped obviously and shuffled up next to Wilson. "Is that… *blood?*"

Wilson rolled his eyes. Dealing with the stubborn chief inspector's change of heart was one thing, but now blood made him squeamish? What would he do next, turn into Barnaby?

"Aren't you the chief inspector? Of course, it's blood," he whispered, following the blood that smeared the tiled floor leaving a trail around the kitchen counter to the adjoining room. Perhaps the scullery?

A woman whimpered from beyond the threshold, and he recognized the pitch. He took a quick breath. Mrs Tilcott was still alive, but were either the governor or Miss Lauretta as fortunate? They were about to find out.

Clink! Clink!

The rattle of what could only be chains sent Wilson throwing stealth to the wind. Heat flushed throughout his body at the thought of what Mr Talmage was about to do to those poor innocent souls. He cocked the hammer of his pistol and raced towards the sound, preparing to shoot him on the spot.

"Stop right there!" Wilson shouted when he rounded the corner but stopped in his tracks.

A lamp swung from the ceiling, the dim light flickered across the room, casting shadows across Mrs Tilcott and another prisoner Wilson couldn't make out, both shackled to the drainpipes that lined the dingy back wall. But it was the prisoner, gagged and hanging by his wrists to a chain secured to the ceiling, that caught Wilson's attention. The prisoner dangled above a metal basin placed on the floor beneath him like a pig for the slaughter. He took a step closer and gasped.

"Mr Talmage?"

The businessman's head jerked up, halting his struggle against his shackled wrists. His eyes narrowed back at him and fought against the gag against his mouth, probably cursing Wilson for his dreadful miscalculation. If Mr Talmage wasn't the killer, then who was?

The chief inspector shuffled in behind him, out of breath and froze when he spotted Mr Talmage. "What? How's he chained up? I thought he was our murderer!"

"Yes… I thought…" Wilson shook his head. This didn't make any sense.

"Well, don't just stand there. The poor man looks to be on the verge of passing out." Plundell shook his head, about to push past Wilson when Mr Talmage's eyes bulged.

"MMM! MMM!" Mr Talmage cried against the cloth that muzzled him.

"I wondered when you'd come," a woman cackled from behind them, sending a shiver down the detective's spine.

The chief inspector spun around, but before he could react, an iron pot smashed into his skull. He collapsed in a heap on the cold stone floor.

Wilson's hands shook as he lifted his gun up to the cloaked figure who tossed the pot aside.

The woman let out a throaty laugh and stepped over Plundell's limp form towards the detective. "Follow me in frightful pleasure while I tell you of the bride's old groom!"

Wilson braced his finger against the trigger and pulled. The blast filled the small room making his ears ring.

"Fret elum." The cloaked figure waved her hand, and the bullet froze in midair.

Wilson blinked. Did his eyes deceive him? Had his mask loosened? Before he could investigate this, the cloaked figure moved with an unnatural speed towards him. He stumbled back to put as much space between them as possible, but it was too late. Her ghostly hands latched around his neck.

"Schlanus!"

As soon as the words escaped the cloaked figure, Wilson's whole body went still, and his vision blurred. He blinked against the sudden onset of slumber, but no matter how much he fought it, darkness closed in all around him. Suddenly the stone floor grew closer. His eyes rolled back into their sockets as he fell unconscious.

19
ONE LAST HOPE

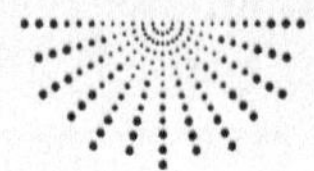

Deadman's Island

The sun had already begun to wane by the time the circus and the Engels made it back to the campsite, but even longer to calm down from the disastrous morning. Their clothes still reeked of sweat and char, but this was the least of their concerns.

With Mr Roderic and Miss Gertrud's shop burnt to a crisp, no one had any clue how they would catch Frau Percht's spirit now. The ingredients Mr Roderic needed to conceal their magic were all destroyed, and now they were back where they started; hopeless and divided.

"I could try searching for her on my own again," Emma suggested as she paced in front of the firepit while Artus attempted to light it. "I could use my new power to force her into the mirror and then maybe bury it?"

"That's much too dangerous," Franziska said, glancing up from the compendium she was hunched over alongside Mr Roderic.

The two of them were studying it in the hopes of finding an alternative plan but had yet to garner anything from their efforts.

"Yeah, for her, maybe," Emma muttered under her breath, knowing it was a longshot to suggest a solo mission.

"Besides, what if someone were to find it?" Franziska added, but Emma was still confident her plan was their best option.

They were concerned for her safety, but in reality, the only person who should be was whoever was possessed by Frau Perchta. Through the torture of her transition, the fire had burned away all the self-doubt she'd once had for her power and, in its stead, was a newfound strength. A control that surpassed any she'd gained from Antoine's lessons on containing her ability.

"We can figure out how to destroy the mirror once she's trapped in it," Mr Roderic said, turning the page of the compendium. "First, we must figure out how to find her, but there's nothing more in here that can help us."

Franziska turned the page. "We'll find something eventually, I'm sure of it."

"Why are we even discussing this?" Artus stoked wood until it finally lit.

Emma's fingertips tingled from the energy she smiled to herself. It reminded her that she'd conquered her fears.

"Because if we don't," Mr Roderic replied. "She'll never stop killing until all are dead,"

"Perhaps that's what this town deserves after what they did." Artus threw a log into the fire, sending a flurry of sparks at Miss Gertrud, who sat nearest the fire.

The poor woman jerked back at the sudden flames. Her eyes were red and glassy. Emma's heart ached for her. She must've still been in shock. The fire had taken her home and their entire livelihood.

Emma couldn't understand how anyone could have so much hate towards an innocent soul like Miss Gertrud. It stirred within her the desire to tear through the town and destroy everyone who'd committed this horrible act against the Engels. But she knew this wouldn't make things right again. The damage was already done.

"Artus, how can you say that?" Franziska cried. "If we all got what we deserved, then none of us should be standing here alive."

Artus bit back a response, one Emma was sure he'd regret. He shook his and made his way for the woods in search of more firewood, flanked by Absinthe and Kizmet.

Emma kicked at the snow while Franziska and the others returned their attention to the compendium, soon distracted by a page on various magical scents. As Mr Roderic and Miss Gertrud went back and forth explaining the multiple notes, she was struck with a sudden idea on how they could help the Engels.

Without hesitation, she marched over to where Antoine and Timur were, who worked on mending the caravan parked a few paces away. It was a miracle they were even able to get it back to the island, given the state the wheels were in. One had nearly fallen off during the trek back.

"Antoine," Emma began, her chin lifting in determination. "Once this is all over, you must offer the Engels a place with us."

Antoine glanced up from behind the wheel. A look of concern flickered across his grey eyes. "I'm not even certain yet where we'll go next. How do you know that's what they'll want?"

Emma tilted her head to the side. "Did you give that same consideration before asking me?"

"That's different," Antoine grunted as he tried to pry the screw securing the damaged wheel off.

Timur smirked when it wouldn't budge.

Antoine sat up and tossed the wrench at him. "Here, why don't you give it a try."

With one swift turn, Timur unscrewed the rod. The wheel groaned but snapped off easily with a single tug.

"Show off," Antoine muttered, dusting the snow off his silk trousers.

"How was my situation any different?" Emma crossed her arms when Antoine turned to face her.

"Because your power comes from the same world as ours."

"What, magic from the human world isn't good enough to offer our freedom?" Emma glared at the tall, pale ringleader. "They've done nothing but help us, and what do they get in return? They've lost their home, and everything they own save for that book. We can't just desert them when it comes time to leave."

"That's not what I meant. Listen, we won't desert them, but I can't promise—"

A loud whistle from the road leading into town gained their attention, and in a split second, everyone sprung to their feet and stood protectively between the vehicle and the Engels.

Emma's breath hitched as the sound of hooves drew closer, and she crouched, ready to unleash the power that kindled within her at anyone who rounded the corner. Timur took a similar stance beside her, flashing his brilliant fangs, while Artus and his panthers dropped the firewood they were carrying and sprinted to join them.

When the hansom cab jostled up to the campsite, Emma met the driver's stunned expression with a steady gaze. Her hazel eyes flashed gold, and she stretched a hand towards the firepit.

The flames shot up and wrapped around her hands,

crawling up her arms, sending a static pulse of energy rushing through her. She flexed her fingers and channelled the fire into a ball. It lapped into motion, hovering between her palms.

"Wait!" A voice from within the cab cried. "Driver, let me out this instant!"

With a shaky hand, the driver pulled the lever, and a harried Barnaby stumbled out. He winced when he landed too hard on his injured leg, leaning on a black rod for stability.

"Detective Barnaby?" Emma waved her hands, and the ball of fire vanished and raced up to greet him. "What did the doctor say? And why aren't you home resting?"

"I'm fine, just a little sprain. But that's not why I'm here." Barnaby started to hobble towards them, and Emma looped her arm around his to help him across the snow. "I know who's possessed by Frau Perchta."

Emma stopped in her tracks. "What? How?"

"I'm afraid there's no time to explain that, but I know where to find her."

Everyone stood for a moment in silence until everyone burst into a slew of questions and protests all at once.

"Where?" Franziska asked, her brows raised in hope.

"We'll need to figure out a different way to disguise our scent," Antoine added. "Not to mention another means of transportation. Unfortunately, the caravan is in no shape to be moved just yet."

"You can't be serious about going after that spirit again, can you?" Artus shouted above the rest. "After what it nearly did to Emma in the cemetery? It's too risky. I won't allow it."

"You won't '*allow*' it?" His older brother scoffed, his pale cheeks flushing in a fit of anger that was quite uncharacteristic. "I'm growing quite weary of your constant opposition to what is right."

"And who are you to say what is right?" Artus taunted, glaring down at Antoine, who stood a few inches shy of him.

"If you won't help," Barnaby shouted to match everyone's volume. "Then I'll have to go on my own. My colleague's life depends on it."

But no one seemed to hear as they continued to argue amongst each other, save for Emma, whose heart skipped a beat at the sorrow etched in the detective's voice. A man she'd come to think of as a friend. Though his colleague was one she had a complicated past with, she knew that he meant a lot to Barnaby. Any friend of his was at least deserving of their help.

"SILENCE!" She screamed, her whole body spiking with heat before igniting her skin with a layer of flames.

Everyone froze to stare at her.

"I believe," she began when she was confident she'd gathered everyone's attention. "That I've come up with an alternative plan to disguise our scent. But we must all be in agreement.

We shall help Detective Barnaby because he is my friend, and if you do not"—she gave Artus a meaningful glance — "then I will no longer be able to call you mine."

A look of guilt flickered across Artus's emerald eyes, and he hung his head in defeat.

"If I may ask," Mr Roderic piped up, all eyes turning to him and his sister, who stood near enough to overhear everything. "How do you propose accomplishing this?"

Franziska scratched her head. "Yes, Emma, I must ask that as well. We've searched the book from front to back without any success."

Emma quirked an eyebrow. "Don't you remember the barrels?"

"Absolutely not." Artus gagged as if reliving some horrid memory. "I'll not be doing that again."

The panthers grumbled in agreement.

Barnaby glanced around as all the circus members' faces soured. "Would someone please explain to me what's going on? How could barrels possibly help against Frau Perchta?"

"It's a long story," Emma replied, patting him on the arm. "But it's safe to say there's a chance all of us with magic will be able to get close enough to the witch undetected. That is if you might be able to call in favour with your friend at the docks?"

The detective furrowed his brow and shrugged. "I think so."

"Good." Emma turned to the owl-eyed shopkeeper who still clung to the compendium. "And once we have Frau Perchta trapped, is there any way you could still perform the enchantment on the mirror?"

"Well, maybe." The petite man shifted his stance. "I'll need a few ingredients, which might be hard to procure."

"Make the list," Emma said with a smug smile.

After all the pitfalls, Barnaby finding Frau Perchta was the miracle they needed and, if Emma's plan went accordingly, they'd be able to rid the town of its killer before Yuletide. She just needed to get everything set into motion before it was too late.

Yes, there was a real chance they wouldn't survive, but her fear was overpowered by a desire to do what was right. Leaving without putting an end to Frau Perchta's evil ways would be the opposite, of that she was sure. Besides, if she was the light as her family called her, then she had to be a force of good in a world of darkness.

20
WITCHES ARISE

WILSON COUGHED, slowly coming to. His chest ached as if bludgeoned, and his body fell slack, held up by something hard secured about his wrists. He blinked several times, the filthy washroom coming into view, and he suddenly remembered where he was.

He shot upright only to gag at the stench of spoiled food that wafted through the air from the drainpipes. There he hung, his feet barely scraping the sticky floor while his wrists were shackled just as Mr Talmage was next to him, with shackles chained and secured to a beam that ran the length of the ceiling.

His heart skipped a beat. This couldn't be happening. He rattled the chains to try and pry his hands loose. They hardly moved a centimetre, and his blood pumped loudly in his ears as the realization that he was trapped set in.

That blasted Plundell should've been watching their backs. Instead, he was too busy making silly accusations to notice the killer sneak in from behind. Where was that buffoon, anyway?

Scanning the dim scullery for his captor, the image of her

face flashed before his eyes, and he shivered. At first, he only saw her disguise, a bluish spectral with hollow cheekbones, which was preposterous as ghosts didn't exist. He'd wondered if his protective gear deceived him.

A mass of brown ringlets and piercing blue eyes glistened from underneath the hood, and it dawned on him who the true killer was. But how was it possible? It meant that she had to be in two places at once, which was a notion he refused to entertain.

"Are you awake?" A familiar voice cooed from the adjoining room.

Wilson straightened, his goggles fogging up as his breath spiked. The ghostly apparition stepped into the room, a bluish haze lapping at the black robes from an invisible wind as if a window was opened. Which was illogical. There couldn't be a draft down here in the basement.

"Don't come any closer!" He cringed when his voice cracked, his throat suddenly dry.

"Or what?" She cackled, leaping over Plundell's body which lay slumped on the ground, his head resting against the leg of the table in the centre of the room. "You'll have the inspector here arrest me? Oh, officer? Excuse me, officer!"

She poked him in the chest with a crooked finger and cocked her head to the side as if to listen for a response. The inspector remained unconscious, and she chortled, hopping on her toes and waving her hands about as if to make fun of his incapacitated state.

Wilson's lip twitched, bothered at how she moved as if disjointed from her body over the chief inspector. He cleared his throat, summoning as much courage as he could muster to distract her.

"I-I know who you are."

The cloaked woman froze for a second before she jerked her head to face him.

"So smart you are, *detective*," she hissed, crawling towards him inch by inch.

Wilson's heart skipped a beat as she slithered up to his side. The instinct to run and flee twitched through his legs. It was pointless. There was nowhere he could go while strapped to the ceiling like a mere animal.

"Then who are we?" She ducked around his body, tickling his side, and he cringed back.

A musty pine and sweet spice tickled his nostrils, and it struck him then why all the victims smelled like Frankincense and Myrrh. It was in her perfume.

"I should've known all along it was you." He licked his dry lips and whispered through gritted teeth, "Miss Lauretta."

She stepped around the other side of him. Her irises flickered from underneath her hood for a moment before she yanked the hood back with one swift movement.

"Who, me?" Miss Lauretta batted her doe-eyes up at him for a moment before she chuckled, a harsh staccato with thin the confines of the small scullery. "I did wonder how long it would take you to put it together, my pet."

She brandished a curved blade and danced about her hanging victims as if she were at a ball.

"I'm just sorry I hadn't figured it out sooner." Wilson craned his neck for any sign of his weapon.

He had to find a way to get them all out of there before she gutted them, but his heart fell when the only gun he spotted was next to the chief inspector, who was still out cold. Perhaps he could distract her while speaking loudly enough to wake Plundell? It was worth a shot.

"I know why you did it!" He said, raising his voice above her hissing laughter just as she brought her knife to Mr Talmage's stomach.

She paused, swivelling her head towards the detective who suddenly regretted his plan.

"I can see it all now, quite clearly." His mind raced as he tried to piece together a plausible story, praying the chief inspector would wake up soon. "The poor daughter of a brightsmith who fell in love way beyond her class. An outcast."

A *tsk* escaped her lips as the old crone with hollowed cheekbones and slivers for teeth glimmered across her face as if she were possessed.

Wilson squeezed his eyes shut, repeating what he'd once told colleague within his mind and repeating it like a mantra.

Magic. Doesn't. Exist.

"Go on," Miss Lauretta taunted, and Wilson peaked out from beneath his eyelashes just as she turned her blade onto him.

He gulped. *Please, inspector! You must wake up!*

"You think you know why I killed Madam Onay, hmm? Why I slit her stomach and left it in the church for the Talmage? Please, *detective,* do tell."

Her hot breath hit his cheek, and he grimaced. The world suddenly tipped on his edge as he realized the inspector would never wake up. But what could he do? He couldn't just hang there while this woman killed him. Then he remembered his analysis of her first victim, Madam Onay. She'd been poisoned first, and her heart had stopped long before she was gutted. And poison was notoriously slow. He smiled to himself at the proud realization that he had time. Not a lot, though it might be enough to free himself from these shackles and get help.

"Well, I think it's rather obvious." Wilson took a few breaths to slow his breath, hoping she wouldn't see behind his bluff. "You lost everything that day when Mr Talmage's only son and heir was murdered—your *fiancé*—and though John Walsh was apprehended for the doing of it, you too knew he had a conspirator, Just as I did."

Her head tilted at that, and she slunk around him. He bit down on his bottom lip that trembled as her cold blade trailed along his waist.

"Tell me more," she whispered in his ear.

He jerked back at the wetness of her tongue on his lobe. "I-I'm not sure how much there is to tell."

"Oh, there's more." She brought the knife to her lips as she backed away from him.

"Well, when you lost your father, there was still a small hope of transcendence after the Talmage's son asked for *your* hand in marriage"—he wiggled his thumb, pressing as much weight as he could against the shackles that bound him without making it too obvious — "Everything was going according to plan until Irvin Talmage, Jr called off the engagement just before his untimely demise. He found out about you and his father."

Miss Lauretta stopped abruptly, her back to him, and he knew he'd hit a nerve, so he pressed on. "You were having an affair with your very own, soon to be father-in-law and poor Irvin Talmage, Jr just couldn't get over it."

He pulled down even harder against his restraints, sweat trickling down his cheek as his joints strained against the pressure as he continued his facade of deduction.

"Without Irvin, tossed aside by his father, you had nothing left. So, you took your rage out on a plan of revenge, though you couldn't commit it fully with John Walsh in prison and all, you settled for murdering Madam Onay for her involvement. Then there was the issue of how to go about it without anyone suspecting you?"

A whimper escaped Miss Lauretta, and Wilson halted his struggle.

"He loved me," Lauretta moaned in a hushed tone, more to herself than to anyone else. Her voice twisted and morphed into the cackle from before. *"No. He left you, but I won't. I'll never deceive you like the others."*

Wilson furrowed his brow. It was as if there were two voices within a single body which was inconceivable.

"He's here now so we can be together forever," Lauretta's quiet voice returned until her head shook, and the crone's voice replied, *"Your new lover came here to kill you. To cover his tracks in avenging your old groom's death. He'll never be good enough for us."*

The knife clattered onto the table. Miss Lauretta turned to face Wilson, a sneer spread across her youthful face as red veins crawled up the side of her cheek.

"You think you have it all figured out?" She shook her head, and her petite features flashed once more to the hollowed old skeleton as she prowled towards the detective. "I don't care what anyone says. I never once slept with this man before his son's death."

Her voice changed again, and the crone returned. *"Why does it matter, pet?"*

"Because!" Lauretta growled to the empty room. "The truth needs to be known."

The detective's breath caught in his throat as she neared. He yanked and pulled to no avail. His arms still remained high above his head.

"And our little rat isn't going anywhere until he's heard it. *Fret elum!*" She waved her hand, repeating the words she'd spoken moments before the bullet froze, and suddenly Wilson's body went cold.

He tried to blink his eyes, but they were stiff like icicles. He swallowed, though nothing moved, and when he attempted to take a step forward, his foot crunched to a halt. It was as if he'd fallen into the Halifax Harbour and solidified into ice. The pain of it was excruciating, and he would've screamed, save for his lungs wouldn't budge.

"Despite my class, Irvin did love me." Tears stung the young girl's irises. "It was only when I revealed what I truly was that he left. And if he told the town, it would ruin me!"

Wilson struggled to ask, yet he couldn't form the words. Miss Lauretta shook off the sudden onset of tears and replaced it with a smirk.

"I know you're wondering how I do it." She twirled back to where she left the knife on the table. "I've been practising since I was a wee one. Little witch in a mortal world."

Miss Lauretta caressed the blade with her index finger, her brown ringlets falling over her face.

"But no spells worked, not until he came to me. The angel!" She gazed upward, raising her hands up to the heavens. "Showed me the way he did. Told me how I could get my revenge and where to find the mirror. He showed me the way to *her* and gave me the powers of the almighty!"

Wilson could barely keep up with her rant as his lungs clenched in attempts to gasp for air, but nothing. If she didn't give him the antidote to whatever she'd done to him, he was sure to pass out.

"You were right about one thing, though, *Detective Davies*" —the madwoman wagged the curved knife at him with a grin — "I did kill Madam Onay for revenge. How could I not? I was beside myself with grief. However, it was only at the bequest of one Irvin. Talmage. Senior!"

She lunged at Mr Talmage, who still hung beside Wilson. Black dots speckled his view but could just barely make out the businessman who cowered back in his peripheral vision as Miss Lauretta slashed his shirt across the chest.

Wilson lost sight of the crazed woman as the darkness enclosed all around him. He kicked himself for not making a better mask, though it was too late. The drug in the air had already taken its toll on him.

"Oh, you can't die yet, *my pet*," she murmured in his ear.

"Not until you've heard how I did it."

His vision blurred, and just when he thought he couldn't take anymore, Miss Lauretta chanted something else he couldn't quite make out. His lungs contracted, suddenly pulling in the air he'd been trying to breathe. His eyes bulged as he gasped for air.

"Wakey, wakey!" She slapped his cheek a few times.

"What did you do to me?" Wilson croaked.

"Shh." She tapped the tip of her knife against her pursed lips. "I'm not finished yet. Now, where was I?"

Miss Lauretta crossed her arms for a moment before a grin spread across her face, revealing sharp fangs. "Oh, that's right. The part where Mr Talmage seduces me, *tricks* me into agreeing to kill Madam Onay in return for his undying love."

Chills swept down the length of Wilson's arms as he finally put the pieces together. He'd been right. Mr Talmage was the killer. He just hadn't been the one to wield the knife.

"He brought her to me like a present, and I held my part of the deal." Miss Lauretta scowled at Mr Talmage.

Sweat poured down the old man's forehead as his attempts to protest were muffled by the gag about his mouth.

"And when it came time for you"—she jabbed the knife once more at the old man — "to leave your wife, you wouldn't even come out to tell me to my face. YOU COWERED!"

She heaved a sigh, wiping a tear from her cheek.

"Then, when I tried to frame you, you had your little secretary cover up the tracks." She let out a harsh laugh. "Then the Governor, well, that was more for me and my father. Still, to see you jailed for his murder would've been a bonus. Even when I tricked you into being at the scene with all that blood, no one could see how you were the real monster. The town's favourite gentleman who could do no wrong."

Wilson eyed the weapon once again. He took slow movements while she was focused on Mr Talmage and inched closer to it.

"But no matter. I now know how to deal with men too lazy to do their own dirty work." She muttered something else under her breath and, with a wave of her hand, brandished a vial. "Drink up, *my pet*."

The room filled with Mr Talmage's desperate screams as his gag ripped itself away from his mouth, and the vial floated through the air at him. Wilson blinked in utter dismay as he watched the contents of the vial force itself down his throat. It wasn't possible. None of this was. A vial couldn't fly through the air on its own, just as a bullet couldn't freeze midair. So, what the hell was happening?

The detective shook his head, his ears ringing as he tried to make sense out of it all. What sort of airborne narcotic could make him see such elaborate things? It was certainly more potent than the devil's root. An opium mixture, perhaps? However, it didn't smell like the bitter ammonia substance.

Nothing made sense save for one explanation. Still, he refused to even mentally form the word.

"Now, your turn." Miss Lauretta's head turned towards him without moving her body, and Wilson gagged at the bizarre sight.

The word he tried so hard not to consider slipped loose, and suddenly he found himself spiralling into an abyss of questions. Was it true? Could there be *supernatural* forces at work?

He suddenly wished he'd lost consciousness earlier. At least then, he would've died not knowing the truth about this case. That he'd been right and completely wrong all at the same time.

She snapped her fingers, another vial appearing in her

hands. This time, she uncapped it herself and skipped to the detective's side.

"Such a shame to kill such a beautiful face." She stroked the stubble at his chin but froze and sniffed the air. "Is... is that *fish*?"

A fire sparked from behind her, and she turned to face the doorway. Two panthers with emeralds for eyes flew in, all reeking as if they'd just come from the fish market, and ploughed into Miss Lauretta, knocking her to the ground. She shrieked, fighting against their strength.

Wilson squeezed his eyes shut for a moment before reopening them in the hopes of ridding himself of the ridiculous hallucination. Little good it did. No sooner had the panthers pinned Miss Lauretta than the red-headed circus girl burst in after the panthers.

He would recognize Emma anywhere, and if Barnaby hadn't convinced him not to arrest her, she would've been in custody. Only now, to Wilson's horror, she was completely on fire, and what were those feathery things sticking out from her back? Did she have... wings?

Miss Lauretta shrieked, shoving at the panthers who pinned each of her arms to the sticky floor. Emma crouched over her and yanked something with a handle from her satchel. A *mirror*? Wilson scoffed. If his colleague had sent this girl to save him with just that, he was done for.

The woman kicked the smaller of the two panthers off her with a strength beyond what her size allowed.

"*Inmetivit!*" Miss Lauretta cried, waving her hand at the smaller panther, sending it flying through the air towards the back wall.

"No!" Emma halted her advances and, in a split second, dove in front of her pet just as the self-proclaimed witch waved her hand again in its direction.

"*Brechteram*." Miss Lauretta sneered as tendons cracked.

The red-headed girl's face fell slack as some unseen force snapped her shoulder out of place. The larger panther's hold on Miss Lauretta loosened, and she took advantage of the distraction. She leapt to her feet and backed around to Wilson's side, putting him between herself and her assailants.

"Ha! Your power is no match for me." The madwoman flashed a smile, sliding her snake-like teeth across her sharp fangs. "Didn't I prove that last time you tried to come after me?"

The girl with the flaming wings turned on Miss Lauretta. Though one arm hung slack and pain flickered across her eyes, her good hand still gripped tightly around the mirror. She widened her stance, wielding the silly looking glass like it was a sword with a confidence Wilson couldn't comprehend. What good would that do in a fight?

"That was then." She flexed her muscles and winced, but the force sent another wave of fire zigzagging through her feathers. "Now, I'm not alone."

The panther, who wasn't knocked out, growled in agreement and crouched. Both the girl and the giant cat appeared ready to pounce.

Miss Lauretta's head fell back as she let out a throaty laugh, shoving Wilson aside and stepping up. "Come on, then. Let's see what you and your kitty got."

The girl narrowed her golden eyes before she charged. Wilson shielded his eyes as the two women clashed into one another. Emma dodged a blow from Miss Lauretta, lifting the mirror up to reflect not the brown ringlets Wilson was expecting but a balding monster with a crown of ram's horns.

A hiss escaped Miss Lauretta when she spotted her new reflection. Emma then began reciting strange words Wilson couldn't understand.

A crazed look flickered across Miss Lauretta's face as she

bellowed. The war cry shook the ground. She hurled herself into a sprint, the bluish apparition of the horned woman peeling from Miss Lauretta's body as if she were splitting into two.

Sparks shot out everywhere when Miss Lauretta rammed her arm into Emma's chest, sending her slamming back against the ground. Emma hit her head against the hard concrete, skidding out of her grasp and across the floor.

"You can't get rid of us that easily." Miss Lauretta spat in the girl's face, the ghost shimmering back into her body.

Miss Lauretta slammed her fist towards Emma's face, but the girl somersaulted out of the way. Her wings flapped, slinging a ball of fire into the air. It hit Miss Lauretta's shoulder, the skin blistering red before melting into char. The woman bellowed, swatting at the flames to smother them. The panther bit into the woman's leg, dragging her back to the ground.

Emma grabbed the mirror and lifted it once more. "Rechna erit, Hexenspiegel! Take that which does not belong!"

Miss Lauretta kicked the large cat with her foot and lurched for Emma, but instead, the ghost emerged from her once more, this time breaking free and hovered above her.

"NO!" Miss Lauretta screamed in unison with the ghost as it flickered and whorled for the mirror.

"From here to eternity," Emma continued her chant, the apparition melting into a hazy mist. "I curse Frau Perchta to this Hexenspiegel!"

The bluish haze swirled into the mirror's reflection, and it trembled as if absorbing a great force. The room fell silent for a moment before Miss Lauretta threw herself at Emma in a fit of rage.

Wilson's breath hitched. It was now or never. He tiptoed as far as his chains would allow in the direction of the gun.

He grunted through the pain of the metal digging into his wrists, toeing the barrel. He was so close.

His eyes watered from the smoke that filled the room as the two battled one another, too distracted to notice his attempt at arming himself.

With one last inch, he managed to hook his foot around a corner of it, but a tremor sent his leg kicking it into the inspector's side and further away. Plundell merely grunted but barely stirred.

"Balls!" He cried, falling back against his restraints.

His head hung, the last sliver of hope vanishing along with his sanity. Just when he thought things couldn't get any worse, the iron chains above him moved on their own. He looked up and jumped when he met the gaze of a slender woman, crouched on the ceiling like a cat. Her snow-white hair pinned in curls atop her head triggered a memory of the circus, and he remembered her name as Franziska. He wondered if all of them were here. But where was Barnaby?

Before he could ask, Franziska lifted a finger to her lips. A crash echoed throughout the chamber, and suddenly a shadow zipped across the room towards Mr Talmage. It moved too fast for his mind to process, but seconds later, the man's chains were severed. The businessman fell to his knees, his face ashen as if he was about to vomit.

Out of the corner of his vision, he saw yet another glimmer, and in the blink of an eye, the smaller panther who had fallen unconscious was gone.

What about me? He thought. Then metal clinked above him, gaining his attention.

The shackles around his wrists snapped open, and he sighed with relief, pulling them into his chest and rubbing them gingerly.

He glanced up at the chain just as the woman on the ceiling slunk down beside him. Moisture sprung to his eyes when he realized the very people he'd once thought of as the enemy had just saved his life.

The fair-haired woman winked at him, and before he could thank her, a wind whipped around them, and both her, the panther, along with the girl and the mirror vanished.

He stood there for a moment, dazed and unable to think clearly. Then, a grunt reminded him he wasn't alone, and he scooped the pistol up, clicking back the hammer and aiming it square at Miss Lauretta, who was about to escape.

"Halt!" He ordered just as a loud bang shook him.

His ears rang from the blast, realizing too late that his trembling finger was on the trigger. The bullet zoomed in front of Miss Lauretta, barely missing her head, and she froze.

"Back away from the door." He motioned for her to stand in the corner.

She mumbled something, but from the way she glanced at him and furrowed her eyebrows, he could tell whatever she wanted to happen wasn't.

"Why doesn't it work?" Her lip trembled as she moved ever so slowly towards the corner. "Why's the magic gone?"

He kept the gun trained on the woman, who muttered to herself while he glanced down at Plundell.

"Inspector." He nudged the man's leg with his boot. "Chief Inspector Plundell, I order you to wake up!"

He sent a kick into the officer's shin, and suddenly, the man jolted up.

"Huh? Ow!" The chief inspector massaged his neck. "What'd you hit me for?"

Wilson widened his eyes, tilting his head towards Miss Lauretta and Mr Talmage.

Plundell raised his eyebrows in understanding. "Oh, right."

He picked himself up, wincing when he stood a bit too

quickly. Just as he was about to reach for his handcuffs, men shouted from the other room.

A constable in uniform dashed into the small scullery and skidded to a halt when he spotted them.

"Chief inspector! Are you all right? We were warned you were in danger." The man ducked his head out of the room and hollered, "They're down here!"

"Yes, I'll be fine, but fetch the doctor for the others. And for this one"—he jabbed a finger at Mr Talmage, who heaved, the contents of his stomach lurching forward — "eck!"

The businessman gasped, swaying on his knees as he fought to stay awake. "Poison! I… I—"

Before he could finish the words, his chest collapsed onto the floor.

Chief inspector grunted, straightening his collar. "Well, his stomach will need to be pumped, and then it's off to the brig for these two."

The room around Wilson soon swarmed with officers. Some saw to the wounds of Mrs Tilcott and the Governor as they waited for the doctor to arrive, while others handcuffed the murderous duo.

"Death is coming for you!" Miss Lauretta cried as she struggled against the two officers who escorted her out. "He's watching and waiting, and he's coming."

But none of this registered to the detective. So, there he stood, frozen like a statue. He didn't even notice when the pistol slipped from his hand and clattered onto the floor. And then he did something he'd never once done before, nor would he ever do again.

He brushed the dust off his frock coat, popped his collar, and, with his head held high, he marched from the crime scene without a single utterance of his deductions. Because the only thing he could ascertain from this abominable crime scene was this; that magic might exist.

21
TIDINGS OF COMFORT AND JOY

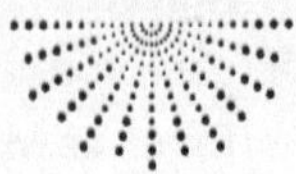

BARNABY PACED the length of the sidewalk that lined the back of Mrs Tilcott's house, often stopping to peek over the fence.

"They'll make it," Antoine said for the hundredth time.

He sat in the driver's box of the caravan parked just out of sight from where the officers would be. Barnaby checked his pocket watch and huffed. They would arrive any minute, but Emma and the others had yet to emerge from the house.

"How do you know?" Barnaby waited for an answer until he realised he already knew it. He sighed and continued his pacing. "Do tell. Your power seems quite suspect. Are you ill or something?"

"Or something," Antoine said, more to himself than to anyone else.

Barnaby chose not to press him on the issue, getting the impression that it was a sore subject. Instead, he took his frustration on the delay out on the snow and kicked bits of it up with each step.

Where were they? He peered into the tiny backyard again to no avail. It'd seemed like hours since they'd entered the house, but if he were being honest, it must've only been minutes. But still, he couldn't help but be nervous. What if someone got hurt? What if they couldn't trap Frau Perchta in the mirror? What if the constables arrived while they were still in there?

All sorts of scenarios flooded Barnaby's mind while he waited for the rest of the circus to complete the final piece of Emma's plan. It was brilliant in its simplicity, and his heart swelled with pride that it was Emma who came up with it.

Barnaby's job was to warn the brigade that the chief inspector and his colleague were after the killer and required backup.

Antoine, of course, drove the getaway caravan while the Engels siblings set up everything needed for the enchantment within the vehicle.

They only needed two ingredients to complete the ritual and solidify the mirror into a tomb, therefore banishing Frau Perchta into the spirit realm: Frankincense and Myrrh. Two rare spices to find at just any old store.

Luckily, Barnaby knew precisely where to find them, and, to everyone's amazement, it was all thanks to Roderic's lessons on their aromatic qualities. During his morning visit to Dr Larson's, Barnaby had recognised the scent and spotted the perfume bottle left on his secretary's desk.

Artus had already returned from procuring it and was now huddled up in the caravan with the Engels, helping them with the final touches.

That left the rest of them waiting restlessly while Emma, Franziska, Timur, and the panthers completed the final piece of the puzzle. Which was for Emma to capture Frau Perchta's spirit into the mirror, Franziska to save Wilson, the panthers to keep everyone from escaping, and Timur to use his vampire speed to ensure everyone got out in time.

The only problem was, they had yet to emerge. Emma and the rest of the circus needed to make it out before the police arrived. They were all wanted criminals. He'd seen the fliers in the city jail when he delivered his message to the inspector's second in command. The charges against them were for instigating a riot, which was preposterous as they all knew that wasn't true, and the destruction of public property, which, again, hadn't been entirely the circus's fault.

Barnaby had snatched a copy of the notice to show Antoine, and though the likenesses sketched on the page hardly matched Emma and the circus, the panthers were hard to miss.

A loud crash from within the house sent him slipping on the ice as he tried to come to a complete stop. He held his breath, watching the solid oak door like a hawk.

Another boom followed, and finally, a blur burst out of the house. It whooshed the wind around Barnaby until Timur came to an abrupt halt with a giant bundle of black fur in his arms.

"Absinthe!" Antoine hopped down from the driver's box.

The caravan's door swung open, and, as if Artus knew his panther was hurt, he raced to Timur's side.

"She's okay," Timur replied in a thick accent. "Just a bit bruised."

Absinthe fought against Timur's strength and finally let her go. As soon as she was on her feet, the vampire vanished towards the house in a whirl of wind.

Barnaby watched in amazement as first Franziska appeared on the sidewalk as if out of nowhere, followed by Kizmet and Emma.

"You're safe!" The detective raced to the young girl's side but stopped in his tracks when he noticed her arm.

"I'll be fine, Detective Barnaby." She forced a smile as if that would be enough to keep him from worrying.

"We must get you inside. Get Roderic to work his magic." Barnaby offered her his arm.

"No, first the enchantment first." She swayed, handing him the mirror that flickered blue.

"Quick!" Antoine cried, hopping back into the driver's box and gripping the reins. "The constables are on their way."

Whistles neared, punctuating their dire need to get out of there. Barnaby waited as everyone piled into the caravan, pausing by the door for a moment and glanced back at the house.

He prayed that Wilson would do as predicted and return to the flat after ensuring both Miss Lauretta and Mr Talmage were arrested. He wished he'd had more time to explain everything to his friend, but he hoped witnessing Miss Lauretta's exorcism was enough to believe. Either way, he trusted that Wilson would do the right thing in the end.

With that, Barnaby hopped into the cramped space within the caravan. The growing band of misfits sped off down the street to rid the world of an evil spirit and enjoy what was left of their Yuletide together.

The detective's flat,
Grafton Street

Emma grimaced and rubbed her shoulder, still sore from being forced out of its socket. She was still in awe that her plan had worked, even after the unexpected wounds. But, thankfully, her shoulder was already healing, and Absinthe had only sustained a small bump on her head, though she whined like she'd broken her arm.

With Frau Perchta safely exorcised from Miss Lauretta's body and all those involved apprehended by Chief Inspector Plundell, she could finally relax. They returned to Detective

Barnaby's flat, and within the hour, so did his colleague. Emma half expected Detective Wilson Davies to toss them out into the street, but he was in such a daze she didn't even think he noticed that they were there.

From the way he repeatedly shook his head and mumbled something about it not being possible, she knew he must've still been overwhelmed by it all. As anyone who'd experienced the supernatural for the first time would, of course. It had taken much more for her to accept that magic was real. In fact, if she hadn't had powers herself, she might not have ever believed. Especially if she'd nearly been killed by a witch possessed by an ancient spirit that was supposed to be a myth.

If she were candid, they all must've been a little shaken not only from the first-hand experience of the wrath of Frau Perchta's spirit but also from nearly losing everything at the hands of the townsfolk. In fact, some of them already had.

Emma watched in awe at Miss Gertrud and her owl-eyed brother as they sang carols in their native tongue along with Franziska while they cooked a Yuletide meal. It was as if nothing had happened. They conveyed not a sliver of resentment, hatred, or sorrow of loss, but instead, they were the very picture of joy. This was something Emma admired in them and hoped she too could emanate.

She then pondered where they would go next. They all knew their time in Halifax had come to an end. But as the shock of the day's events waned and Christmas day neared its end, she realised there was no other place in the world she'd rather be in this moment than right here; surrounded by her family, friends—both new and old—and the delicious notes of the peppery roast wafting from the kitchen.

Her thoughts were interrupted by Absinthe's loud snore, and she giggled at the panther who took up most of the couch beside her. And she was the smaller of the two. Her legs shuffled from whatever dream she was having while she rested off her bruises.

Kizmet had joined the brothers and Timur in search of the perfect fir tree upon Franziska's request. Perhaps it was more of a demand as she was determined to make their first Yuletide together a special one. It would commemorate their journey here as well as their future.

Though there was only a small chance anyone would recognise them from the flier Detective Barnaby showed them, they were still instructed to stick to side roads just in case.

Emma's heart clenched as her thoughts returned to where they might go next. Would they finally go to America? Or would Antoine's visions take them elsewhere? She quickly swallowed the idea as the flat door burst open.

"We're back at last!" Artus exclaimed a slender hand gripped around the top of the fir tree while the other swept his wild black hair out of his emerald eyes.

Antoine followed behind him, carrying the stump of the magnificent tree. They placed its base into the tub of sand Franziska had prepared next to the fireplace, and Emma stood. She'd never seen a tree so tall. Its top grazed the ceiling and filled the flat with a fresh sweet aroma.

She gasped, resting a hand on one of the soft green needles. "It's beautiful."

A clunk on the doorframe made them turn just as Timur entered with a basket that overflowed with apples and pinecones.

"Sorry." Timur grimaced, scooping one of the apples up that had fallen and taking the basket into the kitchen.

Kizmet followed, sniffing the fruit still on the floor. His whiskers crinkled as if the apple were sour and let out a growl which startled Barnaby from his sleep.

"Gah!" Barnaby snorted as he sat up from the wingback

chair next to the window where he'd been napping since they arrived.

Emma held back a grin. "Are you alright, Detective Barnaby?"

"Erm, yes… never better." He blinked his drowsy eyes and adjusted his bandaged leg on the footrest. "My, what an excellent tree! Wouldn't you agree, Wilson?"

"The spirit? Is she back? Where?" Wilson leapt to his feet, a crazed look in his eye as he brandished a letter opener.

His ordinarily neat and tidy necktie was off-kilter, and his dress shirt clung to his chest in a damp sheen. Emma had never seen him like this, though with him spending most of the time she'd known him hunting her and her family, she wouldn't say she'd paid much attention to his appearance. She wondered if this experience might change him or if he would soon return to wanting her and her family arrested. Her throat constricted at the thought. Was it even safe to be around Detective Wilson? Could he be trusted now after everything they'd been through? Surely saving his life had to count for something.

"Wilson, would you give me that before you hurt yourself?" Barnaby groaned as he picked up the pitcher of Glühwein the Engel siblings had made off the coffee table and filled two steaming mugs. "Come, have some of this spiced wine with me and relax. It's Christmas, after all."

Wilson pursed his lips, glancing between the mug his colleague offered him and the panther lounging on the couch. His whole face went stark white as if he were about to faint.

"It's all real… isn't it?"

Barnaby looked to Emma for her to respond, but she jerked her eyes back to the branch she held. He sighed. "It is."

"But this means all that I've believed my whole life has been a lie."

Emma couldn't help but peek at the two detectives from behind her lowered lashes. The dazed look returned to Detective Wilson's otherwise expressionless face as he sat back down at the desk with the rigid posture of an aristocrat at church. It appeared that Barnaby's words had finally settled in with the detective, and perhaps he was moving past his denial.

Wilson tossed the letter opener down. It clattered against the wood of the desk.

"Dinner is served!" Franziska called from the kitchen, followed by the Engel siblings and Timur, carrying various delicacies trays.

Emma licked her lips as platters of peppered apple, sausage stuffing, and garlic potato dumplings accompanied the roast. She could hardly wait to dive into this miraculous Christmas meal, and her stomach rumbled in agreement.

They all sat cross-legged around the coffee table, ignoring Barnaby's moans of apologies for not having more seating at the table. It didn't matter that they weren't eating with the nicest silver or that they hadn't a single ornament for their magnificent tree. In fact, to Emma, it was so much better to throw formalities aside and what one might've thought proper. She was blessed to be able to sit side-by-side with both feline and man as equals.

"A toast," Antoine announced, lifting his glass of glühwein, and they all followed suit. "To this blessed Yuletide feast!"

"Here! Here!" They all cheered.

"And to new partnerships, as we grow together on our return journeys." Antoine gave Emma a wink.

"Huzza—wait, what?" Artus stopped mid cheers.

Emma's heart hitched at the ringleader's implication. Could this mean he would extend the invitation to join them to the Engel siblings? She prayed it was so, but before she could prod for answers, a knock came from the door. Her nerves quivered at the sound. Everyone remained motionless, each one glancing at the other in confusion. Had they been expecting anyone else?

Barnaby flushed. "I would get it, but my leg."

"Of course not. I'll get it." Franziska leapt from the floor and rushed to answer the mysterious visitor.

Emma leaned around the two panthers to see who it was, but Franziska's piles of white ringlets blocked her view. When she returned to the table, she held a letter in her hands.

"It's for you." She handed it to Detective Wilson, and, for Emma believed must've been the first time ever, he looked Franziska straight in the eye.

He furrowed his impeccably trimmed brow at the letter for a moment before taking it. "Thank you."

"What does it say?" Barnaby leaned in to try to look over the top of the paper.

"It's..." Detective Wilson trailed. "It's a message from John Walsh."

Emma's eyes widened as she glanced between Antoine and the rest of the circus.

"Who's John Walsh?" Mr Roderic asked, adjusting his half-moon glasses.

"I'll tell you later," his sister whispered just loud enough that Emma could overhear.

Barnaby gasped. "Why on earth would he be writing to you?"

Detective Wilson tossed the letter aside with a scoff.

"He's summoning you back to London, isn't he?" Antoine asked, gaining everyone's surprise. "I only ask as this is where my visions show us travelling to next."

A fork scraped loudly against a plate, and Emma turned to Artus, who was obviously making a racket on purpose.

"Not this again," Artus mumbled under his breath, shovelling a dumpling into his mouth.

"What was that, brother?" Antoine asked.

Artus glared at his older brother and sat a bit taller in his seat. "We can't return to London. We have no reason to go there."

"Yes, we do." Antoine lifted his chin and met his younger brother's stare with a determined eye. "I've foreseen it. And it is from this vision I've come to discover that John Walsh's power is too great a threat to mankind. We must save him from himself."

"What, like *kill* him?" Artus cried.

"No, brother. We will remove his powers."

Emma gulped. He said this so calmly, but was it even possible to remove someone's powers?

"Oh, is that all?" Artus rolled his eyes. "And I suppose the detectives and Franziska's German friends will be tagging along, will they?"

"Artus, stop!" Franziska glared daggers at the pale man who sat opposite her. Artus winced in response, but Franziska pressed on. "You know how your brother's visions have been? How unpredictable they are? And with Emma's new powers, we can't do this alone. The Engel's have agreed to help us, and in return, we've offered them a home among us."

Artus's emerald eyes glistened, and Emma could tell he regretted his words but made no other response.

"It's all right," Mr Roderic piped up, pushing his half-moon glasses back up his bulbous-tipped nose. "I always find change a bit frightening, but we don't want to be an imposition."

"It's not," Franziska replied, her eyes still hard on Artus, who looked down at his plate. "If you're still willing to travel with us to London, we would love to have you."

"No, no, no, no!" Detective Wilson tossed his napkin onto his empty plate. "None of you will be going to London. After today we will be parting ways. I want nothing to do with your… your demon ways."

Emma jerked at the offending word. They weren't demons. If anything, they were angels, flaws and all. They'd even saved his life. Had he already forgotten?

"John Walsh is my case, and I won't allow any of you to mess it up. I will be going to London alone, and that is all."

"That's it." Barnaby gasped. "It's exactly what he wants."

"Sorry?" The detective glared at his colleague.

They all looked to Barnaby with curiosity. His wide eyes conveyed he'd just had an epiphany.

"He wants you to chase after him." Barnaby let out a nervous laugh. "He knows you don't believe in magic, and he used this town to pull you further away from us. He wants you in London. Alone. For whatever reason, I can't figure it out, but it's the perfect plan."

"How, dear Barnaby? How is this even a plan? This sounds more like utter nonsense spewed from someone who is clearly injured."

"I'm fine," Barnaby snapped at Wilson. "It's perfect because he orchestrated all of this to mess with your mind. To make us look crazy for believing in magic and lure you to London—Wilson, you cannot go there alone. It's a trap!"

"Well, of course, it's a trap," Wilson replied, his tone dripping with arrogance. "But I don't see how this has anything to do with you or this bloody circ—"

The detective froze. Emma glanced between the two detectives for a clue as to what was going on, but it seemed Wilson had returned to the confines of his own mind.

"You see it now, don't you?" Barnaby broke the silence. "He's the one who first put you on the case that led you to Emma and the circus. And then his first victim—*my* nephew,

God rest him—is what brought you here through me. Everything points to some bigger plan with you at its core."

"It can't be…." Wilson continued to mumble under his breath as he shook his head repeatedly. "I mean, I did recognise him… and the scar… his voice… it was all familiar…."

"Exactly," Barnaby agreed.

"If this is true"—Franziska turned to Antoine questioningly — "what can be done?"

Antoine raised his mug once more. "My toast before wasn't solely for the Engels. It was to all-new partnerships, including that with the detectives. John Walsh may have bigger plans for Detective Davies, but he will never suspect our collaboration."

Everyone gasped, save for Detective Wilson, who was still off in his own world.

"You'd really do that for us? After everything, he did to you in London?" Detective Barnaby was without words, and so was Emma.

The thought of returning to London made her heart skip a beat. The last time she was there, she'd been running for her life. Could she not only return but travel alongside the very detective who'd been hunting her? And where would they stay?

"It is what is to be." The ringleader gave Detective Barnaby a decisive nod.

Detective Barnaby scratched his head before lifting his own mug. "Then we're forever grateful to you. To friendships, both old and new!"

The others raised their mugs and toasted, some with more enthusiasm than others. Emma couldn't help but wonder how they would all travel together. And once in London, would they all fit in their already cramped caravan? Or would they grow so large that they'd get their own train?

"Don't worry," Barnaby whispered to her as if he'd read

her mind. "I know a wealthy detective with a townhome in London that has plenty of rooms to spare. After all, he does owe me."

Wilson snapped out of it at that. "Wait, what? You can't mean *my* townhome?"

"I won the bet, didn't I?"

"You most certainly didn't."

Barnaby smirked. "I knew from the beginning it involved the supernatural, and you were so certain it was not, which led to your being nearly killed. My theory is what allowed everyone in this room to save your life."

"That wasn't our arrangement."

"I've changed the terms. Besides, I don't see what other choice we have."

Wilson glared. "Oh, why you...."

"Look!" Franziska interrupted the two bickering detectives and pointed to the window.

Emma gazed up just as snowflakes trickled down beyond the glass and followed the others to admire its magnificence.

"How beautiful," Miss Gertrud gasped, laying a hand on her chest. "You know, they say that when it snows on Yuletide's day, it's a sign the white goddess is making her bed, and the snowflakes are the feathers spilling down from the heavens."

"Gertrud!" Her brother scolded. "Don't speak of Frau Perchta."

"I wasn't. I was merely speaking of her before she became the witch. Goodness, Roderic, don't you believe that despite the bad, one must focus on the good?"

This sparked a good-natured debate between the two on the meaning of Christmas. It was then, while Emma peered out at the tiny specks of white snow that glittered against the setting sun, that she wondered if perhaps this was what Yuletide was all about? A time to put differences aside and for second chances. Not only for oneself but for all.

She let the thought linger upon her heart like the snow coming down, blanketing the little town of Halifax in a fresh layer of white puff. Though she couldn't say she would miss this place, the uncertainty of their future back in London made her content to be right where she was at.

Detective Barnaby patted her on the shoulder. "Merry Christmas, Emma."

"Merry Christmas." She smiled back, knowing she would cherish this day for many years to come.

There weren't any presents under the tree or stockings over the fireplace, but what was important was that she was surrounded by the ones she loved the most. It was all she could've ever hoped for on this Yuletide day.

MORE TO DISCOVER

GASLAMP FANTASY & MYSTERY

The Unforgivable Act

The Detective's Nightmare

The Yuletide Killer

DARK URBAN FANTASY

Tompkin's School (A Supernatural Academy Trilogy Book 1)

Tompkin's School (A Supernatural Academy Trilogy Book 2)

Tompkin's School (A Supernatural Academy Trilogy Book 3)

CLEAN PARANORMAL ROMANCE

Timur's Escape

For more on the books of the Transitioned Universe visit the OFFICIAL website at www.TabiSlick.com

JOIN THE UNIVERSE

Paranormal* | *Historical* | *Urban Fantasy

Join my monthly reader's group to stay up to date on all of my new releases, giveaways, book news, and receive personal updates from behind the scenes of my writing strategies.

www.TabiSlick.com/Join

www.ingramcontent.com/pod-product-compliance
Lightning Source LLC
Chambersburg PA
CBHW031956040826
48979CB00041B/16

* 9 7 8 1 7 3 4 5 5 6 8 8 9 *